The Dying Realms

Annie Harper Trilogy, Book One
- The Golden Fleck Series

Hil G Gibb

Haruki Publishing

For Louise Wiles

Copyright ©2024 by Hil G Gibb

All rights reserved.

No part of this publication may be reproduced in any form or by any means – graphic, electronic, or mechanical, including photocopying, recording, taping or information storage and retrieval systems – without the prior permission, in writing, of the author.

The right of Hil G Gibb (Hilary Gibb) to be identified as the author of this work has been asserted by her in accordance with the UK copyright, designs and patents act 1988.

No portion of this book may be reproduced in any form without written permission from the publisher or author, except as permitted by U.S. copyright law.

Contents

Chapter One	1
Chapter Two	10
Chapter Three	20
Chapter Four	27
Chapter Five	31
Chapter Six	42
Chapter Seven	57
Chapter Eight	71
Chapter Nine	78
Chapter Ten	94
Chapter Eleven	103
Chapter Twelve	121
Chapter Thirteen	140
Chapter Fourteen	155
Chapter Fifteen	161
Chapter Sixteen	173

Chapter Seventeen	181
Chapter Eighteen	196
Chapter Nineteen	203
Chapter Twenty	217
Chapter Twenty-One	227
Chapter Twenty-Two	232
Chapter Twenty-Three	239
Chapter Twenty-Four	244
Chapter Twenty-Five	248
Chapter Twenty-Six	255
Chapter Twenty-Seven	265
Chapter Twenty-Eight	271
Chapter Twenty-Nine	287
Chapter Thirty	290
Chapter Thirty-One	301
Chapter Thirty-Two	313
A Word from Hil	322

Chapter One

The Necropolis in the heart of Glasgow, peppered with thousands of headstones, was deserted under the autumn sky — aside from the permanent residents buried beneath the soil and the occasional raven perched on a branch or atop a stone cross.

It was 'the city of the dead'.

A dry and somewhat lopsided muffin squatted at the foot of a particularly ornate monument. The muffin had been thrown out into a Costa bin in St. Vincent Street. It was just one in a crumpled bag full of old and similarly lopsided muffins. Without anyone noticing, the bag had been snatched away by a pair of small, quick hands.

Now, the remainder of the bag sat safely nestled against the denim pant leg of a young woman celebrating her eighteenth birthday, all alone in a graveyard.

Annie Harper sat straight backed and cross-legged in front of the monument. With great precision, she carefully pushed a single, bright blue-and-white-striped candle down inside the top of the muffin's puffy pinnacle. She then sat back, satisfied that while the muffin was lopsided, the candle was straight. She dug a lighter out of the deep pocket in her jacket and sparked it. After three attempts, the flame remained alight and took on a satisfying yellowy-orange glow.

After carefully lighting the wick, Annie sat the muffin back down on a mossy patch of dirt and thought long, and hard about her birthday wish.

There were quite a few options to consider:

1. A wish for a reliable roof over her head — something she had wondered how she would achieve each night for the last two years

2. A wish for food — something that most would think was the norm, but for Annie was never a given and, on many occasions, was considered a luxury

3. A wish for a good and loving mother — something she'd given up on years and years ago

4. A wish for an adventure — but what sort of adventure?

Seriously? she thought. *An adventure? Hasn't my life up until this point been adventure enough? Realistically, it's been less of an adventure and more of a modern-day version of Dante's Inferno.*

Growing up with a barely functioning, alcoholic mother, decimated by drugs and mentally tortured in a way that Annie simply didn't understand, Annie had, to all intents and purposes, brought herself up. She thought it was inevitable that she would come away somewhat scarred.

Her mother, whose diet was primarily based on cheap Baileys alternatives, always increased her drink quota once Annie's stepfather had beaten her mother's body black and blue — in all the places where it wouldn't show once dressed. Over time, her mother had turned to drinking before receiving a beating — something Annie later understood was an effort to prepare for what was coming. When the stepfather left, rather than improving, the drinking simply got worse.

Looking back now, she knew that her mother had somehow been self-medicating. She had seen this a lot among her homeless community. In this community, she had seen an uncomfortably large number of people in emotional pain, simply doing what they could to get by.

When Annie was morphing into a teenager, like many her age and stage, her emotions often got the better of her. There would be bouts of shouting matches with her mother. Suddenly kitchen cabinets would fly open of their own accord and bang shut, wildly. Soup in the microwave would spontaneously explode despite the socket being turned off. When her mother joined in with the shouting, such unexpected, unexplained things simply multiplied. It would be at this point that her mother would suddenly go quiet, go still, and go for the gin.

Once, Annie unwittingly created a smoothie disaster when she found her mother trying to make 'just a quick bloody Mary' before taking Annie to school. It was as if some of the 'happenings' were a way in which Annie was trying to help her mother.

Annie started walking to school on her own from that day forward.

She was five.

She would pretend to the teachers that her mother had walked her most of the way and was watching her from around the corner. For some reason, her teachers never questioned her story.

Wish option 5. Annie could make a wish to never be homeless again, but she was homeless by choice, and had been since just before she hit sixteen. Anything was better than the unsolicited, unwelcome, and unsavoury advances of her mother's boyfriend of the time. What made it even worse was the fact that her mother knew about it and did nothing.

No — Instead of options one to five, Annie opted for a sixth wish. She made a shy, self-conscious, barely audible, whispered wish to herself.

"To love and be loved."

Here, sitting alone on the cold, partially frozen earth, surrounded by vast, ornate monuments, and with dark clouds hanging overhead, Annie still couldn't help but think this wasn't the worst birthday she'd ever had.

No, that accolade would go to her sixth birthday. She had no recollection of the ones before that, so she couldn't make judgement of them. When she was close to turning six, Annie had painstakingly written out invitations to everyone in her class, using those party invites that were pretty much written already out for you. As per tradition in primary schools up and down the country, the teacher handed them out at the end of a school day.

On the big day itself, she had scraped her hair up into lopsided bunches with mismatched ribbons, knelt on the sofa so she that could see out of the window, and waited.

Waited... waited... waited.

No one came.

Not even her mother had remembered, or if she had, she did nothing to acknowledge it.

There were no cards, no presents, and no party games.

No love.

That night, she had cried herself to sleep, her hair still in lopsided bunches.

After that, Annie didn't really make anything of her own birthday. She went on to set the birthday bar so low that it simply lay on the ground. She had vowed never to lay herself open to such disappointment again, and a small, gilded cage locked around her heart with a teeny tiny clunk.

But this, her eighteenth birthday, marked her official graduation into adulthood. It warranted some acknowledgement. She could now vote. Although she couldn't vote with no permanent address. She could now legally consume alcohol. Although, why would she want to when she'd witnessed, first hand, what it did to her fellow homeless folk?

No, on balance, in contrast to many others, this birthday was sound. There were no expectations. Tick. There was no unwanted attention. Tick. There was a birthday cake, of sorts. Tick. And, after all, she had an entire bag of muffins to scoff as party food. Double tick.

The day tipped into dusk.

Annie played with the wick of the candle, now more exposed by the wax melting away. Waving a couple of fingers around the heat of the flame made it extinguish, then flutter back to life again. Annie did this a few more times before leaving it lit.

She had never really acknowledged or explored whatever 'powers' she seemed to possess. The occasions they had come into action, they had proved to be unruly and woefully flawed. When she was little, she thought that everyone could move things around without touching them, and that when someone was crying, it rained, just like it did with her.

Once at school, she soon came to realise that what she thought was normal was distinctly abnormal and something most likely to be feared. She quickly ceased any path to discovery, let alone mastery, of her 'gift'.

Annie closed her eyes tight, made her tentative wish, exhaled a quick puff of air, and blew the remaining tiny stump of candle out.

When she opened her eyes, a long tendril of smoke was curling skywards. As she looked past the tendril, Annie spied something at the base of the next gravestone, in amongst the long grass. It glinted in a rare beam of dying sunlight that pierced the clouds in the early evening. Squinting curiously, she stood up and went over to it.

It was iridescent and glinted with a rich, and unusual blue-green tone.

As she got closer to inspect it, it looked to be a piece of ancient jewellery, the size of her fist. The centre stone, set in what looked like hardened clay with fragments of gold leaf, was dazzling and practically glowing, amongst the dying October weeds.

Most of the time, tourists or visitors of the Necropolis' residents would drop an item accidentally — a pair of sunglasses or a single glove. Some might even intentionally leave a little keepsake in the grass on an ancestor's grave — perhaps a newly discovered ancestor. It didn't need to particularly be their ancestor. It could simply be a gravestone that a visitor felt drawn to.

This item, however, looked like something someone would very much miss. Upon peering closer, she realised that it was carefully cemented into a low plinth at the base of the gravestone. While the jewel looked valuable, the gravestone itself was modest when compared with the many monoliths and monuments. The Celtic cross was beautifully ornate, but Annie couldn't make out the carved inscription in the dim and dying light.

Someone has taken great care and placed this here with the intention of it staying put, she thought.

The large stone in the centre of the piece was a beautifully rich colour and Annie could feel it almost beckoning to her. She felt a surge of energy flow interwoven with expectation as she approached the item — like a lioness creeping up on her prey.

She reached for it hesitantly, as if reaching for something that might spark, or shock her. She didn't understand what made her both curious and, at the same time, reticent.

Just before her fingers were about to curl around and brush the blue-green stone, Annie heard shouting. It was pretty dark now and a flashlight illuminated her face, and her surroundings for a brief moment before shifting away, and sweeping from side to side.

Adrenaline raced through her as she realised a night guard may have seen her. She shot bolt upright and scrambled for balance. She hoped to grab her few belongings and make a getaway before anyone could collar her.

As panic surged through her, so did the recognisable feeling of inner electricity. It buzzed as it filled every atom of her being. Above, dense clouds rolled in, butting up against one another, darkening the skies even more. They moved across the bright, full moon that had taken up residence for the night.

It was as if she'd willed the weather to give her an assist, as Annie ducked down into the darkness between gravestones. Gasping for breath, she heard a shout for her to,

"Come out here now or there will be harsh consequences."

Stuff your consequences, thought Annie as she ducked further down. Her heart pounding, she grabbed on to an unseen gravestone for balance.

The moment her fingertips grazed the soft, green moss, blanketing the rough stone, Annie's vision swirled fast before her. She fell forward into the gravestone — literally *into* it.

Instantly, it was as if she'd been unceremoniously thrust into a rollercoaster carriage that was midway through an inverted loop. She was steeply rising, falling, and somersaulting. She was completely out of control. Momentary flickers of memories sped past her in chronological order. Sometimes she was looking down on herself, observing what was going on, listening in. Sometimes she was looking through her own eyes, feeling every second, replaying those past emotions in the now.

She couldn't grasp and hold on to any of them. Suddenly, the images before her slowed down. Annie felt a brief moment of relief, thinking her dizziness had come to an end. But then came the deconstruction of everything.

The distinct edges and boundaries between objects, surroundings, and the people in her visions started to evaporate. Everything became pixelated and reverted to their atomic-level components.

It was impossible for Annie to process the information. There was just so much of it. She could see everything, smell it, taste it, and hear it. Her senses were overloaded. She couldn't tell where one thing ended and another started. Holding her hand in front of her, it too, pixelated. She couldn't see where she ended and everything else started.

There was a brief moment of blackness, where the sounds, smells, and tastes simultaneously stopped.

There was nothing. Nothing at all.

Then Annie hit the cold, unforgiving earth.

She hit it hard. Really hard.

Chapter Two

A piercing ringing jangled in Annie's ears. It muffled the sounds of animals, a number of animals. Annie's stomach felt like it was in her throat, her throat felt like it was jammed up into her brain, and her eyes were clenched closed.

Groaning and sucking air in through her teeth, she painstakingly rolled over onto her side, having hit her shoulder blade on an unyielding rock. Her eyes screwed up tighter as she felt for, and found, the painful 'sweet-spot' in her shoulder.

"Oh, come on," she hissed to herself, at her stupidity and clumsiness for having fallen.

Feeling around to lever herself upright, Annie realised the ground felt quite different from that between the gravestones and monuments. There was no moss or wet leaves turning to mulch. It was drier and scratchy. It poked into her skin through her worn leather jacket. Confused, she willed the screwed-up muscles around her eyes to relax. Gradually, she was able to jack her eyes open, and she glanced upwards from her position on the ground.

"What the hell?" she murmured.

This was not the Necropolis.

Behind her, Annie could see that the sky was still grey and gloomy. However, it looked more expansive and, somewhat ironically, there was a whiff of death in the air that wasn't to be found in the Glasgow graveyard.

Here, it was daytime.

Just a second ago it had been night.

As she scanned around her surroundings, Annie saw that the ornate monuments and monoliths were gone. They had been replaced by stupendously tall trees. They stood bare, lifeless, thin and weak. They reached up to the sky as if in desperate pursuit of nourishment.

The only familiar feeling was that of late October. It drove the cold straight through her bottle green, worn out sweater, through her oversized jeans, and through her scuffed brown boots that had once belonged to her mother. She gave the faintest of smiles as she remembered how the laces had been chewed by the long departed family dog.

The cold drove through to her bones.

Sitting up to get a better look, she saw that she was in a small clearing, densely populated with elegant horses, most of which were saddled. Because of their proximity and confinement, many of them fidgeted and jostled about, becoming irritable with one another.

What the hell is this place? She wondered. *Where's the Necropolis?*

Without warning, a large and hefty object flew past her.

Had Annie not already sat up, it surely would have struck her squarely in the head. Her eyes searched wildly, left and right, for what it was. She felt large, heavy hooves stomping into the ground next to her. Her searching eyes widened when she looked up to see a man, astride a horse dressed in ornate leather and metal armour. His long-fingered hand was outstretched towards her. His hair shone in the sunlight that flickered due to the swiftly moving clouds. His eyes were full of an increasing urgency as he stretched his arm further out to her and bellowed,

"Grab my hand and jump up if you want to live!"

Sore as she was from the fall, Annie sensed his urgency and, without hesitation, jumped up, and grabbed on to the rider's hand. He pulled her up with ease, and Annie swung her leg over the saddle, wrapping her arms around his waist as she did so. Her unexpected rescuer clicked his tongue and squeezed the horse's reins, signalling for him to make haste. Squeezing one leg onto his mount's rib cage, he deftly turned his horse around, and the three of them galloped off into the woods.

Shocked about her fall through the gravestone, the near death experience with the fleeing horse, and the unexpected rescue, Annie held on for dear life. As they sped between the trees, following a riderless horse galloping and whinnying ahead of them, she surmised that they were on a mission to capture it. This rogue horse, livid with its rider, had reared up, dumped its payload, and galloped off at full tilt. Annie's face blanched as she realised that she'd very nearly been fatally clipped in the head by its hooves.

The rider to whom she clung, moved them expertly through the trees, adeptly leaping over jagged, broken tree stumps and fallen branches that were sun-bleached white. They finally caught up to the horse and came alongside. Annie watched out of one eye as her rider carefully reached out with one hand and grabbed the reins of the panicked horse, as they flapped about in the wind. Expertly, he slowed both the rogue horse and his own ride down to a controlled trot.

As they circled back around, Annie felt utterly windblown and bewildered. Her sleek, long blonde hair was now knotted and she was too shocked to begin to understand what had just happened.

Still, ever-proving she had her wits about her, Annie took the opportunity of their slowing down and shifted her body towards the other horse. She was not in the habit of trusting strangers who hoisted you onto their horse and made off with you into the woods. Without a moment's hesitation, and no former experience of horses or riding them, she sat behind her rescuer's saddle and leapt sideways. She struggled for a moment, but made it onto the other horse's back. She scrambled for the reins, trying to gain some control.

What the hell am I doing? she mentally shouted at herself. *I've never even ridden on a horse, let alone taken over the steering of one that I've just blithely leapt onto!*

"What in Fen'Harel's name are you doing?" yelled her mystery rescuer. Even though he had saved her from most probable and gruesome death by horse, she was understandably freaked out, and habitually suspicious.

"Who the hell are you and where am I? And... and how is it that I'm on a bloody *horse* right now?" she emitted a scream-cum-squeal as her ride, picking up on Annie's emotional state, nervously trotted backwards, snorted anxiously and continued to foam profusely at the mouth.

"You are in the Sun Elven Realm," he answered her, with surprising calm. "You are... a human, are you not? As for what is going on with the horse... Well that rather looked like your own choice."

Annie scoffed, too confused and scared to be offended by his sarcasm. She looked at him quizzically before answering.

"I don't feel like I'm human most days, but sure, of course I am. What are *you* then? Are you some sort of a mediaeval reenactment kind of guy, or something?"

Evidently, it wasn't beneath him to be offended.

"If I knew what a mediaeval reenactment kind of guy, or something were, I would guess, that I am probably not. I am Prince Carric, son of Peren, King of the Sun Elven Realm, second heir to the throne of said kingdom."

Annie's jaw went slack in disbelief. She stared at him, careful not to make too many sudden movements that might set the rogue stallion haring off again.

Seriously? You have got to be kidding me!" she thought.

"An elf?" she scoffed aloud. His unwavering stare told her that he wasn't kidding at all.

"Okay, then," she said, tight-lipped and uncomfortable with how he was looking at her — her mind racing.

"I'm just going to... take this... horse, and... and go find a bus station..."

"Find a what?" said Carric as he dropped his reins and held up his hands. They were pale, like fine pearls, and his fingers were long and slender, yet strong. For the first time, in their silence, with only their heartbeats pounding between them, Annie saw that he was beautiful.

For a moment, they simply stared at each other — the strangely willowy yet strong rider, through his almond-shaped eyes and Annie, through frightened, wildly alarmed blues, her golden fleck writhing, distrustfully. It did that sometimes, the golden fleck. Well, quite often actually. She only had one, in her left eye. One was quite enough. It moved in different ways and speeds, depending on Annie's emotional state. Sometimes, Annie thought its movements were reflective of what *it* was feeling or thinking. It was like she and it were in a symbiotic relationship of some sort. Annie had grown used to it and, as a child, she often thought of it as some sort of pet — with personality traits more akin to a cat than a dog.

Splitting the unwavering tension between them, Annie yelled,

"Who the hell are you, *really*?" Much to her alarm, both the horses jostled a little at Annie's sudden outburst. Carric chuckled softly, lowering his hands and picking up his mount's reins. It was the warm, good-natured chuckle of one who is at ease in one's own skin.

Being so at ease with oneself, she thought. *That really is only the stuff of dreams.*

"My name really is Prince Carric. I really am an elf and you are obviously a human. I can see by your poor posture on that stallion, among other things," he said, tapping the tip of his ears to indicate another clear difference between them. Grinning, he asked,

"Are you unharmed? You landed through your portal quite hard and with no grace whatsoever."

Annie stared at him like he had grown two heads.

"Landed through my what-al?"

Like, seriously, can this guy's questions get any weirder? she thought.

"It is how you arrived here in these Elven Realms. In the Sun Elven Realm, to be exact. Welcome! Apologies that it is not a little more... breath-taking," he added bitterly, gesturing to the open expanse of splintering, dying trees, dried-up waterbeds, and thirsty grass.

Annie tried hard to think logically as she watched him. On the one hand, this man could be completely truthful and really be an elf, sitting atop a beautiful black stallion, dressed in thick leather and shiny metal riding gear with a long, luxurious red cape that draped over his broad shoulders and the haunches of his mount. But, on the other hand, she had hit the ground pretty hard and thought maybe she was concussed.

Or dreaming, or in a coma, she added to herself.

"You're an elf," she finally uttered quietly. "You're an elf and a prince. And I'm awake and...lucid... and sane?"

"Why, yes," said Carric nodding. "Leaping onto a flighty stallion with no prior experience of riding aside, you appear to be lucid, but not necessarily sane. Now, come along, we need to get your steed back to its rider and the event."

Annie would have laughed in his face, had they been at the same level of confidence, elf prince or no elf prince.

"I'm not going anywhere with you!" she replied incredulously.

Carric sighed dramatically. He dropped his hands to his sides and barely held back from rolling his eyes in exasperation.

"You do not seem to know where you are, my lady, so perhaps you should stick by my side. After all, I could have just left you in the horse pen, at the mercy of their hooves. I will take you back with me, where there are no Shadow Elves. Where it is safe and you can get that shoulder tended to. I may even allow you to watch the event."

Annie huffed.

You'll allow me will you? She thought. *Allow me, my arse!*

"So what event will you be *allowing* me to watch?" she asked, massaging her shoulder. It did hurt from when she had landed on that rock and, on balance, this apparent 'prince' had rescued her and did *seem* nice enough.

"The event occurs annually, in the Elven Realms," he replied with thinly veiled zeal. "The best riding archers in each shire of the Sun and Woodland Elven Realms compete to determine who is the very best of the best."

"Don't tell me," she said in sarcastic, flat tones that appeared to completely pass him by. "You're one of those competing."

"Naturally," he grinned, now circling her mount and clearly eager to get back.

Having just been saved by this 'elf' and with absolutely no idea of where she was or how, or why, Annie was actually considering him to be her best option.

In a quieter, more tender voice and smiling warmly at her, Carric said,

"Forget the event. Please, let me take you back to the palace. You are clearly confused and our Wise One can assist you."

Annie wrestled to hold back a laugh.

So now we have a Wise One in the mix, she thought. *Of course we do.*

Pulling herself together, she asked,

"But what about the competition? Surely you'll miss your spot and forfeit your chance to be champion."

"It is about time someone else won the competition," Carric replied casually with the fleeting hint of a cheeky grin.

"So, let me guess. You've been the reigning champion for what, three or four years? Why am I not surprised?" said Annie, rolling her eyes.

"Actually, for som one hundred and eighty moons now," said Carric, not wanting her to under-estimate the longevity of his prowess. "Look, you are not the first human to be confused in our realm. Two humans have been among us before you. I would like to help you."

Annie studied him. She had to. From a very young age, it had become part of her nature to be distrustful of people. Time after time, she had been let down, especially by those who should have made her feel safe and loved: by her mum, her stepfather, her teachers. Naturally, when this stranger was offering to help her and willingly forfeiting an obviously well-loved event, Annie felt uneasy. It didn't matter whether he was elven, royalty or even a commoner. Such self-sacrifice and kindness was alien to her.

So, standing there, in some random place, in the company of a man with pointed ears, speaking of "Elven Realms," she made a split-second decision to go with him. Her gut and fluttering fleck were telling her how to survive, and this "Prince Carric" seemed to be her only way home.

"Well... all right. I guess you're my only ticket to get home," she conceded, clumsily dismounting her horse and stepping towards him. Languidly, Carric gave her his hand. Once more, he hoisted her up with ease and she swung her leg over the saddle. Without a word, Carric took each of her hands and guided them gently around his sides. After she'd firmly clasped them around his waist, he clicked his tongue, prompting his stallion and the riderless horse to move along at an instant canter.

Chapter Three

Annie could hear the enthusiastic, yet reserved clapping and call of the crowd at the arena ahead of them. Their voices and applause whistled through the bare trees on the crisp and breezy wind, clear and unmuffled by anything green or lush.

When they came to a slow trot just outside the line of trees, Annie peered around Carric's shoulder and gasped. Just beyond the arena where the crowd were engrossed in the competition, a magnificent, literally breathtaking, palace stood tall and proud on the hill ahead of them. Against the dying brown and grey of the earth, the palace's brilliant, blanched-almond colour was a stark contrast. It was as if a master sculptor had fashioned the whole building from one, gargantuan piece of marble. The carved wonder was peaked with slender spindle towers, sculpted to look like white trees, and wrapped in grandiose balconies. Detailed statues and gargoyles inhabited every alcove that were scattered across its surface.

The arena was laid with scorched grass and edged with cobbles. Pillars wrapped in lifeless vines, once lush and crawling skywards, delineated the dimensions of the rectangular area that Annie guessed was some two football pitches long. To one end, there were two competitors. Their horses' pelts shone and their manes, and tails were braided in intricate designs. Both the horses and their riders jiffled impatiently. The audience, a spackling of elves in various dress robes and armour, stood tall and lithe, each one of them beautiful in their unique way.

Annie took notice of their skin: some almost golden, some practically translucent, and rest were everything in between. Every single one of them had shell-like ears that swept up into fine points. Despite the suspense and intensity of the contest before them, they clapped lightly, as if moving any quicker would break delicate bones.

As Annie looked around, in awe of her surroundings, a younger, handsome elf, slender yet muscular, approached. His skin was like copper and simply beautiful. Walking alongside this mesmerising elf was an almost replica of him. Her skin was a slightly redder shade of copper. Her long brown hair flowed past her waist. Sections of it were braided into fishtails and decorated with leaves and small flowers. A smirk crossed her thin lips when she caught Annie's eye with her own bronze ones, and she nodded in silent acknowledgement.

"Your Highness!" greeted the first elf, crossing a closed fist over his chest and bowing deeply to this prince of the Sun Elves who, in response, nodded to him.

"Who is your guest?"

Carric dismounted and assisted Annie, placing a supporting hand on her waist — a touch that made Annie instinctively flinch.

Carric took note and released the pressure on the small of her back. Annie instantly relaxed and gave Carric a slight, yet grateful smile of gratitude.

"Finwe, Elva, go to my father," said Carric. "Tell him that yet *another* human has entered our realm."

Yet another human, thought Annie. *Charming.* In response to Carric's tone, her concern grew. *Who were the other humans? What did they do with them?*

Finwe looked to the elf beside him. Annie could see they were closely related. Perhaps twins even. The female shot her another look, and Annie could see their eyes were the same deep bronze, shaded with curiosity and wariness.

"A human?" Finwe gasped. His sister frowned and tugged on her brother's arm to do the prince's bidding.

Two other elves stood nearby. Their armour was equally detailed as the prince's, but their metal was silver plated rather than gold. Their weapons were sheathed but their hands were placed on their hilts, held at the ready. One of them, a more sturdy and muscular elf with a deep, milk-chocolatey smooth voice, spoke first.

"We must escort her into the palace at once."

Habitually mistrustful, Annie felt ice-cold shivers of fear shoot through her veins.

Escort me? That sounds formal, threatening even, she thought and briefly wondered if it might be best for her to turn on her heel and run right back into the woods.

To do what, exactly? She thought. Where I'm at appears to be the least worst option for me... for now.

Having weighed up her limited options, she cleared her throat instead of making a break for it.

"Excuse me," she said in a voice that was bolder than she actually felt. "But, what the hell is going on?"

The four elves turned to stare at Annie, with menace. She shrank back, thinking it better to not speak up. She straightened herself defiantly, but remained silent. Out of the corner of her eye, she noticed some of the crowd had begun to stop and stare at her. They looked somewhere between worried and angry. A couple of young elf children stood behind their parents, jumping up and down as they tried to get a better look at the human woman.

The sturdy elf approached her.

"I am Lucan, chief commander of the Sun Elven army and protector of this kingdom. Unfortunately, you have entered a realm in which you simply do not belong. What is your name, human?"

Lucan had a commanding presence, and with his large hands on his hips, he towered over Annie, dwarfing her in an instant. He looked down his large, straight nose at her, clearly wary but unafraid of her. He, too, was handsome.

Are there really no elven uglies? Annie thought, smirking to herself.

Lucan's features were square and strong. His thick black eyebrows arched sharply over deep-set and utterly earnest eyes. While he distrusted humans, he wanted to connect with them, to better understand them. To his mind, studying and knowing your potential enemy was always a sign of a fine soldier.

Annie felt slightly calmer, despite being surrounded by these heavily armoured elves, with swords and arrows and goodness knows what else. She glanced between the four that stood before her, and then to Carric, who had dismounted and come to stand at her side.

"Annie. My name's Annie Harper," she answered, looking back to Lucan, who nodded.

"Lady Annie," he said, looking at her with concern. "Not just any human arrives here. Only humans with additional... gifts. You must come with us, so we can assist you in getting back home."

Annie grimly thought about exactly what kind of 'home' she would be going back to. While she knew next to nothing about this place, if it proved to be real, it could be an opportunity for a new start. Maybe she would prefer to stay. Might that be something she could do?

Again, she thought, *What happened with the other humans?*

Elva broke the edgy silence by speaking up.

"My brother and I will get you back home," she vowed, holding a closed fist to her chest in solidarity. Then, following his sister's lead, her brother did the same.

Nodding to the Woodland Elves, the second warrior spoke up, facing Annie with a little glint in his eye.

"The needs and goals of the Sun and Woodland Elves are aligned. I am Varis of the Sun Realm and second in command of the Sun Elf army. Lucan and I will join the 'party'."

With basically no idea regarding the "needs and goals" of which Varis spoke, Annie gave a slight nod and smiled politely. She was hungry, sore, cold, and confused. She thought that she'd possibly slipped and knocked herself out at the Necropolis.

A thought struck her.

"Wait, if you are all elves, how come you are all speaking English?"

The members of the group exchanged looks of confusion.

"Why Lady Annie," offered Varis. "It is you who are speaking Elvish."

Annie took a step back in surprise.

OK, I did not see that coming, she thought.

"But I don't know a single word of Elvish," she protested.

"It would appear that you do. A great many words in fact." said Finwe, chuckling.

The elf called Elva stepped forward.

"It would seem that only humans with magic within them can travel here and speak our language. At least that is what we discovered with the two humans that came before you."

There it is again, thought Annie. *Who were these humans?*

Her head was rhythmically pounding now. Carric could see that Annie was finding all of this utterly overwhelming.

"Let us not be too hasty in sending this human back to whence she came," he said, with a cheeky quirk of his mouth. "If my brother Adran were here, he would undoubtedly insist that we be more open-minded and welcoming of anyone who is other to us."

With the gentlest of touches to her waist, Carric carefully steered Annie and started guiding her away from the assembled group. There it was again. A tender, almost intimate touch. This time, Annie was surprised that she didn't instantly flinch away. In her living memory, touch had, more often than not, been unwelcome, unpleasant or painful — or sometimes a combination of all three. Annie's modus operandi was to mitigate against such negative experiences by avoiding the touch of another if at all possible, at all times.

"Before taking Annie to King Peren, I shall afford this human a short tour of where we live by taking her to 'The View'," he called over his shoulder as the two of them rounded a corner and disappeared out of sight.

Chapter Four

"You don't have to do that," said Annie, looking up at this statuesque elven man. *Are all elves so tall?* She wondered. *I'm starting to empathise with Gulliver when he came across the Brobdingnagians in his travels.*

"It is true that I do not have to do anything, Annie," Carric explained as they walked down through what Annie could only assume were the formal gardens of the palace grounds.

"Rather," he continued. "I want you to have a greater understanding of the expanse of the elven realms before you return to your human one."

There it was again. The idea that Annie would be returning to her old life. While she'd only been in this realm for the briefest of times, she was increasingly favouring it over the realm that she'd left. A small voice at the back of her mind would not be silenced:

You're also increasingly favouring the touch of this eleven prince. Where has your guarded mistrust of others gone?

It hasn't gone anywhere, she protested to herself. *It just seems to have lowered with regard to this particular person... I mean, elf.*

They stepped outside of the formal gardens and headed up a steep bank of what obviously used to be long, lush grasses. Once on top of the bank, Annie's jaw dropped at the view before her.

The sweeping vista of undulating hills before a backdrop of magnificent, jagged mountains extended as far right and left as Annie could see.

"This is all of the elven realm?" Annie asked.

Carric smiled at her and she could feel her golden fleck do a happy little, acrobatic backflip.

"This is but a fraction of the four elven realms," he explained. "Further east than you can see, there is the Shoreland Realm that wraps around the edge of the sea." Seeing Annie was taking a genuine interest, he carried on.

"The coastline that meets the ocean is extensive, some eighteen thousand leagues." Carric now gestured to the mountain range ahead. "Just past the Mountains of El Brogé, is the Woodland Elven Realm, where Finwe and Elva hail from."

Suddenly, Carric turned to face Annie. His eyes were filled with an intense sadness.

"Our realms are dying, Annie."

"Why?" asked Annie, uncharacteristically placing a sympathetic hand on his forearm.

"It is all because of the theft of a sacred object that ensures our realms live and thrive continuously. The Sun Elven and Woodland Realms have joined forces and are constantly on the search to find ways to retrieve it."

Hesitantly, Annie asked, "Do you know who stole this object?"

"Apart from that it was a female human, no," Carric snapped. Then, realising the harshness of his tone, he adjusted it and continued. "We have left no stone unturned, but to no avail. It is as if the culprit simply spirited away. And she probably did, through the portal and back into your Human Realm."

Carric looked lost in his own thoughts and Annie searched her mind for something to change the subject.

"And beyond that," Annie asked. "Is there anything beyond the Woodland Realm? Is beyond there the fourth elven realm?"

Unfortunately, Carric's smile failed to reappear. If anything, his face took on an even more grim expression. "There is the Shadow Elven Realm. A place that you should be extremely grateful that you did not land in."

Annie felt that pressing Carric for more details would be ill advised. Instead, she looked out upon the Sun Elven Realm. While the sight filled Annie with awe and wonder, she saw that closer to the palace, the land was bare. Trees were dying and closer hills were carpeted in dried-out, scorched grass. A hazy fog clung in the air, and where the rich sounds of birds and insects should be, there was an eerie silence. The wind whistled for a moment, rustling the dead, brittle leaves, and then Annie heard absolutely nothing. Standing there for a moment, she felt it would be almost peaceful, if the silence were not caused by the ominously pervading devastation all around them.

Carric's voice snapped her out of her darkening reverie.

"Come," he said in almost a whisper.

He led the way down the other side of the bank. He strode ahead leaving Annie several strides behind and trying to catch up. With their backs to the palace and their faces into the wind, both Carric and Annie failed to see or hear the unnatural movement in the grasses behind them.

Without warning, a pair of large, strong hands gripped Annie's slender shoulders and fiercely yanked her backwards.

Chapter Five

"Did you seriously think you could get away, Meredith?" hissed the owner of the gripping hands. "You are coming with me, now."

With the air whipped out of her, Annie wheezed in exasperation,

"Who? Who's Meredith?"

Already tired of not really having a clue about what was going on around her, this abrupt abduction left her feeling completely out of control and her golden fleck spiralling. In this instant, the hazy fog thickened menacingly.

Annie struggled and wriggled so hard that she was able to wrench herself out of the grasp of her captor. She slipped out from his hands that were damp from holding Annie under her arms as she thrashed about. She stumbled forward and toppled into the tall grass. Landing hard, she acquired green-brown grass stains painting her face and streaking across her hands, and knees. Panting hard, she rolled over quickly to brace herself against further attack.

But no attack came.

Instead of being reached for and grabbed hold of once again, she watched as the angry elf, his expression full of disdain and his eyes almost spitting fire, had no chance to touch her. Carric, standing right behind him, had run his sword straight through her attacker.

Annie watched, mouth agape and eyes flooding with tears of shock, as Carric's blade slid slowly out of the elf's back. The moment that the sword was retracted, the elf crumpled to the ground, moaning, barely alive and bleeding profusely. Annie watched as this elven prince, who had just come to her rescue for a second time, knelt down. He carefully bunched a handful of this now-dying elf's clothing, and gripped his powerful hand into a fist, pulling him up by the neck so that he was almost off the ground.

Moaning, gurgling, and bringing up blood, the Shadow Elf winced as Carric leaned into his face and spoke in a low, even-toned voice.

"Why are you and your filthy comrades here, Shadow fiend?"

The blood-soaked Shadow Elf sneered for a moment before his face slumped in exhaustion, along with the rest of his body. Only Carric's grip was holding him upright now.

"Tell me," Carric insisted. The Shadow Elf responded, breathlessly, spitting blood with every word.

"That... human thing... belongs to... Tathlyn..."

Carric whipped his head back to stare at Annie. She caught his gaze, fiery and impassioned. His focus was intent on everything, as if he could tune into each and every present detail separately, while keeping each of the previous ones in a mental background mirror, never not watchful of his full surroundings. He was like an enormous sparrow hawk, Annie marvelled to herself.

Now, looking back at her, he commanded,

"Run to the safety of the palace. I will take care of this soul-eating oaf. Keep your wits about you, Annie. There are bound to be others. These cowards only ever hunt in packs. I will meet you at the palace, in the throne room. You will be safe there."

Annie wasted no time in protesting his rudely demanding attitude, or who he thought he was to be telling her what to do.

The only thing that matters is that I escape these people... elves...that are chasing me, her inner voice shouted. Wasting no more time, she scrabbled to her feet, silently thankful that she had on her trusty, worn-in Doc Martens instead of the holey sneakers she'd nicked from a fashion boutique three years earlier.

The deep tread of her boots broke up rocks and dust as she set off, scrambling up the bank and running back the way Carric had brought her. Blissfully unaware of the violence that had just occurred at its edge, the palace stood majestic, in all its dazzling, ivory-white glory, cool to the touch despite the two hot suns beating down upon it.

Annie had absolutely no time to stop and acknowledge or admire them.

Without looking back, she ran at an inhuman speed, unaware that her heavy boots never once actually touched the paths of the formal gardens. She screamed to a halt outside one of many courtyards that fringed where the palace met the ground. Panting, she stepped in. It was uninhabited and quiet. She felt she'd put a safe distance between herself and her would be attackers, for now.

Annie stopped to take three long breaths in and three longer breaths out in an attempt to steady her heavy, erratic breathing. She took a moment to look around and assess her surroundings. It was something she had become highly practised at across her eighteen years. So practised, in fact, that it had become her natural default setting for whenever she entered an enclosed space. The courtyard was edged by long stone benches and clearly exhausted, drooping plants. Evidently, this place was taken care of by a gardener who was unable to stem or surmount the difficulties presented by the poor, nutrient-starved soil. Some of the benches had even split from the softening of the soil that was unable to hold the weight of them any longer.

Within a slow blink of her eyes, Annie could see how splendid it had once been. Unlike the formal garden that she had just run through, this was made beautiful through the variety of plants with different leaf shades, shapes and sizes. Trees that were similar to the Japanese maples of the Human Realm, provided a glorious splash of bright burgundy.

But with the opening of her eyes, it was gone.

Even the flagstones the benches lay across were cracked and had, in places, collapsed into the weakened earth foundations.

It was a sorry sight.

As Annie continued to take in her collapsing surroundings, she tried to keep quiet and hidden. She tucked her long blonde hair into her jacket and pulled her hood up over her head, zipping it up so it fit nice and snug. She felt the need to be sleek and stealthy, well aware that she had just run away from danger and was now possibly heading back into danger, albeit of a different sort.

But the prince had told her to run here. He said she would be safe here. He had seemed kind enough, trustworthy enough. And Annie knew that, if she could never trust any one thing again, her acute judgement of character always stood fast — at least in her own world.

Whether it can in this one still remains to be seen, she thought as her sense of imminent threat refused to die down.

Remember, she advised herself. *I'm not in my Human Realm — like I could forget that small detail. Having said that, I'm not completely out of my comfort zone here. I can't rely on anything or anyone, so that's still a constant companion of mine.*

Keeping to the edges of the courtyard, Annie knew that this was not the time to take a stroll through the palace grounds. It was imperative that she wasn't taken by these — what were they called? Shadow Elves? According to Carric, this man, this elf — who had already saved her life not once but twice — the palace was her only source of safety right now.

And right now will just have to do, she thought. Living off her wits wasn't the least bit alien to Annie, even if her current surroundings were.

She took a deep breath, closed her eyes, and pretended she was back in her adopted hometown of Glasgow, and that it was just like every other day she had known. Annie knew how to proficiently sneak into and out of places. Over the years, she had done it a million and one times.

Yes, but this is a palace, her inner voice insisted, reminding her of the difference to her norm.

That's not helping, she retorted to herself. She carefully made her way along the final stretch of courtyard wall and darted through a small, oak like door set into a much larger one.

The vast and ranging building was densely populated with high archways that dripped with ornamentation similar to that of the human Rococo period; something Annie had read about on her many visits to her local library — a haven of quiet from the noisy chaos of home.

Despite the suffering of the realm's natural features, the palace itself maintained a testament to light-flooded, decadence and elegance. There was an exuberant use of curving natural forms and ornamentation. The decor was almost frivolous and playful. The intricate patterns and serpentine design work displayed elaborate and precisely executed detail. A thick gold trim highlighted the curved edges of the ceiling, which was covered in elaborate, asymmetrical artwork, looking down upon the palace's subjects in muted pastel tones.

Annie had no idea where to go once she'd entered these hallways. Each held a large opening out onto further gardens and courtyards, every ten feet or so. It caused light and shadow to cast itself, one right after the other, creating a gentle strobing effect. Annie watched and moved furtively, slipping into the shadows of the archway walls, and darting across the floodlit, open arches in the wall, in the hopes that no one would spot her.

Much like a Shadow Elf would do, she thought wryly. She had no idea if there was, right now, an elven bow and arrow trained upon her or an elven chambermaid, ready to hit her over the head with a bedpan, in defence of the palace. Either way, she instinctively knew that she had to keep going. She had to get to the throne room. She had to get to the king. His son, who was possibly fighting off a potential horde of Shadow Elves, needed help.

The mouthwatering scent of fresh bread told Annie that she must be near the kitchens. Or, it would have been mouthwatering, had Annie's mouth not already been so irretrievably desert-dry from nervous tension. As calm and collected as she remained during her escapades of sneaking around places she shouldn't be, the air of excitement always left her with more adrenaline than she could handle and a terrible case of cottonmouth. She was also finally coming round to the idea that it wasn't merely adrenaline that coursed through her, but something else. Something extra to being human.

What had Carric said? Something about humans with gifts?

She knew for certain that she had gone through a kitchen entrance when she heard many elves chattering amongst themselves to the backing track of them chopping, peeling, and tenderising meat. While it was mainly talk about palace life and their families, Annie heard phrases like, "Fetch me two mixing bowls," and "The king will have my head if these mastas aren't out in time and cooked to absolute perfection!"

So as to remain unnoticed, she kept low and slow, and quiet, as she skulked around another corner, where she could see into the kitchen itself. It was a large room full of stoves and large ovens, with brass pots and pans hanging from low hooks, and piles of fresh fruit and vegetables everywhere. In one corner, a couple of piglike creatures hung, possibly ready to be prepared as the centrepieces of a feast fit for, quite literally, a king.

Bright lights shone above a magnificent white marble slab positioned in the centre of the room. A handful of elves stood gathered around it, all wearing tidy aprons, their other-worldly, or rather, this-worldly, silky hair pulled back into braids and buns. Each of them clearly had a set task as they threw and tossed, and slammed enormous balls of a raw dough-like substance onto the surface of their workspace, kneading it as they went, their deft fingers sprinkling a bit of flour over it every so often.

Annie dipped lower under a bench by the wall. Watching carefully, she saw four elven women, all dressed in long, crisp, pristine aprons. They were clearly making their way out of the kitchen. In perfect synchronicity, they each picked up a large tray, piled high with different-coloured dishes, each emitting a magnificent aroma. They formed a straight line and marched out into the halls beyond the kitchen. Annie decided to follow them, thinking that, most likely, where there was food of this quality, there would be elves with some authority and maybe even the king. Surely there, she would find some degree of safety.

However, she remained cautious and painfully aware that her clothes, and appearance didn't exactly blend in. Unlike the tall willowy maidens she crept along after, Annie was short, attaining five foot four on a "tall day", and dressed in jeans, and dirty combat boots. Catching her reflection in a long mirror, she noticed that her hair was sort of up in the messiest of messy buns.

Well that's just typical, she thought.

She couldn't have been less like the sleek, clean, and shiny appearance of the elves. Thankfully, all four maids were intensely focused upon the job in hand and seemed blissfully ignorant of an addition to their ranks.

Annie followed them into what appeared to be a ballroom. It was cavernous with wall-to-wall sleek marble floors and rich red-curtained walls. The curtains fell in sheets of the deepest crushed velvet against the white stone, and Annie took the opportunity to hide among their generous folds. She soon realised that the elven maids had marched on and she was alone.

Rather than following the maids into the safety of a crowded room, albeit crowded with elves, both the maids and their trays had marched straight through the ballroom and out the other side. As she snuck out from behind her cloak of curtains, Annie listened for footsteps, chatter, clattering, any sort of noise at all. Without the relative protection of the marching maids, she was aware of her heightened vulnerability.

She wondered if she should try to find someone trustworthy-looking to speak to and explain her situation.

Maybe that Finwe or his sister Elva, she thought. *Perhaps Commander Lucan or his side-kick Varis.*

"I've come on orders from your prince," she'd tell them when they confronted her, imagining the group of elves, suspicious and angry at the apparent disappearance of their royal friend. She imagined them picking her up and roughly tossing her into the damp and fusty dungeon that she assumed was somewhere below her feet.

Those feet, that were desperately trying to keep her heavy boots from clunk clunk clunking, and echoing throughout the entire palace as she tiptoed with no real sense of which way she should go. Those same heavy boots led her into yet another chamber. The smell told her that this room was the destination of those prim and proper maids. This room was longer, but far more narrow that the ballroom. It was like the long galleries that were to be found in stately homes of the Human Realm. Such galleries were used by the aristocracy to promenade along when the weather was inclement. A long, powder blue runner rug ran, like a stream, from the door to a large platform area at the far end, upon which there sat two ornately carved, golden and jewel encrusted thrones that were the very definition of opulence. Enormous octagonal chandeliers dripped with multitudes of crystals that reflected and split the light of hundreds of candles, to create indoor rainbows in every direction. More vast, rich red and velvet curtains cascaded to frame huge, diamond-cut windows and every alcove in the walls was occupied by life-size statues of figures that were probably both famous and infamous elves throughout history.

She approached the thrones slowly, as if trying not to wake a sleeping and potentially hungry tiger. Glancing around her, she winced as she noticed the dried mud trail that her boots were leaving behind her on the pale carpet. There was a substantial dining table against one wall, made of a dark oak like wood, that could have seated up to twelve elves. For all its length, it held just one place setting. An elaborately carved and jewel-encrusted chair, that echoed its counterpart thrones, sat before an uneaten plate of food. Deliciously red and plump tomatoes were surrounded by wild rice and grain. In the middle, as if presented like some sort of art installation, was an entire small poultry bird of some sort.

On closer inspection, Annie could see and smell that the food was still hot. Steam curled up from the meat, still juicy and glistening on its gold-trimmed plate.

She knew what this meant.

Whoever was about to tuck into such a meal would be entering the room, soon.

Suddenly incredibly nervous about what kind of reception she would get from someone of an elven royal household, her eyes widened in dread. Annie's blood pressure had taken a sharp upturn at that point. There was nowhere to hide and she felt utterly exposed.

Get out of here, Annie urged herself as she turned to head back up the carpet stream for the door. But, as she turned on her heel, a tall, lavishly-dressed man — *elf, you idiot!* — stood directly in her path.

Chapter Six

They stared at each other in tense silence for what felt to Annie like centuries. The edges of his older, much *much* older eyes drooped where the skin had begun to lose elasticity and sag. They showed absolutely no smile lines or proof of having ever laughed. Instead, signalling some weight of sorrow, there were heavy, dark circles under lurking under them. At least half a dozen lines struck deep across his forehead, as clear as the lines on notebook paper. In the centre of this weary face, were those eyes, which, unlike the rest of his face, remained sharp with a burning intensity. Annie could feel his gaze stinging and burning her while he searched her face. It was as if he remembered her but couldn't place her.

How could that possibly be? She thought. *You can't remember a person that you've never met... can you?*

He spoke first. His voice was calm and even, and deep, but with a razor-sharp, cutting edge. He had a commanding voice that somehow remained soft within their close proximity, and yet still bounced off of the walls in an echo.

"And who are you, maiden?"

Annie found it difficult to reply. Her mouth was still desert-dry and she didn't dare step forward in any sort of friendly greeting or offering of a handshake. There was no mutual respect established here, that was clear. And it didn't look like there ever would be. She had, after all, snuck into this palace and into this throne room, and now she would likely be thrown in a dungeon, left to rot, and forgotten about.

Alone and unloved like always, she thought. And then, with resolve, she thought, *And like always, I've got this.*

Clearing her parched throat, Annie straightened, squared her shoulders, and looked straight at him, unabashed — well, maybe a little abashed.

This is ridiculous! She told herself. *I'm in some other realm — a word I'd never normally utter —, I'm being called a maiden — I mean seriously, me... a maiden? — and I'm royally winding myself up about some imaginary dungeon, which may just be that — imaginary! I've sneaked in and out of plenty of places, and this enormous, beautiful palace, inhabited by actual elves, is essentially, no different.*

In a voice somewhat louder and sharper than she'd intended, she announced, "My name is Annie... Annie Harper. I've come on the orders of Prince Carric."

Now the mood shifted, and the elderly male elf took a step forward, his guard lowering only slightly, but enough to pay attention to Annie's explanation.

"Prince Carric?" he asked, concern briefly flashing over his face. "My son?"

"Your son?" Annie repeated. *I'm such a dummy*, she thought.

It all made sense. This intensely powerful elf was strikingly tall and dressed in silken, artichoke-green robes. His silver hair was in waterfall braids to keep it neatly tucked away and his equally silver beard was trimmed and groomed to a double point. A heavy, jewelled chain was hung around his neck and his fingers sparkled with elaborate rings. He was clearly the only other thing meant to be in that throne room, and he was clearly the only one with the right to be sitting upon the throne.

"Oh," said Annie as it dawned on her. "You're... you're the king."

In a move which she expected would win her some brownie points, she lowered her head in respect. She decided against an attempt at a curtsy that would, knowing her, inevitably go horribly wrong. Annie continued since the king had no intention of filling the conversational void.

"P - Prince Carric saved my life today, twice actually. A ... I'm not sure exactly. A *shadow elf*? A shadow elf sneaked up through the long grass on our blind side, attacked and —"

"Shadow elf assassins in my realm?" hissed the king, lips pressing together in barely suppressed rage. "Again?"

Just then, Finwe burst through the large, heavy doors of the throne room's main entrance and came to the side of the King. Panting and puffing, Finwe bowed in deep respect to the Sun Elven King, even though he was not Finwe's own sovereign.

"Greetings, your fine Majesty," said Finwe with a great flourish of his hand. He face then drop slightly and tried to cover up his alarm, when he saw that Annie was standing right behind the king. "Ah, I... see you have met... what was it, again?"

"Annie," she replied bluntly, slightly annoyed that he'd forgotten her name already.

It's not like you're overrun with humans, she thought.

Finwe nodded hurriedly, as if he was in a rush to brush her off, in favour of tending to more pressing matters. Turning his attention back to the king, he said,

"King Peren, it is always an honour to see you. You may well have already noticed that this Annie is a... a human."

Annie instantly clasped her hands to her ears. Peren's eyebrows very nearly met with his hairline in shock.

He must have thought me to be an ungainly, impudent and unusually short elf, thought Annie.

Before the king could say anything, Finwe pressed on.

"Prince Carric discovered her and, before bringing her to you, he took her to see "The View". I am guessing he took her to demonstrate the extent of the damage that one human can do."

One human? Thought Annie. How can one human do all that? And why would they want to?

King Peren quickly regained his wits. He stormed right up to Annie, towering over her, his hot breath on her face.

She noted that it smelled oddly pleasant, like a freshly lit Turkish delight candle.

Are all elves like this, or just the royal and higher ranked ones? She wondered. Her brief musing was cut short as King Peren spoke harshly right into her face, demanding answers she really didn't have.

"Why have you come here? What is your game and where is my son?"

His voice boomed now, bouncing echoes off the walls that pounded straight back, into Annie's head. She tried not to flinch, but failed.

"Coming here wasn't my choice. I don't have any game and as for your son," she was gaining some courage now, feeling her golden fleck triggering the familiar sparking of fire in the pit of her stomach. "Your son has saved me from a careening horse and a Shadow Elf assassin, and could well be fighting off more of them as I speak. He is the one who told me to run here. To run here to safety."

Although King Peren visibly relaxed a little, Annie could tell by the look he threw at her that he would never, ever trust her. She suspected that the feeling would be mutual. Once again, he stared at her as if somewhere in the depths of his mind, he knew her, but couldn't quite place her. He tilted his head and squinted as if she was a half remembered quote from an old book that he longed to recite. He eyes methodically scanned over her and stopped abruptly at her left wrist. It was around this wrist that she wore her bronze bangle.

Her mother had given the bangle to her on the day she was born, as a keepsake. It was old, very old. Her mother had made up stories of how it had passed along their female line for generations. She had worn it every day since the age of thirteen, when it finally fit her. For Annie, it was the one possession she never took off, never pawned, and had never lost. It was her one prized possession. Was that a flicker of recognition in the king's eyes? King Peren suddenly looked shocked. He swiftly looked away, as if the sight of the bangle had stung him in some way.

"She cannot stay here," he said dismissively, turning away from Annie and confronting Finwe, who did not the least bit shrink away from the King's strong, commanding gaze.

"She came here on the prince's orders, your Majesty," said Finwe, reiterating Annie's explanation, but the king would hear nothing of it.

"While that may be so, I am the king, and I say she cannot, and will not, stay within my palace walls. Return her to her own dicrad realm at once!" he shouted, his voice an inexplicable mix of anger and desperation. His outburst left the large, airy room feeling hot, stuffy, and cramped.

"The king, and also my father," said a confident voice from behind them. "My father who trusts me to put the good of the kingdom before anyone or anything else, yes?"

King Peren's eyes glazed over. He instantly recognised the voice of his youngest, spoilt, and reckless son. He was not at all like the dutiful, selfless, and fine Prince Adran, his first born. Peren chose not to bother facing his son, and only turned his head slightly to reply over his shoulder.

"Carric, the next time you find a human in our realm, who is being hunted by our enemies, perhaps you will not stupidly send her in the direction of your king. Yes?"

Silence held its breath for just a beat before Carric relented and looked a little deflated.

"Yes, Father," he sighed.

Before anything more could be said, others showed up behind the prince, who resumed his more confident stance. Commander Lucan had entered the room with his second in command, Varis, and Elva, the Woodland Elf, right on their heels.

"We heard about the Shadow Elf assassin, Carric," said Lucan, while bowing to his king. "Were there others?"

"None that dared show themselves," said Carric. "I left the carcass of the hapless attacker out beyond the bank, for the wild narmo and huarda to feast upon."

While the others didn't even bat an eyelid, Annie felt a little queasy about the Shadow Elf being left out for the wildlife to dine on.

While Carric and the others continued to discuss the assassin's attack, King Peren moved uncomfortably close to Annie once more. She shifted a step back before clearing her throat, intending to speak up, but the king cut her off before she could get a word out.

"This cannot happen again," he hissed, looking down at her and almost through her. It was as if he was seeing other scenes from another time, playing out before him. "I know who you are. The last human took the heart of one of my sons. You are not going to steal the heart of another, even if he is just my spare."

The last human, again? She thought. While Annie had not one clue what he was talking about, the king's bitter cocktail of anger, fear and venom was painfully palpable.

"How can you know who I am?" Asked Annie, finally finding her voice and possibly foolishly, matching the king's tone. "Nobody is stealing anybody's heart and, although I can't really believe I'm saying this, I can't think of anything better than getting back to my *bloody realm*."

Peren sneered and waved a hand, dismissing her reply.

"You will be taken to the precise spot where you were discovered," Peren continued. "From there you can create your brùkling portal and leave mine and all elven realms... *forever*."

"But I don't know how to create mine or any portals," Annie blurted, a little desperate. "I just kind of stumbled upon it and fell through."

"Typical," he sneered. "It is of no surprise that you are just as ignorant as the last one."

"What is it about this last one?" Annie asked, but was flatly disregarded. "Who was the last —"

Peren swooped in, completely invading her personal space, and abruptly cut her off in a threatening whisper.

"Hush your human mouth."

Moving away and struggling to rearrange his cragged face back to one of complete ambivalence, the king barked out his orders.

"Fetch our ancient Wise One. The rest of you, leave the room immediately and prepare to return this human to her portal."

<><><><><><><><>

The statuesque Wise One entered the throne room and broke what felt like many hours of tense and brooding silence that swirled around both Annie and King Peren. In fact it had only been the equivalent of a small handful of human minutes.

Without the requirement of an invitation, the Wise One glided silently across the room toward them. Her robes, long and dark crimson, swept across the silk thread carpet behind her, trailing after her like a faithful pet snake slithering this way and that. Her long titian hair cascaded down her back in beautifully languid curls, as if untouched by her great age, and her skin was of an equally youthful appearance — as if there was cream pooling beneath the surface, illuminating it from the inside out.

Again, thought Annie, rolling her eyes. *Even an elderly Wise One has to look like she's just stepped out of a Cosmopolitan photo shoot.*

As the Wise One came to face Annie, there was another brief moment of surprise and recognition. She quickly re-composed herself, but Annie had already seen the silent communication.

But how can you recognise me? She thought. *We've never met...have we?* Annie felt like she was once again at risk of losing her grip on reality. To be honest, she was surprised that her encounters with elves hadn't sealed her mental unraveling process earlier.

Knowing and concerned glances passed covertly between the Wise One and King Peren.

"And just look at *this*," announced the king as he snatched Annie's left wrist up high and forcefully shoved it under the Wise One's nose.

Pursing her lips in distaste and calmly pressing Peren's arm downward to replace Annie's wrist by her side, she simply said,

"Yes. I see."

"See what?" Annie demanded. She was getting tired of all this cloak and dagger behaviour. Annie favoured up front honesty, a value that ran straight through her. She'd always found her moments of deceit and stealing at the very least, uncomfortable, and had reconciled them as being acts of necessity.

Ignoring Annie, the Wise One turned to Peren.

"I understand that you have fears about this human," she said.

Fears? He's afraid of me? Annie wondered. *How can I be bringing a king to feel scared?*

Peren began to protest, but with a gracefully raised finger that insisted that the king hear her out, the Wise One went on.

"What of Prince Adran? Surely he needs to know that the —"

"He needs to know nothing at all," snapped the king, visciously. "This human needs to go back from whence she came without Adran ever knowing about it, and she needs to go fast! You are to instruct her as to how, just as you did the last one. Because," he sneered towards Annie, "just like the last one, she has not the slightest clue."

Without any hint of subservience, the Wise One replied, "As is your wish, my king."

The Wise One unhurriedly turned back to Annie.

"Sit with me child and I shall explain how you can create your por —"

Peren's frustration at the Wise One's calm manner boiled over.

"Never mind all this sitting and explaining shéat. The less she knows, the better. Take her to Carric's skor-like gaggle of elves, get her to the very spot where she appeared, and get her gone!"

<><><><><><><><>

With barely a word spoken among them, the Wise One, Lucan, Varis, Finwe, and Elva rode out from the palace in a formation that surrounded Carric. Annie was sat behind him with her arms tightly fastened around his waist. She had declined having her own horse, deciding that horse-womanship wasn't a newly emerging goal, much less a desire, for her.

They were headed back to her point of arrival and were acutely aware that more Shadow Elves could be readying themselves to intercept and prevent their current mission at any moment.

Annie's mind raced with questions that her exchange with King Peren had provoked.

How can this royal elf, or any elf for that matter, claim to know who I am? Did the other human know Peren's son? What happened between them? How did I create the portal? How can I create it again? How can one human cause the elven realms to die? Why would anyone want to cause all this devastation?

The thoughts just wouldn't stop curling around on each other, over, and over, like a nest of newly-hatched snakes.

The Wise One rode on Annie's right-hand side. She felt that this elf knew the answers to the questions that were swirling around in her head, constantly vying for attention.

"I think that you know what's going on with me," she said to the august elf who, unlike any of the rest of the group, rode side saddle with complete composure and easy grace.

Without even looking at Annie, the Wise One replied. "Your thinking is accurate."

"So tell me," Annie implored. "Please help me to understand."

The Wise One slowly and smoothly turned her head to look at Annie. Her eyes unhurriedly searched every detail of Annie's face. Finally, looking straight into Annie's eyes, she radiated a generous amount of compassion that was then overshadowed by a little sadness and an unwilling resignation.

"Regretfully, this I cannot do. The king has forbidden it. While I have the highest autonomy, it does not exceed that of the king."

"But surely," said Annie, desperate to get any kind of foothold on understanding what was going on. "If you have the highest autonomy, yours is right up there with the king and you can decide for yourself to tell me. He doesn't have to know. I certainly won't be telling him. Apparently, very soon, I won't even be here."

There was a flicker of a smile at the corners of the Wise One's lips. "You have razor sharp wits about you Annie. While I would prefer to explain everything to you, the king's wishes — no, demands — must be honoured, whether I like it or agree with it, or not."

The Wise One turned her face back towards the direction they were riding. Annie felt bitterly disappointed. Without thinking, she rested her cheek on Carric's back and found comfort in the rhythmic, nonchalant swaying of the horse's hips as it walked . When Carric spoke, it made her jump and blush profusely at having done something so intimate.

"I am sorry that this is happening to you," he said. "My father has fixed, granite-like views on this matter. In fact," he added with a bitter edge to his voice, "my father has fixed, granite-like views on *every* matter."

Placing his reins into one hand he gently place his free hand on Annie's. To her surprise, she didn't flinch away. Instead, she let his long fingers envelope her hands that were still clasped around his waist. A small, almost shy, warm glow started up in the pit of her stomach. Then her heart sank a little.

Typical, she thought. *I finally find someone that I feel I may begin to trust and I have to spirit myself away through a portal to a different realm, literally worlds away. Just how many barriers to joy can one girl survive?*

"I believe we are almost at the spot, my prince," Lucan called back to Carric.

"Yes," Carric replied, removing his hand from Annie's. "It is just around this next sharp bend."

The company dismounted and let their horses graze freely on whatever scraps of nutritious grass they could find.

The Wise One took Annie's arm gently and led her a little distance away from the group. The bunching up of Annie's sleeve as the Wise One took her arm, revealed the bracelet once more. The Wise One's eyes alighted upon it and her expression shifted again to one of remembering with...

Is that regret? thought Annie.

"I can clearly see that you want to tell me about this," she said, looking intently into the Wise One's face.

"Wanting to and being able to, are two very different things," came the reply in heartfelt tones. Shaking herself out of the thoughts of things remembered and back into the case in hand, the Wise One continued.

"This is the place where you will create the portal and return to your realm. In order to do that you need to —"

The Wise One's explanation was abruptly cut short by an ominous rustling close behind them. Annie whipped her head around and was shocked to see nine more elves emerging from the trees.

They were nine more Shadow Elves.

Chapter Seven

The six males and three females were all clothed, head to toe, in a coarse, ebony fabric. With only parts of their faces and wrists uncovered, there were glimpses of silvery, almost papery skin. Annie would have been mesmerised by the way their skin shone like metal fish scales, had Carric not shouted to alert his comrades. Evidently, Carric had also seen the Shadow Elves and had turned to face off with the two that were closest.

"Back off!" he barked, adding a growl. "Announce yourselves! Are you simply low life degenerates and thieves, or have you been sent by Tathlyn to disrupt our mission? Are you here to assassinate us and try, once more, to take this human?"

One of the Shadow Elves at the head of their diamond formation sneered with disdain.

"We have no obligation to answer your questions, prince."

One of the females, a tall, sinewy elf, stepped forward, brandishing a short sword with a silver hilt that glinted. She pointed it at Annie.

"The human," she hissed through her mask. "Give her to us, now."

Carric guffawed in her face, throwing his head back as he did so. His shoulder-length hair shook against his broad shoulders as they bounced with laughter.

"You can try, you impudent, feeble creature," he replied, thrusting the words impudent and feeble, home. "But I can assure you, your attempts will be thwarted," he added, unsheathing his sword. It also glinted, but with a jewel encrusted hilt, perfectly shaped for his grip, and with a blade that was freshly sharpened.

"Surrender or flee to your dismal realm, you *succum cocotte*," he said with a sneer, pointing the tip of his sword directly at the female Shadow Elf. She smirked at him from beneath hooded eyes. Before she could speak, there was a sharp whistle, and heads turned.

Commander Lucan had come to stand at Carric's shoulder. He smirked devilishly at the group of enemy Shadow Elves. His tone was light, but edged with warning.

"It is a far way to come, from your Shadow Realm to our glorious Sun Elven Realm."

"Glorious, Commander Lucan?" scoffed another Shadow Elf, coming forward from the back of the pack. "It does not seem too glorious around here lately now, does it? Your lands are becoming as barren and thirsty as ours."

"So you know who I am," retorted Lucan, advancing on his enemy one extended stride, in a tacit challenge. The Shadow Elf shrank back a little, but shot an eager, almost hungry look at Annie, who was feeling the beginnings of abject terror. The horror rumbling within her was now echoed by the dark, heavy clouds that rolled in at a pace across the previously clear sky.

What can they possibly want me for? she thought, feeling frantic. *Why are they so intent on capturing me?*

"Go back to your realm or there shall be more trouble than you can handle." said Finwe. "You are outmatched in fighting skill and fighting mind." He now stood at Carric's other shoulder, his chest puffed out in a plain, unequivocal challenge. He looked as if he might spring up at one of them at any moment.

"We are not going anywhere," hissed another female Shadow Elf while locking her glare onto Annie. "Not without the *human*."

"We are here to protect the prince and right now, the prince seems to be protecting the *human*. Therefore, it would seem that we protect the human," Finwe quipped.

Now Varis appeared at Finwe's free shoulder.

"There must be something very important about this human for you to initiate such a blatant attack, so deep within the Sun Elven Realm."

"So we are not going to allow you to have her," Elva chimed in. Her bow was drawn as she appeared at Lucan's free shoulder.

Carric, Lucan, Varis, Finwe, and Elva had formed a lethal elven wall in front of Annie. The Wise One in this moment of stand-off, nimbly sprang onto her horse and galloped back to the palace to raise the alarm.

There was a long moment of strained, silent tension in the air that snapped in less than a blink of an eye.

With a shared, screaming battle cry, the Shadow Elves attacked.

At once, Carric turned to roughly grab Annie by the shoulders and forced her to run over to the horses, who had been faithfully standing by, grazing near a brittle tree. In one swift movement, he hoisted himself and Annie up onto his horse. Had it not all been so terrifying, she would've been in awe of his strength, and enjoyed the feel of his muscles rippling through his arm as it wrapped around her.

The others were locked in combat with the Shadow Elves. Both Lucan and Varis swiftly despatched two of the male Shadow Elves with single, diagonal blows across their chests. Elva mortally wounded another with an arrow through his thigh that split his femoral artery. Within moments, a fatal loss of blood had sealed his fate.

The rest were not so easy to dispatch and they had the advantage of numbers.

Carric reared his horse and landed a blow to a Shadow Elf darting towards them. Dinner plate hooves connected with his head as Carric brought the horse down to trample the elf. Clinging onto Carric, Annie shut her eyes, but couldn't shut out hearing the sickening crack and crunch of the Shadow Elf's skull.

Suddenly, Annie was being viscously yanked down out of the saddle. She screamed and kicked her legs as another two Shadow Elves grappled with her. They brought her to the ground before another of them dragged her off backwards towards the cover of the woods.

Still screaming, Annie watched as Carric swung his sword, fighting off two other elves on the ground. He thrust his blade through the belly of one then sliced the back of the knee of the other before piercing him between the vertebrae in his neck.

Yet more Shadow Elves appeared, emerging from the protection of the trees and shedding their expertly camouflaged cloaks.

Finwe let fly arrow after arrow, each finding its target in the chest or throat of a Shadow Elf. Once out of arrows, he unsheathed his long dagger and sprinted forward.

"The human, Annie!" Carric called to his companions, who immediately began scanning the area for her. "Do not harm her. Rescue her!"

Varis spotted Annie and alerted Finwe with a nod of his head. Finwe had been injured by a Shadow Elf blade and his copper-like skin, now sliced across the arm, seeped a blood that resembled precious liquid metal. Despite his injury, Finwe sprinted after Annie and her captor. He passed Carric and landed blow after blow. He tackled the Shadow Elf who was dragging Annie backwards, taking him down to the ground. As a result of the sheer force of his tackle, Finwe and Annie rolled over, and over until they hit the base of a tree.

"Ow!" Annie grunted, wincing at the force with which she had collided with the tree trunk.

Finwe, similarly winded, now lay on top of her.

"Greetings," he said lifting his head and offering a quirky grin. This salutation didn't at all befit the current situation. As if to underline the behavioural faux pas, he lifted a gloved hand to do a little sheepish wave.

"I'm Finwe, remember? And I do not not quite remember your name, he teased. "You are?"

"*Suffocating!*" Annie gasped, pushing his weight off her. In one swift movement, Finwe rolled onto his back and jumped to his feet in front of Annie, just in time to find yet another Shadow Elf standing before him, wielding a sword that pointed at his chest.

"Hand her over," he demanded. Finwe only smiled and shook his head.

"Absolutely not," he replied, cheerfully.

"Look out!" screamed Annie, but Finwe had already been struck over the head with what looked to Annie like an oversized mallet. A Shadow Elf had dropped silently from a lower branch of the tree hanging just over Finwe's head.

Finwe's body instantly slumped and remained eerily still on the dusty ground. Annie gasped and scrambled for something with which to defend herself — a rock, a stick, anything she could get her hands on. Even a handful of dirt to throw in their eyes would distract her attacker long enough to let her run. But it was too late. The two Shadow Elves who had ambushed them at the base of the tree, grabbed Annie roughly under her armpits and pulled her up to her feet.

The taller of the two pulled Annie close and looked at her directly, as if specifically searching for something. His gaze shifted wildly, precisely scanning her face. After what to Annie felt like an eternity, he smiled a mean smile and shoved her hard into the arms of his comrade. This Shadow Elf caught her and held on tight, digging his nails into her upper arms.

"It is her," the first one said, adding with a sinister sneer, "take the human, Meredith, back to Tathlyn's Tower. King Tathlyn will want to see her, immediately."

<><><><><><><><>

Not again, thought Annie with a small squeak as she felt herself falling once more. Another portal was propelling her at a breath-taking speed, through to yet another realm, but she instinctively knew it wasn't of her making. Once again, there was the rollercoaster loop-de-loop — the steep rising, falling, and somersaulting. Moments of memories sped past and she noticed that this time, they were not her own. Sometimes she was looking down on a scene of Shadow Elves, observing what was going on and listening in. Sometimes she was looking through their eyes, feeling every gruelling second. The memories were occasions of violence, aggression, and fear.

She anticipated the moment where everything dismantled and became their constituent parts. And there it was. The dizziness stopped and the deconstruction started.

The distinct edges and boundaries between objects and surroundings vaporised. Everything became pixelated and reverted to their atomic-level components. It was impossible to tell where one thing ended and another started. Holding her hand in front of her, it once again pixelated.

This time when she hit the ground, it was harder, colder and she landed flat on her back.

It winded her, comletely.

"Okay... that... hurt... a lot," she muttered through gritted teeth as she slowly, one by one, moved each limb to ensure it was still at least vaguely functioning. The Shadow Elves, who had performed a controlled landing, picked Annie up by the arms and shoved her forward.

Turning her head to take in her surroundings, Annie discovered that she was in a tower with dark walls and a dank, musty smell as if wet dirt permeated every cold, damp stone. Looking up, she estimated the tower was at least ten human storeys tall, but it could have been taller, as she couldn't see as far as the ceiling.

Without warning, she was shoved back down onto the floor. The stone floor was shockingly freezing to the touch and shivers shot through her body. Annie's breathing became increasingly erratic when one of the elves knelt down in front of her and tightly grabbed her wrists.

"Please. I'm not Meredith," she whispered, wincing. "I'm Annie. I just want to go home. I don't want to intrude on your world. I won't tell anyone about it. I swear. They wouldn't ever believe me even if I did."

The Shadow Elf merely sneered at her with thin lips that met in a cupid's bow. He silently moved his hand in a circular motion around her wrists. In doing so, he tightly wrapped an invisible rope around them. She could feel her skin being cut, as if she was being tied up with the thinnest twine.

"Ouch! That *really* hurts!" she cried, but the Shadow Elves paid her no heed. Gingerly levering herself up, Annie sat bound and helpless against the inner wall of the tower's chamber.

A single open window allowed her to look up and see outside. It was approximately thirty feet up and there was no other obvious exit, not even a door to run out through. To one side of the chamber was a tall mirror with an ornate black frame covered in eleven figurines in twisted poses of agony. It brought to Annie's mind the tortured souls of Dante's Inferno. It was leaned against the crumbling brick wall that was slick with earlier rainfall that now trickled down through the cracked mortar, feeding the black, dry vines that still clung to the stone by their filigree roots.

A large, padded, and overstuffed throne sat against another wall. It was surrounded by tall and twisted, iron candelabras. Short stacks of books sat on a long, dark walnut table to the left of the throne. The table was covered in frantic elven etchings, carved into the wood, like notes thought up and jotted down by an unsteady mind with an unsteady hand. Annie noticed the shape of what looked like an unusual eye with two pupils, carved in several areas of the table legs.

"Where have you brought me?" demanded Annie, glaring up at them. The Shadow Elves looked at each other and laughed, harshly. Their voices sounded like rusty nails being scratched down a blackboard. It was eerie, the way their skin appeared so delicate and yet everything else about them was so ugly.

"You will never escape, so what does it matter where you are, *human*?" said the taller elf, sneering and revealing his yellowed and jagged teeth. "Only Shadow Elves can jump through portals out of, and into our realm. Unless you have a Shadow Elf with you who is willing to let you tag along, you are three hundred leagues or more away from the Woodland Realm, never mind the Sun Elven Realm. But no one of our kind would help a disgusting, pitiful creature like you, Meredith."

"Like you can call me disgusting," retorted Annie, her fleck thrashing and boosting her bravado. But Annie was puzzled. He'd spoken to her as if he knew her, but he, like her first attacker, knew her by another name. She shifted in her kneeling position.

Who's this Meredith? She thought.

"Wait! Just wait a minute!" she yelled at them as they turned to leave her. "That's not my —"

Slam!

The elves had already left through a large hatch in the floor that had been covered with what looked a lot like a bear skin, except, that is, for its two heads. They had slammed it closed after them and, as they did so, a large, formidable looking padlock magically appeared to seal her in.

She had to get out of this tower. Struggling to her feet, Annie jumped several times to piece together a view of what was out there. A myriad of ancient tree tops occupied the entire expanse of what she could see. Their trunks branches several feet thick and their tortured broad branches twisted this way and that, intertwined and bare.

I... need... to get... out... of... here, she thought as she jumped over and over, frequently losing her balance, due to her hands being tied.

Before she could even devise a plan, she heard a voice and whirled around. A tall, heavyset Shadow Elf stood before her, draped in long, velvet robes of a deep plum. His skin was muted, its shine lost in the shadows of the tower. He stepped forward slowly, almost cautiously. A sinister expression spread across his face, pushing up his sunken cheekbones and pulling his sickening, thin-lipped mouth into an ominous smile.

His long, white hair was draped elegantly over both shoulders and Annie in a brief, and completely inappropriate moment of humour, wondered if conditioner was compulsory in the Elven Realms. Everything about him seemed fragile yet powerful, like most poetry.

Not thinking it was possible, Annie found she was on an even higher alert than usual. She was aware of the water running faster down the walls. The way this elf slunk towards her made Annie's skin and fleck crawl. She shifted from foot to foot, standing square-shouldered and straight-backed, intensely feeling the disadvantage of her bound wrists and small stature. In truth, Annie felt completely nonthreatening and completely vulnerable.

So this was Tathlyn.

He was the high king of the Shadow Elves, loathed and mostly feared throughout the other realms. He was born out of darkness and drew his energy from vast emptiness of the soul, and the life force of others. His voice was as silky as his robes and as smooth as his movements, but as untrustworthy as a serpent. He spoke to Annie in the coolest of tones.

"Despite being dishevelled, you are still as beautiful as the day you left me," he said, his head tilting slightly as he gazed at her with... was that... affection? He looked at her as if he knew her and Annie felt her lip curl up, instinctively.

"Am I?" she replied, flatly. Annie's sense of survival kicked in, hard. She knew that being this "Meredith" person might be the only thing that would keep her alive.

Tathlyn's ardour practically bounced off Annie. He wanted to touch her, to look deeply into her eyes, to lose himself in them for hours, to hold her, to have her. Annie forced herself to remain neutral while every fibre of her being was screaming,

Eww! Now I'm completely freaking out!

Just as swiftly as his ardour had risen, it ebbed away, and a very different, threatening look occupied his face.

"Where is it, Meredith?" He asked, his nose millimetres away from hers. "Where's the amulet?"

Annie shook her head vigorously, her brow furrowing as she answered,

"I don't know what amulet you mean. Is it important?"

Tathlyn's lust and menace were instantly replaced by rage. He took several steps back and swinging his arm, accompanied by a low growl, he pushed some invisible force forward, and tossed Annie into the wall behind her. She hit the rough stonework and crumpled to the ground, wincing in pain.

"Where is the Labradorite Amulet?" he hissed, baring his teeth. Although his voice was still steady and quiet, it cut like a knife against Annie's ears, puncturing what little confidence she had to reason with this insane ruler.

How can he think he knows me? What's this amulet? Who's this Meredith? Her mind was reeling.

Tathlyn persisted, his voice barely above a whisper. In one bound, he swept over to Annie where she lay on the ground, shielding her face. His meanly thin lips were practically touching her cheek as he hissed into her ear.

"I am Tathlyn, the greatest King of the Shadow Elves. I rule the entire land in which you now pathetically lie and snivel. You will tell me what you have done with the amulet, Meredith, or I will be forced to kill you, my love."

Annie's fleck moved in an alarmed and jagged pattern across her eye. She felt an all-too-familiar surge of energy emanating from the pit of her stomach and coursing through her veins. The candlelight flickered increasingly around the room as her fear and anger increased. She was furious and indignant at everyone, and everything.

In his peripheral vision, Tathlyn noticed the candlelight as it bounced from wick to wick, spurting now with flames and burning faster, and faster. Candle wax began to run down the iron candelabras, dripping into puddles on the ground. Far from being fearful, he looked practically nostalgic. He smirked at her with an almost boyish grin. As he opened his mouth to speak again, he was abruptly stopped. His right shoulder was thrown back by a great force and Annie saw that an arrow was now pierced right through him.

Tathlyn roared in complete surprise and pain, and he haplessly grasped at his shoulder. Annie watched, wide-eyed, as he casually choked the only other Shadow Elf in the room. As the dead elf dropped to the ground, Tathlyn's body transformed into a cloud of dense, black smoke, before dissipating entirely in front of her eyes, and the arrow dropped to the ground.

Chapter Eight

Rooted to her current position, Annie whirled her head around in the direction that she thought the arrow had come flying, and instantly came face to face with Finwe. His caramel-brown head of hair had popped up through the frame of the window and he was now peering inside. He made sure it was all clear before signalling down to others who were out of Annie's sight.

"Good evening, princess!" Finwe said with a bright grin. He jumped down from the window and give her a quick, comical bow.

Despite her most recent experiences, Annie's mouth contorted into a lopsided smirk as she struggled to her feet.

"It's daytime, and I'm not a princess," she said in a mock, snarky tone. She was more than ready to get out of her binds and shifted uncomfortably as Finwe climbed through the window, and dropped down into to chamber.

Dusting himself off, he chuckled and looked around before replying,

"Prince Carric said that King Peren agreed that you are in need of rescuing. And so he got the lot of us here to do just that."

Annie's heart swelled a little at hearing this. She had never had anyone show up for her — to have her back. Having always relied primarily on herself, it would have made her tear up in any other circumstance. Right now, however, she was only focused on getting free and away from her current surroundings.

"How did you do that?" She asked. "He turned into... Tathlyn just went... he went poof!" Annie exclaimed.

Finwe chuckled again at Annie's exaggerated and demonstrative movements, limited as they were with her hands bound.

"It was not I that did it to him." he explained. "King Tathlyn did it to himself. Although Tathlyn has no magic within himself to draw upon, he does have skill and mastery of it. He also has a seemingly unlimited source of animals and elves to use in order to achieve such mastery of magic."

"Well that doesn't sound sinister at all," Annie snorted.

"Oh I am afraid that it is very sinister," replied Finwe, not grasping her sarcasm. "It is very sinister indeed."

Hearing a noise behind her, she spun round and looked back to the window.

"It's you," she exclaimed brightly when she saw Prince Carric climbing in. Dropping down, he hurried over to her.

He knelt down in front of Annie and clasped her small hands, which remained bound, in his.

"It is Shadow magic," he said to another Sun Elf, who now stood beside him. Annie remembered him as Commander Lucan, and the elf called Varis was also with him. "You will be all right, but first we must break these dicrad binds."

"There is an archaic Sun Elven incantation that will, most likely, dissolve these," said Lucan, studying Annie's wrists. To her human eyes, her wrists looked free of constraints. However they felt weighed down, as if by heavy chains.

Silently, Lucan removed his gloves and cupped his own hands over Annie's right wrist. Then, nodding to Carric, he waited as he too, removed his gloves and cupped his hands gently around Annie's other wrist. Closing their eyes, Commander Lucan began whispering an incantation in Old Elvish.

While the words were obviously foreign to her, and she couldn't tell where one word ended and another began, Annie could feel their meaning. Slowly, the pressure linking the heels of her hands together was relieved, syllable by syllable, until the enchantment finished. At the very moment that the invisible cuffs broke, Annie pulled her hands apart. With a sigh of relief, she let her tense shoulders slump and then wiggled her fingers as if practicing on an invisible piano. She looked gratefully at them both, her gaze lingering more than a little longer on Prince Carric.

"Thank you," she said. "Now, let's get out of here."

She went over to the window expecting to be given a leg up or some such.

"We will not achieve an exit through our means of entrance," explained Varis, feeling the walls for any hidden exits. "The jump up to the sill on the outside of the wall was far less than the one on this side."

"What about this?" asked Finwe, studying the padlock that had materialised earlier. His copper-skinned fingers ran over the large lock on the trapdoor that took up a sizeable portion of the floor.

"It appears Tathlyn feels he needs to take extra precautions and doesn't completely trust his magical skills when it comes to keeping a human," Prince Carric huffed, not realising the padlock had appeared through the means of magic. "Do you have a weapon that can break it?"

"No," Finwe sighed, furrowing his brow. "And Elva with her lock-picking skills is waiting for us on outside the tower."

Thinking for only a moment, Annie announced,

"Let me take care of it."

She was already kneeling down by the door, fiddling with the lock before she had finished her sentence. Her hair, once up in its messy bun, as per usual, was now falling over one shoulder. She had removed the hairpin that had been almost keeping it in place, and was now gently waggling it inside the lock.

"Hurry," called Elva, who had been keeping watch outside the window and was now unsheathing her weapon in anticipation of an attack. "Finwe, it looks like there are Shadow Elf guards coming."

Leaping onto Tathlyn's throne, Finwe tried to get a good vantage point to look through the window for himself, but it was too high, and all he could see were tree tops. He wished he could place a reassuring hand on his sister's shoulder to let her know he was there, and that he had her back.

"We shall hurry to get the prince, and the human, out of here. Meet us in the woods, just over a league back the way we came."

After much twisting and turning of her hairpin, Annie heard the most satisfying click of a yielding lock. Once the lock was opened, its rusted iron creaking as it unlocked, the group made their way down a spiralling stone staircase beneath the trapdoor. The staircase was walled in by cold stone that oozed and leaked dirty water, emitting a musty, and pungent, mouldy smell. The stairs tightly wrapped around a central column, leading them down and down, and down further still.

Weapons unsheathed, Annie was placed tightly between Carric and Varis, who walked behind his prince and this human, all the while also making sure to watch Lucan's back. He closely took in every movement of his commander, who was at the head of the group. One of many things Commander Lucan could count on from Varis was his diligence and watchfulness. Varis never lost sight of Lucan and vice versa.

With fright loudly knocking on the door of her mind, Annie held her breath the entire way down the stairs. She dared not even whisper as they found their way out, assuming that even one inhale or exhale, or an utterance of words would be picked up by a Shadow Elf, and give the game away. Finally they were confronted by a large, iron-strapped door. Surprisingly, it was unlocked and swung open easily.

"It looks like Tathlyn was overly confident in his ability to keep Annie, after all," snorted Carric.

As they emerged from the damp, dark tower into fresher air, Annie noticed that the differences in lighting were negligible. The Shadow Realm was shrouded in a constant cloud of blue-tinted darkness, like a forever-dusk. But at least the air was cool and crisp.

With Lucan giving a silent signal, the five of them slunk around the circumference of the tower. Three of the elves looked in all directions, while Annie was unsure of what to even look for, or what to do. As if he was reading her mind, she suddenly felt Carric's hand rest comfortably on her elbow, guiding her in sync with his own footsteps, his attention solely on her. They came to an abrupt stop up ahead and Annie heard a brief whispering as she peeked around the group, trying and failing, to get a glimpse of whatever was going on at the front of them.

"What is it?" Carric whispered up to Lucan. Lucan turned back to answer him, cupping a hand over his mouth so as to quiet his voice as much as possible.

"It's Elva," he called in a relieved whisper.

Elva had ignored the instructions from her twin brother, and had been waiting for them at the bottom of the tower, keeping watch. When she saw Finwe, a hugely relieved smile spread across her face. She was a picture of strength, like a viking shield-maiden. Her long, hooded, velvet cloak hid most of her leather armour and an abundance of long, lustrous hair that she kept braided. Her smile beamed so much that it looked like she was holding fireflies behind her teeth. She pulled Finwe into a quick hug, firmly patting him on the back with a bistre-brown, leather-gloved hand.

When Annie caught her eye, Elva cautiously smiled at her and nodded in silent acknowledgement. She, too, had made the promise to rescue Annie, the human woman, under the orders of King Peren.

Chapter Nine

They had walked for what felt like hours in the warm, dry, and endless evening. The eerie wind undulated in a strange yin and yang mixture of hot and cold air. Together, they had stolen away from Tathlyn's towers without alerting any Shadow Elves that were on guard. Now they were making their way deep into a forest unlike any other Annie had seen before.

To gain access into the forest, Lucan and Varis had used their swords to cut down thick, dead vines, that had woven an almost impenetrable tapestry between the tall, brittle trees. The vines were covered in barbed thorns, so the utmost caution in slicing and pushing them aside was required. Dark, brittle barked trees twisted upwards, their frail, sharp-ended branches contorted and reaching outwards in what felt to Annie like sickening pleas for mercy. In contrast, the ground was a pale putty colour and felt soft, and uncomfortably yielding under foot.

Annie started hearing whispers all around her. Whispers of the wind rattling through the dry leaves. Whispers of small creatures scurrying this way and that. Then there were the random, intermittent snaps of branches on the ground, splintered under foot by larger animals that remained invisible to Annie's searching eyes. Occasionally, there was the screaming death throes of an unfortunate prey animal.

These sounds combined with the come-down from her adrenaline surge initiated by her abduction, caused Annie to feel panic rise in her throat. By the time they'd found a half-decent clearing to pause and take stock in, Annie's nerves felt completely shot. Her golden fleck was curled up tight, clenched even. It didn't help that her emotions whipped up the wind causing the trees' branches to bend into increasingly disfigured shapes, and splinter. Several times, one of the group had almost been injured by a falling branch suddenly breaking away from its trunk and falling to the ground with a loud, and hollow *thunk*.

"We — and by that I mean more particularly, the human — need to rest and regroup," Lucan ordered, stiffly.

"The human has a name," bristled Carric. "And from now on, I would like you to use it. She is called Annie."

There was a moment of tension as Lucan stared at Carric, weighing up his response to his prince's request.

"Very well," he agreed, eventually and turned to start making camp for the night. "We have put enough distance between ourselves and the Shadow Elves, for now at least. It will be some time before they realise that their captive has escaped."

At Varis's suggestion, they settled outside a damp, shallow cave that sat at the edge of the clearing. Although the cave was damp, it provided protection from attack on that side of them. It gave them a good vantage point should any Shadow Elves launch an attack on them. Finwe walked in a large arc, creating six small campfires. Every little campfire radiated ample heat and light, crackling as though chuckling with delight.

Silently, Varis pulled a bundle of large, earthy coloured capes from a bag typically meant to hang off a horse's saddle. He laid them out carefully, taking time to thoughtfully move away a few larger rocks sticking up out of the earth before spreading them out and smoothing them flat. Elva walked the perimeter around the entire clearing. She used smouldering herbs and spoke enchantments to seal them off from any unwanted visitors as she went.

Noticing Elva's use of rudimentary magic, Annie decided to accompany her as she progressed around the perimeter.

She may be able to help me to understand my own magic, she thought.

She may be able to help you to control and use your magic, she replied to herself.

"Do you need the smouldering herbs to make your magic work?" Annie asked, tentatively. Elva completed her enchantment before turning to Annie to answer.

"I need the smouldering herbs precisely because it is not my magic," she replied and chuckled lightly at Annie's confused expression. "Rather than there being a magic within me, I have been taught to master the magical properties of everything the natural world has to offer. I am not like you, Annie. You clearly have magic within you, as part of your being. I do not."

"I think you might be right," said Annie, blushing a little, not quite believing how casual the conversation was. Not one to enjoy having the spotlight upon her, she quickly turned the focus of the conversation back onto Elva. "I see that your bag is stuffed with plants and packets."

Elva looked down and patted her large satchel fondly, like an old and very dear friend.

"I always bring a variety of dried plants and seeds with me," she said, adding, with a palpable sadness in her voice, "especially since they are far less likely to be found in our surroundings these days."

Annie tried and failed to think of something uplifting to say, so she remained silent and simply observed as Elva completed sealing off their campsite. Elva looked back at Annie.

"If I do not use too much up here, I may just have enough to see us through the long and testing trip ahead of us."

"Long and testing trip?" Annie exclaimed. "I'm not sure I like the sound of that at all! You got to me so quickly. I just assumed it would be just as quick a journey going back."

Elva vigorously shook her head.

"Oh no," she smiled. "This is just the very beginning. We cannot go back in the same fashion that we came, Annie. No Shadow Elf portal will work for us and we Woodland and Sun Elves cannot create our own. If one does not have the natural ability, it involves the use of dark magic and we are sworn never to use it."

"Unlike the Shadow Elves, I suppose," said Annie with a roll of her eyes.

"Exactly," replied Elva. "No. We shall have to go the old-fashioned way," she added with a generous dollop of resolve.

As always, Annie was curious.

"If you can't make portals, how *did* you get to the tower so fast?" she asked, puzzled.

"Ah," Elva said with a sly smirk, tapping her nose and side-eyeing Annie knowingly. "We 'coerced' a captive Shadow Elf to create one of their portals and hitched a ride. We all volunteered when Carric arrived with instructions from King Peren. The commander almost missed out, poor fellow. He would have missed all this adventure!"

From across the semi-circle they heard Lucan at his favoured position in front of one of the fires. He laughed loudly. Annie didn't think the starchy commander had any emotional range, but there it was.

"He would have liked to be at home, in his feather bed, with his sheets that smell of gentle rain, and a flagon or two of hot Perry Berry mead at his lips, but do not think for one minute that he is not enjoying this," Varis explained, with a silly smile that caused Annie and Elva to burst out laughing together.

In this vast, desiccated land, with its strange weather, that she suspected was of her own making, the peculiar creatures, plants, and elves, of all things, Annie felt a unique sense of camaraderie. It was a new feeling and she confessed to herself that she liked it.

Despite having fallen into another realm, been attacked, been kidnapped, been mistaken for someone else, been chained up, been tossed into a wall, been rescued and been told that this was merely the beginning of the journey back to the Sun Elven Realm and home, Annie still looked forward to what the morning might bring.

Hopefully nothing too dangerous or painful, she thought as she took one of the capes for herself. She decided to huddle up on a small mound of dry grass right outside the cave. The cape was fine, like merino wool and it provided a soft, yielding foundation on which to lay down. It was easily large enough to cover over her too and soon Annie felt blissfully cocooned. Stretching out, with her cape neatly tucked beneath and all around her, she gazed up at the sky. It was shrouded in darkness, as if covered by a thin, netted veil that, nonetheless, allowed the sky's smattering of stars and two moons, to peek through.

She felt content enough to at least try for some sleep. She suddenly felt really tired. She didn't know how many hours it had been since she'd last slept — *Or eaten*, she thought, listening to the sudden, protesting growls of her empty stomach. Time in this realm was confusing her internal clock and the idea of breakfast in the middle of the night started to make Annie's mouth water.

As she was snuggling herself up in her blanket and deciding to dream of being a burrito, in an attempt to quell the hunger pangs, she saw Prince Carric out of the corner of her eye.

"I know it is late, but I come bearing a hot meal," he announced, walking towards her. Burrito Annie shot bolt upright in response. She was so hungry that she was certain the sounds of her stomach growling were audible throughout all the various realms. As Carric approached with two bowls full of something that sent forth coiling tendrils of steam and a delicious scent into the air, she pulled her knees up to her chin, as was her habit. When he sat down close next to her, she could see that the bowls were full of a hearty stew.

"How did you —" she began, carefully taking the bowl offered to her and looking down at its contents.

"I thought you may be hungry, so I turned to Elva," he explained, before she could complete her question. "Elva's ability to conjure something out of almost nothing is quite legendary. There are not many elves like her. Perhaps no other elf like her. She and her brother are Woodland Elves, you see, and in their realm, some, like them, live in giant Taura Alda trees. The trees are hollowed out and carved with wooden steps, and shelves for their possessions, which they share. They all exist in harmony with nature. Elva in particular, has quite the impressive knack for harvesting herbs, berries and suchlike, and concocting a soupy stew as delicious as this."

With that, Carric lifted the bowl to his lips and slurped a loud, and satisfied slurp. Annie chuckled into her own bowl and sipped up some of the soupy stew. It truly was as delicious as advertised. It was a complex mix, with flavours Annie couldn't quite put her taste buds on. It was smoky, like firewood crackling in a hearth and a peppery flavour pattered up and down her tongue. It was pleasant and blended with the sweetness of something reminiscent of a succulent plum.

"I'd like to see these impressive sounding treehouses," said Annie after taking and enjoying, a few more sips.

It was a very welcoming last chapter of an extremely extraordinary day and, as the last drop of stew slid down her throat, warming her insides, a fresh wave of tiredness swept over and engulfed her.

"Many of their treehouses were ransacked," Carric explained. "They were burned and cut down by hordes of opportunist Shadow Elves, once the realms began dying. Many began to scavenge in order to survive. Some even went so far as to break sacred, ancient rules. A Shadow Elf burning a Woodland Elf's forest? Well, there are no words that adequately sum up just how despicable an act that was."

They sat in silence for a while.

Carric had finished his soup in half the time that she had and he was now casually leaning back on his elbows. His empty bowl was balanced across his chest and he gazed up at the cloudy sky. Annie looked over at him and watched the bowl move up and down, lifting, and falling in sync with each breath.

This elf is... intriguing, thought Annie as she watched him. His brash, bold ways were a stark contrast to the gentle touches he placed on her back and the way he wistfully watched the sky, in the same way she always did. Without even trying, this contradictory elf beckoned her to him. Annie was more than a little thrilled and, at the same time, a little scared. Being drawn to someone ran counter to her usual modus operandi.

Learning that many of the homes of Elva and Finwe's people were destroyed made Annie's skin go cold. Without thinking, she felt herself naturally leaning towards Carric. His body heat radiated out to her and gently enveloped her.

"Thank you for bringing the stew to me," she said, lifting her bowl in a gesture of gratitude and smiling coyly at him.

Smiling coyly? she asked herself, amazed at her own reaction. Had her golden fleck had them, it would have raised a quizzical eyebrow. *Well this is new.*

Finding words was something Annie had never struggled with before, but now, around this prince, she fell quiet, unable to think of anything to say to him. And it frustrated her to be so tongue-tied and full of butterflies around a man — or rather — a male elf.

He is simply a man — a male elf, she kept reminding herself, even though Annie knew deep down, that was far from the truth. He was an elven male and a prince at that. He was also an elven male who was demonstrating that he cared for her.

"It is important that all of us keep our strength up," Carric replied with a nod. He sat up, taking his bowl as well as Annie's, lifting it out of her grasp without a second thought. She gasped a little as he lightly touching her fingers as he did so. Again, she felt the need to thank him for taking care of her.

Instead, she found her mind drifting towards this other name, this other person that both Tathlyn and the Shadow Elves were convinced was her.

"He was so sure he knew me, but not actually me. Someone else. Over and over, Tathlyn called me Meredith," she said, mouth twisting in thought as she tried to reason out why and how. "He genuinely thought I was her. He was convinced that I was this Meredith person."

Carric looked surprised. He jumped up with both bowls in one hand and held out his other hand in a gesture that said, *Come with me.*

Without hesitation, Annie rose from her tuft of grass and took his hand. A zing of pleasure swept through her as their fingers connected in a hold. She immediately glanced up at him and saw that he felt it too. She didn't want this moment to ever end, but she knew her information about Meredith was somehow important. She forced her hand to let go and prompted the prince.

"He was convinced that I was Meredith."

"Yes... yes," he said, almost imperceptibly shaking his head to get refocused on the situation in hand. "I am not sure why, but I think that this could be extremely important. Come. Let us see what the others make of it."

Drawing the members of the group to sit in front of one of Finwe's fires, Annie told them of the instances of mistaken identity.

"So, you are sure Tathlyn thought you were this Meredith person?" asked Elva as she ladled out more stew for the bottomless pit that was Finwe.

"Not just Tathlyn." Annie nodded. "The Shadow Elves who took me, and the first one who tried to take me near The View, kept calling me Meredith."

The eyes of her companions lit with excitement, silently urging her to go on.

"Tathlyn seemed to be wracked with mixed emotions about her. There was hate, anger, distress and... and, love, I think. But that doesn't make sense, does it? What's so important about this Meredith? He kept asking me about an amulet."

"Meredith was a human that was here many moons ago" Varis explained, recalling the stories of this female human's betrayal. "He must really believe that you are her." He nodded fervently at this thought, adding, "He must be convinced that you are the human thief that took the sacred Labradorite Amulet from our Sun Elven Realm."

Annie felt inexplicably indignant.

"So, the sacred object that keeps the Sun Elven, Woodland, and Shoreland Realms alive and thriving, that Carric told me about, is the Labradorite Amulet? Well, I can tell you right now, I'm *not* her and I'm *not* a thief." Her golden fleck stabbed at her conscience and she crumpled a little, casting her eyes downwards.

"Well, I *am* a thief," she said in almost a whisper. "I've stolen small things and only when I had no options other than to go hungry or cold. I'd *never* take something that would endanger so many and on such a scale. Never. Never ever."

With one long, bronzed finger, Elva raised Annie's chin to look at her and peered at her directly.

"We believe you, Annie. No one here is saying that you actually are this Meredith, but Tathlyn must have mistaken you for a reason."

Despite Elva's kind words of reassurance, Annie still felt a prickling discomfort about the intense scrutiny she was under. Like palaeontologists examining some recently discovered bones, Carric, Lucan, and Varis were looking at her this way and that, squinting their eyes to scour every detail and contour of her face.

"And anyway," she added with the aplomb of a barrister making a pivotal, unequivocal point on behalf of his client, "I wasn't here many moons ago. I've barely been here five minutes. It couldn't possibly have been me."

Suddenly, while pointing at Annie, Varis gave a triumphant shout.

"There!"

Everyone jumped out of their skin. He continued to point excitedly at Annie.

"Can't you see, Lucan? Right there, at this angle, she is Meredith. Meredith the Thief!"

Annie visibly cringed at this title.

"Why, yes," Lucan exclaimed. "What say you, Carric? Once you see Annie at this angle, you start to see Meredith from every angle!"

Annie was becoming thoroughly irritated about this intense inspection and the accompanying accusation. Elva had just tried to reassure her and now the Sun Elves were falling over themselves to spot her likeness to this Meredith.

"How can you know that I look so much like her? Carric said no one met her. Did you see her? How come you didn't jump to the same conclusion as Tathlyn when you first met me?"

The Sun Elves looked at each other and shook their heads.

"We did not meet her as such," Lucan explained. "We merely caught a glimpse of her as she escaped with the Labradorite Amulet. But once you see it, there is no denying that you and Meredith are the spitting image of one another."

"And," added Varis, a light-bulb moment clearly having been lit in his brain, "for you and Meredith to look so very much as one, I am wondering if you are somehow related."

"I have no knowledge of a relative of mine called Meredith," Annie asserted, but then she lost her conviction. "That is, I've never known any relatives except for my mother, so maybe I have an aunt or cousin who is this Meredith."

"Yes," said Varis, with enthusiasm oozing out of every pore. "Perhaps we can use this to our advantage somehow."

"Maybe Annie can help us to get the Labradorite Amulet," Lucan added, hopping on Varis's train of thought. "After all, she can create a portal between us and the Human Realm."

Without the foggiest of knowing how, Annie thought, wryly.

"And," continued Lucan, "if she is related to Meredith the Thief, perhaps she too could hold the Labradorite Amulet and bring it back to us."

"Yes, yes," enthused Varis, almost dancing a jig now. "If she is of the same blood, that would absolutely be possible."

With a single look from Elva, the two Sun Elves checked their joy and self congratulation at having seen the likeness, and made their connections.

"Only the hand that stole the Labradorite Amulet can bring it back," Elva explained to Annie, in a gentle tone and now performing her own impromptu jig. "It is possible that if you are related to Meredith in some way, you may be able to hold the amulet because of your shared blood. The Wise One will be able to confirm this hypothesis."

"Will you help us, Annie?" Carric asked her. His voice rang clear with sincerity and spoke to the part of Annie that longed to trust. She nodded.

"Yes," she promised. "In any way that I can."

"I believe now would be a good time to get some rest," Elva said in a tone that clearly meant it was an instruction rather than a suggestion. Everyone dutifully did as they had been told. Annie marvelled at the respect that Elva commanded from these other elves. It struck her that, within the group, position in life or vocation had evaporated. Now it was a group of equals where each member brought their strengths and was free to apply them.

She was intrigued to find that she was beginning to feel like a member of the group too, rather than an outsider or simply an asset to be rescued. Being a distant relation to the infamous Meredith meant she had something to 'bring to the table'.

Heading back to her grassy tussock, Annie resumed her study of the stars. To her surprise and pleasure, Carric resumed his position beside her, with a flagon of warm mead to share. Many comfortable moments of silence passed between them. Suddenly, a thought came to her. Propping herself up on one elbow, she turned to Carric.

"Is it blue?"

"Is what blue?" he asked.

"The Labratight Amulet. Is it blue?"

"The Labradorite Amulet," he corrected her. "Why, yes..." he answered, looking at Annie now with growing curiosity.

Eyes growing wide, she smiled in disbelief.

"I think I saw it. In my realm... er, my world, the human world... the Human Realm," she was flapping her hands as she became increasingly tangled in her words. "Whatever. I think I saw it in Glasgow."

Taken aback by such a claim, Carric nearly dropped his flagon and spilled much of his mead in his lap. He was so excited by the prospect of finding the amulet that he didn't seem to notice.

"You saw it? Where exactly? Annie, you must tell me. If we know where it is, we may have a chance to retrieve it!"

"The cemetery, in Glasgow. That's where I came through to this realm. It was the strangest looking thing, it almost looked as if it was —"

"Glowing?" Carric interjected and finishing off her sentence.

Annie sat bolt upright beside him.

"We must tell the others," she said while scrabbling to her feet.

Before she could take off from her spot, Carric circled her forearm with his hand.

"I think we can leave this revelation until tomorrow. For now, we all need rest." Carric gave her his disarming smile. "Come back and lay down beside me."

Suddenly her excitement and immediacy about knowing where the Labradorite Amulet was faded away, and Annie folded back down to the blanket to be beside Carric.

The wind that had whipped up instantly died down to a warm breeze and Annie's fleck curled up as if asleep.

Chapter Ten

The suns rose on a bitterly cold group of elves and one young human woman. Annie's wavy blonde locks, windswept and in need of a thorough wash, covered her face as she slept, wrapped up in her soft woollen cape-cum-blanket. As she slept, her nostrils were triggered by the strong scent of something cooking. It smelled vaguely of citrus and chicory. She was pulled out of sleep by the delightful scents and, when she'd opened her eyes, she saw Elva ahead of her, holding a small iron cooking pot over one of the ever-burning fires.

"Good morning, Annie," Elva greeted her brightly, when she noticed her sitting up. She added with a cheery disposition typical of her twin brother,

"Leech tarts and bark tea?"

Leech tart? Oh my God. Leeches? Eww! Annie forced herself to keep her expression at least moderately neutral.

"Absolutely," she answered, with forced enthusiasm. To be fair, leeches or not, it did smell amazing. After brushing a couple of leaves out of her hair with her fingers, she stood up and looked around their camp. The others were busy gathering supplies. Finwe was sat on a boulder, tying his boots up, his bow slack over his shoulder. Prince Carric was nearby, sharpening his longsword on a stone.

Varis, in his warm and soothing tones, greeted her from where he stood nearby, while drinking a cup of bark tea. Its steam rose and coiled from the rustic metal mug he held in his hands. It enticed Annie into drifting over to where Elva sat with the tea brewing on a second fire close to the first, that held the leech tarts.

"What are they preparing for?" she asked, looking around at Carric, Lucan, and Finwe. Elva handed her a cup of tea and a small, wooden plate that appeared to be a simple disk from an old stump.

"Hunting," Carric called over, grinning at Elva. "I'm sick of all of these greens, berries, and leeches. No offence, Elva."

"None taken, Your Highness," she replied, with a light snort through her narrow nose.

"Can I come with you?" asked Annie, turning to look at Lucan, who was sat on a stump, listening to the conversation.

Carric had stopped what he was doing and looked at Annie quizzically before asking,

"Do you know how to hunt?"

"Well, no," she admitted, biting her lower lip. "But, I've lived by my wits my entire life and I'd like to learn."

She wanted to feel more useful. After watching the way Lucan led, the way Varis and Carric protected, the way Finwe fought, and how Elva kept everyone nourished, attended to their wounds, and kept them in check, Annie was beginning to feel that having a connection with Meredith the Thief wasn't enough of a contribution.

I guess I did unlock the padlock on Tathlyn's trapdoor, she thought. *But having skills with a hairpin pales by comparison.* She was surprised to discover that she desperately wanted to be a part of their group, and if that meant learning to hunt, then so be it.

Carric exchanged glances with the others, who all nodded encouragingly. It was settled, Annie would join them on their morning hunt.

When they were kitted out, Annie having laced her boots all the way up her shins, and Finwe having availed her person of a few skinning daggers, they set out through the forest. As dead as it was, the sounds of animals scampering across the forest floor were still plentiful, and it wasn't long before Annie, Finwe, Lucan, and Carric were all crouched in a small dip in the earth. They were peeking over the lip of the dip, spying on a rather large creature stood several feet ahead of them.

"A moosephant," Finwe whispered, practically salivating.

"A what?" whispered Annie, marvelling at what was before her. The animal's silhouette was squat, with short, thin legs, knobby knees and a large, rotund body. From its face came a trunk that often lifted to touch and stroke the enormous antlers atop its head. Annie stared at it, her breath taken away by the creature's unusual features.

"It's one of the most delectable and tender meats in all the realms," Finwe whispered in response, while licking his lips.

While Finwe manoeuvred to get a better shot, Carric explained to her how to hold a bow. He'd handed her his, and now they stood together. Carric placed his hands firmly upon Annie's which, in turn, gripped the bow. She practised pulling it back without any arrows, laughing quietly to herself as Carric encouraged her, whispering in her ear.

"The tracking is the most important part of the hunt," he told her. "You must be a highly skilled tracker to find a beast as elusive as this one. Focus on feeling the bare earth in your feet, working its way up to the very top of your head."

Annie stood, feet firmly planted in the earth. She couldn't help but think it might be better to take her boots off, but she dared not make too much noise, for fear of scaring this prized animal away.

"Perfect," Carric whispered, and they smirked at each other in silence. Then, a branch snapped ahead. It sounded like a gunshot and made Annie flinch. The moosephant had broken a low, dry branch off the tree it stood next to. It wrapped its trunk around it, nonchalantly tossed it into his mouth and chomped down hard.

Focusing their attention on the creature ahead, Annie watched as Finwe took aim, drew back his bow, and let loose his shot. The arrow flew through the air, spinning and whizzing past trees. It found its target, landing straight and hard in the heart of the moosephant. Slowly, it slumped to the ground. Finwe, and the others lowered their heads in silent respect and thanks for the creature's unwitting sacrifice. Annie followed suit and found the whole event quite moving.

"Now for the messy part," Finwe announced, lowering his bow and heading forward to where the animal lay on the ground, lifeless.

Considering the size of the beast, quick work was made of skinning and carving up the animal. Although it was something none of them revelled in, they were clearly highly skilled. Annie stood keeping watch for any Shadow Elves. Everything had to be taken from the site and leaves were spread over the spilt blood. When they had finished, it looked like nothing had happened.

"In order to keep the Shadow Elves off our trail," Lucan explained, "it is vital that we leave no trace."

When the butchery was completed, they had enough meat to feed them all for that evening and several days more. Everyone took a portion of the beast to carry. The mood of the hunters was up-beat and almost carefree as they made their way back to camp. But it changed in an instant when they walked into the clearing. They saw some of the capes strewn everywhere, each fire was out, and Elva was nowhere to be seen. Immediately dropping his parcel of moosephant meat, Finwe sprinted forward, shouting for his twin sister.

"Elva?" he called. "Elva?"

He faintly heard her in the cave, and ran to her. Holding her by the shoulders, he looked her all over.

"Elva! Are you all right?"

The other hunters had gathered around now, as Elva and Finwe exited the cave, their arms still around each other.

"I'm all right, Fin," she said with a smile. "We fought them off."

"So, then, where is Varis?" demanded Lucan, his eyes frantically scanning the area for his right hand elf.

"Varis is hurt," Elva told him, noticing Lucan's searching gaze. "It is just a slightly sprained ankle. He is in the cave resting with some healing tea."

Lucan nodded solemnly, reaching out and touching Elva gently on the arm in silent thanks before moving past them, and heading into the cave to check on Varis. The rest of them followed Lucan into the cave.

"A posse of Shadow Elves, lackeys of Tathlyn, swooped in on us," Varis explained from his seat on a pile of the remaining capes on the floor.

"They must have breeched the protective seal at its weakest point, where it met the cave," Elva continued. "The Shadow Elf that escaped will get word that we are here. We have to keep moving, and quickly. We must pack everything now and go."

Carric held up is hand to halt the members of the group springing into action. He brought Annie to stand by his side.

"We have agreed that we believe she is a relative of Meredith, the first human to step foot in our realm. The Thief."

Elva looked puzzled. "We have had two humans here before Annie, Your Highness, how is this any different?"

"Annie has agreed to help us restore the realms," he announced.

Everyone looked at Annie in great surprise. Carric continued.

"Annie knows exactly where the Labradorite Amulet is," he answered simply.

This elicited a gasp from Elva, who put her hand to her mouth and looked at Annie in astonishment.

"You have seen it? No one has seen it, not for hundreds of moons. It could be anywhere in Meredith the Thief's realm."

"I mean, I think I saw it," Annie said, before thinking better of it and correcting herself. "No, actually, I'm quite positive I saw it. It was beautiful and mes —"

"Mesmerising," Elva finished, a smile creeping across her face.

<><><><><><><><>

That evening, after walking at a steady yet brisk pace for several more hours, they reached the outskirts of the Shadow Realm forest. Setting up camp flanked by huge boulders slick with vivid green slime, the group devised their plan to enter through Annie's portal and into the Human Realm. They would make their way to the Sun Elven Realm and return to the spot where Annie came through her portal on her first day. Their spirits were high and Annie's hopes of helping the group started to consolidate her sense of belonging, a feeling of importance, and of being able to contribute to something worthwhile, and valuable.

But let's be honest here, she thought. *A small and growing part of me doesn't really want to leave these Elven Realms.*

A main area of concern regarding their plan was exactly how they would each get through Annie's portal. Carric told Annie the commonly shared tale of Meredith and how she had been forced into taking growing numbers of Shadow Elves through her portal and back again, using the principle of trial and error. It had initially worked with taking six elves at a time. The trial with seven proved fatal. The seventh elf was severed from top to toe in an instant.

They decided that Annie would link hands with Carric first, making sure that the king's second-in-line to the throne would safely travel through the portal. He would be followed, hand in hand, by their four companions.

"We are very fortunate that we are five elves in total," Varis commented. "There would have been a mighty row and major falling-outs if we had been more and some had to be left behind."

"Yes," agreed Lucan. "Every elf in the Sun and Woodland Realms would want to be on this mission."

To Annie's surprise, all the talk about the risks of travelling through the portal and the mission to retrieve the Labradorite Amulet, didn't scare her. Rather, she was energised and keen to get on with it. This long journey to get back to the Sun Realm, felt like merely a lame starter before a hearty main course.

She settled down to sleep in her cape burrito. Annie felt Carric silently hunkering down beside her, and she could feel a warmth spread through her emanating from the pit of her stomach.

For the time being at least, everything was hopeful and somehow, right.

Chapter Eleven

Upon waking, Annie's first thought was of the smell of cooking bacon. It was, in fact, pan-fried moosephant. Moments later, she sat hunched on a decaying log with a mug of herbal tea clutched in her cold hands, and a plate of steaming, greasy meat precariously balanced on her knees. Annie let the smell fill the hood of her jacket, which she had pulled around her face, preventing anyone from knowing just how groggy and potentially grouchy she was first thing in the morning.

Carric sat himself close beside her and shared his heavier cape. He draped a corner around her shoulder as they laughed about the differences in hunting boars from the Human Realm versus moosephants from the Elven one — not that Annie really knew anything about hunting boars. She simply described what she had seen in films that were set in mediaeval times.

From her tree stump across the way, Elva watched Carric and Annie from out of the side of her eye, while she sat over the boiling pot of herbal tea she was stirring with a stick.

"You have a look of concern, sister," whispered a disembodied voice, and Elva jumped at the closeness of it. She turned her face and found she was nose to nose with Finwe.

He chuckled.

With a smirk, Elva playfully shoved him away and retorted,

"Get away with you. You will knock the tea over." She then added with a huff, "I am not quite concerned... I am... wary. As should Annie be."

Finwe shrugged as he lifted his moosephant horn mug to his lips that were spread in a wide, wolfish smile. "She is in no danger, El. It is the Prince of the Sun Elven Realm. What could he do?"

"Plenty," flatly answered Elva under her breath and she turned her attention back to the pot of brewing tea. "You see me only as your silly sister, Elva, but you forget that my intuition has never been wrong. I am telling you that the 'beloved sunspot' may well be of royal, Sun Elven blood, but I see a deep vein of darkness in him. He has a selfishness and something else that I cannot quite put my finger on."

Patting her reassuringly on the back before he walked away to help Lucan and Varis pack up camp, Finwe said quietly, "You must mind your own business, my very *silly* sister."

Elva laughed to herself, shaking her head as she took one last lingering and searching glance at Annie, and her prince.

They whispered back and forth now. Carric's head was dipped low with his chin pressed lightly against Annie's cheek as he muttered words that were only for her consumption. They were in their own little bubble where everything was good and all was well.

While Elva's feelings hung heavily over her, she could not deny that there was a pleasant crispness to the air that morning. It was light and freeing, as if gravity wasn't weighing them down quite as much, for just the moment. Elva sensed that it was a gift from nature and gave thanks.

Despite the 'gift from nature', the day's journey was rough. The air grew hotter and thicker as they emerged from the cold darkness of the woods, and travelled for leagues across open, barren desert sand which, to Annie's surprise was a deep purple. In addition to the challenge of travelling so far, their walking was hampered by the sand. It fell away beneath their feet, sucking their boots under, and making them feel as if they were made of lead. Each step taken slipped back a little. All of this slowed their progress and made their journey particularly arduous.

Despite being shrouded in a layer of semi-darkness, the vastness of the desert still had Annie in awe. The horizon and everything it touched was tinted in a cool blue as day fell deeper into night. The farther along they trudged, crossing over sand hills and level plains, the colder they became. With nothing to protect them from the increasingly bitter chill wind, talks of finding somewhere to settle for the night began to chime throughout the group.

"I'm tired, hungry, cold, and have I mentioned tired, and hungry?" said Carric, entirely within the stretch of an enormous yawn.

"There are deep caves here in these deserts," remarked Varis quietly. "Ones that go underground and are said to tunnel under much of the Shadow Realm sands. They maintain a pleasant ambient temperature as they are protected from both the high temperatures of the day and the cold of the night. While they could keep us warm," he warned, "they are not without danger."

"What sort of danger?" asked Annie. She was getting a foreboding sense of, *out of the frying pan into the fire.*

"Well," said Varis in a matter-of-fact tone, "while there are the sand cave Brandr Dragons, who will be hibernating at this time of year and will be no threat to us, there are still the Ravbition Worms." Lucan gave a little shiver of disgust. "Providing we do not create to much vibration," Varis continued, "they will not emerge from deep below to eat us. Then there are the Crystal Caves which, as long as we do not disturb them, will not shatter and slice us to ribbons."

"Dragons," exclaimed Annie, bubbling over with excitement. The mention of dragons and the possibility that they were real had turned her deaf to the strong possibility of death by Ravbition Worms or cave crystals.

Carric laughed.

"The Brandr Dragons are not real dragons. They are large and exceptionally aggressive lizards that you would not want to get into a pinch with."

"Oh," said Annie, unable to disguise her disappointment.

"No," Finwe chimed in, grinning. "The real dragons are much further away, beyond the Shadow Realm, up in the Layaimash Mountains."

If it had possessed hands, Annie's fleck would have slapped one on its forehead — if it had had a forehead. *He's pulling my leg,* she thought. *Of course there aren't any real dragons. It would be too much of a cliché.*

Lucan and Varis exchanged brief, knowing glances before Lucan turned to address the group in his capacity of commander of the Sun Elf Army.

"We will risk it, but you must keep your wits about you," he warned. "Everyone must look out for each other, keep calm, and stay quiet."

Annie was acutely aware that Lucan's instructions around keeping calm and quiet, were particularly pointed at her.

<><><><><><><><>

The caves themselves were easy enough to reach. They were just a league off to the north, hidden against a particularly rocky sandhill, whose jagged edges burst through the sand to create tortured shapes. The opening to the caves was wide, a mouth gaping open, surrounded with huge, black, boulders whose surfaces were smoothed by thousands of moons of harsh sandy winds.

It was pitch black as they walked further and further into the caves. Everyone was slow and deliberate about where they stepped, lest they trip and fall, or worse still, awaken a Ravbition Worm. As the cave narrowed into a tight series of tunnels, Annie felt slightly panicked. She hadn't been inside of a cave before, let alone one that was pitch black, quickly descended, and narrowed, and where one false turn could land you, goodness knows where. It was making her feel slightly claustrophobic.

She began to hyperventilate.

Annie's breathing was quickening at an alarming rate and she could feel each heartbeat pound through her chest. Her fingers were starting to feel numb. The roof of the tunnel started to vibrate, and tiny stone pellets began to rain down upon them. The gritty dust beneath their feet started to whip up into swirling, biting peaks. Behind her, Annie heard Varis's warm and encouraging voice in her ear.

"Slow your breathing," he cooed. "That's right. In through your nose and out through your mouth. It's only a bit farther to go before the cave widens out, my friend."

In the darkness Annie nodded, inhaled slowly through her nose, with stilted intakes of breath and let out a shaky exhale. Varis began to breathe in time with Annie, gradually making each breath much longer and deeper. The swirling dust slowed, the rain of pebbles ceased, and her golden fleck settled at the bottom of her iris. She gave a little jump when she heard Elva's voice at her other shoulder, moving her gently to the front of the group.

"Take control of your powers," she urged. "Use them. It is what they are for."

As she continued the process of deeply and steadily inhaling and exhaling, Annie closed her eyes and, instead of trying to see through the darkness, she felt her way, not through touch, but rather, through 'knowing'. She didn't fight, but rather, allowed a flow of energy from her core to pour through her like a glass of cold water, trickling down her gullet. At first, she was hesitant, tentatively reaching out around her to know which tunnel to take, to know when to bend where the ceiling was particularly low, and to know when something on the floor was presenting a trip hazard. All the while she was connecting with the surfaces around her without having to actually touch a thing. Annie's 'knowing' became increasingly confident and she was able to lead the others quickly through the darkness and series of tunnels.

"There are lights!" exclaimed Finwe eagerly, squinting in the darkness. Even his Woodland Elf eyes and their good night vision had previously failed to break through the thick darkness of the tunnel that Annie was leading them through.

Carric, whose hand was laid on Annie's shoulder all the while, gently squeezed it.

"You are doing well Annie," he whispered, his lips faintly grazing her earlobe. "Keep going."

Finally, the tunnel widened out into a massive cave with high vaulted ceilings. Feeling her magic subside, Annie opened her eyes.

The cavernous space was made of jagged crystals. The lights Finwe had seen were everywhere. In all shapes, sizes and colours the jagged crystals were infused with light that covered the walls and ceilings of the cave. They created a kaleidoscope of patterned light that cast across everything they touched, including the elves and Annie. They stood, jaws agape, in awe at this natural cathedral deep under the purple desert.

"It's so beautiful," whispered Annie. She felt Carric's hand wrap around hers and squeeze gently, as if in silent agreement, his voice temporarily taken by the wonder of their surroundings.

"I had heard of this place," said Varis, adding almost reverently, "but I never imagined it was as breathtakingly stunning as this."

Having soaked in the view before them, the group made their way through the crystal cathedral. The crystals looked as if they had exploded out of the walls at odd angles and thousands of them hung above as stalactites. This place was in such sharp contrast to the Shadow Realm deserts above.

"So you're telling me that we've been trudging across desert," Annie said, her voice oozing awe, "and this marvel was below us the whole time?"

"Not at first, but for part of it, yes," said Lucan, who had plenty of experience leading his elven troops across the realms, with Varis always loyally at his side. "Thankfully, your skills with your magic got us through the dark tunnels and out into this place. This route through here should lead us directly to the Woodland Realm."

Finwe and Elva grinned at each other upon hearing this. Finwe excitedly grabbed his sister's hands and encouraged her to dance with him, but Elva only laughed in his face, and playfully shoved him away. Carric couldn't help but chuckle at their antics, as he gave Annie a hand to help her step up onto a large, chartreuse gemstone sticking out of a chunk of the black rock wall. It glowed gently. Annie could have rock-climbed as she used to in her world. To avoid going home after school, she would head to her local youth centre and blag free sessions of whatever activity was going on. Annie smiled to herself and, despite the disturbing memories surrounding those times, she remembered it fondly.

"Best not to jump and dance," warned Varis. "We do not want to be inviting trouble from the Ravbition Worms."

They all instantly stopped dancing and laughing.

While the others stood stock-still digesting the thought of attack by Ravbition Worms, Varis and Lucan explored the cavern. Looking up at the high ceilings that sparkled with gems, they searched for an area that had the least number of stalactites.

"We'll stay here tonight," Lucan announced, and Varis nodded in agreement.

"It's warm down here, but we must remember to remain quiet so as not to attract any unwelcome visitor, Shadow Elf or creature," Varis instructed.

Carric nodded and, thinking of tossing his large, leather satchel aside, thought the better of it and carefully placed it on the ground.

"Very well," he said and with a charming smile he turned sharply to look at Annie. "Would you like to help me gather materials for a fire or seven?"

Annie smirked at him. Her tummy fluttered, performing little summersaults. She was excited to spend some time with him alone. Nodding, Annie took his hands and let him lift her with ease off the crystal-covered rock she was on, and place her gently, *soundlessly* on the ground.

"What could we possibly use for firewood?" she asked, looking around. The ground didn't hold much, other than sparkling black sand.

Placing a hand on Annie's shoulder, Finwe turned her to look at Elva.

"Some of us are always prepared for virtually anything," he said.

Elva was setting down some kindling dug out from her satchel, along with a small, round jar. She unlatched the lid and took a pinch of white powder.

"Elva, what is that?" Annie asked curiously. Elva smiled under her lashes and answered quietly,

"Naur mál. It helps to ignite fires in the most barren of places. I always keep a little on me. Anyway," she added, casting a glance at Carric, "*some* things around here do not require a catalyst to ignite."

Annie was surprised and embarrassed to find herself blushing.

As the group busied themselves with their different tasks, Annie noticed a slight shift in the air, and became uneasy.

"Carric," she said haltingly, placing a hand on his arm for balance. Carric, alerted, stopped talking about his triumphs in hunting and quickly took her small hand in his.

"Annie?" he said, unsure of the look in her eye, but sensing that it was something important. The golden fleck that was always there glinted and squirmed uneasily. She blinked rapidly a few times, as if getting rid of a loose eyelash, but the fleck became increasingly agitated.

"Sorry," she said finally, attempting to shrug the feeling off. "I just feel.. I think it's going to get dimmer here. Any minute now. I think that's a bad thing."

Carric looked around. Elva had yet to start the fires. On hearing Annie, she slowly stood up and walked over to stand with Finwe, who was staring around the room, concerned. Lucan and Varis followed suit.

Annie was right.

Moments later, the immense space, full of sparkling light, lost its glorious glow. Its myriad of crystals faded, as if running off a weak battery life.

No one moved.

Varis, quiet and concentrating, heard the first crack.

Crack. Cr-ack. Crrr-aack!

Like a train, Varis sprinted at full throttle and hit Annie, wrapping his arms around her hips and launching them both across the cave in an expert body tackle. She and Varis flew, landing hard in the sand. Realising he was crushing her, Varis rolled away so that they lay side by side on their backs. Soft and warm as the sand was, they sat up with a groan, wiping the sparkling black grains from their arms and legs. Where she had stood with Carric just moments before, there was now a twenty-foot, beautifully pale, fuchsia gemstone, its snapped razor-sharp edges sticking up out of the ground.

Annie, panting and wide-eyed, looked over to Carric, who was staggering and clutching his hand. As he leapt back from Varis's quick-thinking launch at Annie, he had sliced open his palm on a jagged champagne-coloured gemstone that was jutting out from the wall. He winced, as his hand seared with pain and gushed blood.

"Are you all right, Annie?" he shouted over the sound of another cracking noise from somewhere above them.

"The gemstones must fall when they lose their light," said Finwe, his worried gaze staring upwards, his hands ready to shield himself at any moment.

"Why would they be losing light?" demanded Carric. "Shéat," he hissed, tearing a strip from the hem of his shirt with his good hand and placing one end in his mouth. He emitted muffled groans between gritted teeth as he wrapped the cloth tightly around his bleeding hand.

"They are not losing light, they are losing power," Elva hissed, mindful of any deadly monster worms. Finwe went tearing across the cavern's clearing to help Annie to her feet.

"We must leave," Elva urged. "The Shadow Elves must know this is our only way out. I think that they are draining the crystals' power."

There were more splintering and cracking sounds now. The whole ceiling appeared to tremor causing all the crystals to jangle and tinkle. Had it not been so deadly, it would have been a pleasing sound.

Lucan growled in frustration, looking to Varis, who placed a firm hand on the commander's shoulder.

"There is time to get out. I believe that the cave is free of crystals about half a league from here and then we emerge *victorious*."

"We will emerge into the Woodland Realm," exhaled Elva in relief.

"Best realm in all the land!" Finwe grinned, pulling Annie to her feet and quickly adding, "No offence, Carric."

"Let us move on before someone gets impaled by one of these damned things, shall we?" he replied grumpily, clutching his injured hand then placing an arm around Annie in a gesture of shielding her from the deadly crystals. Together they started to make their way through the cave to safety. Lucan suddenly held up his hand in a gesture for everyone to stop still and be quiet.

"I can feel something rumbling beneath our feet," he said. Everyone focused on the connection of their feet with the ground.

"I feel it too," said Elva.

"Ravbition Worms!" Varis exclaimed, not caring about the creation of vibrations. With the dropping stalactites, being quiet now seemed a moot point.

The six of them ran.

They were accompanied by the sounds of immense gems, splintering, falling, and crashing to the ground. Suddenly, thirty foot, lime-green, faceless worms started to burst through the black sand. Their gaping mouths, with row upon row of serrated teeth, searched for the sources of vibrations in anticipation of a tasty morsel or two. Many were impaled by falling crystals, shedding their citrus-yellow, acidic blood over the cathedral floor. The blood fizzed and bubbled as it made contact with the black sands. Others were expertly sliced to ribbons by the masterful swordsmanship of Lucan and Varis.

Dodging falling crystals and ascending worms, the group made their way to the natural archway at the far end of the crumbling cathedral. Once everyone had come through the arch, Finwe stepped back into the cave and took aim with an arrow that he had been dipping into Elva's fire starting powder. He waited. Annie couldn't tell what he was waiting for. A rumble at their feet announced the arrival of another Ravbition Worm. This was even bigger than the rest. Finwe waited until the worm's mouth was bearing down on him. He let loose his arrow and it disappeared down the worm's gullet. A split second later the worm's midsection exploded and its body slumped, blocking the arch, and protecting them from any further attack.

Elva chastised him.

"You could have been killed going back in there! How did you know that would work?"

"I did not know," Finwe grinned. "I just thought that your fire powder mixed with the worm's acidic insides, would create an explosion. And it did!"

As one, the others rolled their eyes. But, at the same time they were grateful for Finwe's quick thinking and swift actions.

As they moved on, they heard the sounds of shattering, like glass, echo throughout the tunnels. Although not as magnificent as the cavern that they had just escaped, the tunnels also had crystal stalactites. These too were fading and dropping from the ceiling like the leaves as the year turns into autumn. While they were tiny by comparison with the huge cavern and didn't threaten death, they nevertheless promised injury, as they rained down upon them.

At what should have been the exit, the group were faced with a mountain of the fine, black sand. Its tantalisingly soft and glittery appearance belied how heavy it truly was. The mound blocked the only exit that led up and out of the caverns, and into the Woodland Realm.

Lucan and Varis were at the front of the group, and turned back to face everyone.

"We could dig, but there would not be enough time or hands to out-dig the impact of the Shadow Elves draining all the crystals. Technically, we are still within the Shadow Realm, so Elva's rudimentary skills in ancient incantations would not be sufficient," Lucan admitted, though he did not appear defeated.

Instinctively, Annie knew right away, that the only solution was her. She had begun, in some small way, to harness and control the magic that was naturally a part of her, on a cellular level. Although, she wasn't sure how, she knew, deep down, that she would enable their escape. Her golden fleck turned encouraging summersaults in confirmation.

"Stand aside," she announced, mustering her courage, stepping forward, and placing her hands up towards the intimidating wall of sand.

"I... I don't exactly know how this will happen," *Or even if it will happen*, she thought, "so you should all probably shield your eyes or faces or something... or, better still, shield everything."

Her elven comrades looked taken aback. All having been in positions of power of one sort or another, they were not especially used to being told what to do, never mind being told what to do by a human — even if that human was imbued with natural magic.

Still, looking at each other, they did as she asked, and stepped aside to watch Annie work, or at least try to work her magic, on this bigger challenge. Guiding through blacked-out tunnels was one thing, but tackling this sand mountain was, quite probably, quite another level of challenge.

Annie took a few deep breaths and closed her eyes to focus her feelings. Most of the time her magic had presented itself without being asked and she'd had little-to-no control of it. It had been brought on by such things as her anxious or angry emotions, or her negative feelings of abandonment by her mother and never having a family where she felt loved, and safe. But, standing there, with a group of newly found companions who were ready to protect her at all costs for how she may yet save the dying realms, Annie had no negative feelings to draw upon.

Ignoring her doubts and tapping into the feelings that she did have, she did an internal scan, and discovered that she felt the fresh, tender shoots of companionship, and trust, when she thought of Elva, Varis, Finwe, and Lucan. She dared to admit to herself that she felt excitement, warmth, and more than a little surge of lust when she thought of Carric. She noticed that, rather than being agitated, her golden fleck confidently swished in figures of eight. With these combined positive, warm feelings, she felt her magic surge through her, starting at the pit of her stomach.

This time, it was not frenetic but, rather, a calm energy that collected from her stomach, moved into her spine, and flooded out like a cool wash across her body, reaching out through the tips of her fingers. Annie felt filled up and illuminated with magic. And, to her surprise, she felt she had some semblance of harnessing her magic. She felt pretty much in control. She turned and, with this newfound control, focused on the sand barricade. However, her control lasted only a moment before she couldn't contain it. In an instant, the wall of sand violently exploded into a thick cloud of sparkling black dust that coated the entire group as it settled.

The sand barrier was gone.

Covered in the dust herself, Annie looked around her at her fellow travel companions. Their eyes fluttered and blinked through their sparkly coating. Finwe coughed a couple of times, spraying glittery sand dust in all directions before saying,

"Well, that worked."

"Let's go," commanded Lucan, without even a flicker of acknowledgement of Finwe's quip.

Outside felt like the first time the early morning suns had ever graced their faces. Smiling, Finwe and Elva embraced, with puffs of sand glitter exploding off them as they did so. They were overjoyed to be in their home realm.

According to Elva, the extent of the barrenness in the Woodland Realm had increased. The once lush foliage and dense cornucopia of nature was now left naked and withering, as if trapped in a forever late autumn. Crisp, curled, browning leaves broke and reluctantly let go of their trees. They drifted quietly to the dirt ground below, where emerald-green grass once grew. Now, the woodland floor was only dried mud and rotting moss.

Despite this sorry state of affairs, the air was not still. It continued to hum and thrum with insects and birds who were trying to adapt to their unfamiliar surroundings. The air moved with a gentleness that the group of six companions hadn't felt in days. The suns beamed down, warming their stiff, cold, and bruised bodies. For the first time in a while, Annie felt something like close to normal and she could tell that her companions felt the same.

The urgency to get Annie back to the Sun Elven Realm and through the portal still remained, and so, without resting, they set out once more.

Chapter Twelve

The suns were still bathing the six travellers as they made their way through the Woodland Realm forest, dense with bare trees. It was difficult to trudge through, as the ground was covered in thick layers of rotting leaves, interspersed with boulders of various sizes whose edges were softened by carpets of moss.

"After the Shadow Realm, this is delightful," remarked Annie, kicking up a tuft of crimson and burnt sienna gold leaves, and watching them scatter through the air before settling back down to the sticky earth.

"Hmm... like fiery autumn sludge," Carric grimaced. He was holding Annie's hand and helping her to balance as their boots sank deep into mud with every third step.

"Welcome to my home!" exclaimed Finwe, throwing his arms up into the air in a grand gesture to their surroundings. His sister nudged him with her elbow and he quickly corrected himself, saying, "*Our* home."

"Has your home got any food?" groaned Carric, gripping at his taut stomach to indicate his intense hunger.

"Indeed, Your Highness," Finwe replied with mock obsequiousness. He stopped at a tree and jumped to expertly land, and balance, on one of its lower branches. It groaned and creaked under his weight, but managed to hold fast.

"We once had the finest game and greenery in all the realms. Now, we have only a few dozen flocks of Water Hens and herds of Lúg Elk, that roam the land in search of plant life."

"Many of us in the Woodland Realm," Elva chimed in, "have increased our consumption of insects, that still seem to thrive, as if in an attempt to compensate. But the nutrition in a Lúg Elk steak would take far too many insects to equal."

Finwe pulled a funny, grimacing face.

"And no matter how hungry you are, a Fungulus Beetle will never, ever come close to being as delicious as a Lúg Elk."

At that, he made everyone laugh as he clutched his throat, stuck his tongue out in dramatic disgust, and fell backwards out of the tree. All but Elva gasped in fear of his potential injury, but they needn't have worried. On falling backwards, Finwe flipped his long legs, did a graceful summersault, and deftly landed on the ground without a sound. The others laughed and clapped. For a brief moment, they could forget the peril that themselves and the elven realms were in.

They walked on.

<><><><><><><><>

Listening to Carric, Elva, and Finwe talk about the current conditions of both the Woodland Realm and the Sun Elven Realm, it hit home to Annie, just how much the food sources were growing scarcer every day. The realms were dying, and with them, their wildlife and their population, and all because this wretched amulet had been stolen.

Damn my ancestor!

Annie's thoughts were cut short when she heard Carric groan loudly.

Whirling around at the sounds of distress, Elva immediately marched over to the prince. He was wincing in pain and grasping his hand. His blood had already seeped through the temporary wrap that he had made in the Crystal Caves. Elva removed the dressing slowly and carefully, much to Carric's chagrin.

"It is throbbing like I have been brutally grasped by a Lúkts Gamp," he hissed. When the makeshift bandage fell away, his pain increased tenfold. The cut was jagged and ran deep. But the most concerning thing about it was the stinking black ooze which was separating from his blood like oil from water.

"In Phylin's name, what is *that*?" exclaimed Carric, looking repulsed at the sight of it. He quickly looked away and growled in frustration, angry that he'd been injured, and might be less valuable to the group.

"You must heal it," he insisted. "One injured animal weakens the whole herd."

In her quick-fingered, warm hands, Elva held his large, open hand, palm skywards. She studied the wound carefully before answering.

"It is infected. I think it is Shadow Elven dark magic, from the gemstone that cut you. I believe that I can heal it, but I require a few things."

Without waiting for a response from Carric, she turned to her brother.

"I am going to need Cinnaflower petals and a sprig of Lasyel. Hurry, before it spreads and *kills* him."

"*Kills* me?" Carric blustered, but no one was listening to him.

Finwe nodded to Elva, brow furrowed in determination to save his companion, who happened to be a Sun Elven Realm prince. While he was not *his* prince, Finwe had vowed to protect his group. He found he couldn't be as suspicious of the prince as Elva was. It just wasn't in Finwe's nature. Although, he *could* see the concern about Carric in his sister's eyes.

Annie stepped forward, putting a firm hand on Carric's shoulder.

"I'll go, too. I can help look. I'm good at finding things." She was shocked that Carric could die, but being shocked wasn't going to help him. Taking action could.

They were in agreement. Lucan and Varis would join the hunt for the necessary ingredients. As he knew the forest far better than the commander, it was agreed that Finwe would lead them. Elva would remain with Carric, expunging his wound as best she could until they returned.

Before they set out, Annie gave Carric a brief kiss on the lips, much to his and everyone else's surprise, including herself.

"You'll be fine," she assured him, in a less-than-assuring tone that sounded more like a plea or a prayer. Carric simply nodded. He smiled after her as they left, growing ever smaller as they disappeared farther into the trees.

Annie walked in a synced stride with Finwe — two of hers to one of his — and, in an attempt to take her mind off the danger Carric was in, took the opportunity to bring up the topic of breakfast. She'd noticed that, aside from Carric and Finwe, the other elves had become accustomed to eating less frequently, sometimes not at all. Like Carric, her human stomach was having none of it. It had been consistently and persistently growling for some time.

"What was your favourite food before the amulet was stolen?" she asked conversationally.

Without hesitation, all three elves replied,

"Lúg Elk meat."

"Er, what is a Lúg Elk exactly?" she asked.

She heard Lucan and Varis ahead of them, chuckle. *Will they ever stop being amused by the humans?* Annie wondered. *Probably not,* she shrugged in response.

By means of explanation, Finwe said, "Lúg Elk is the less dangerous cousin of the Lúg."

Annie looked at him with a blank expression. He accompanied his further explanation with exaggerated gestures to the point where Annie thought, *So I'm going to understand what a lúg is through the art of interpretive dance? Seriously!*

"A Lúg is a huge, winged, scaled lizard that has deadly breath when riled, or just when it feels like it."

A light went on in Annie's brain.

"Oh, here we go," she said sarcastically. "I know this one. You mean it's like the *dragons* that are in the Lammash Moutnains."

"The Layaimash Mountains," Finwe gently corrected her, while missing her sarcasm entirely. "And no, just like the sand cave Brandr Dragons, the Lúg are not real dragons. The Lúg projectile vomits acidic spittle. It doesn't breathe fire."

Once again he was moving this way and that, and moving his hands as he continued explaining enthusiastically. Annie had noticed that he seemed to do everything with unbridled enthusiasm.

"Lúg Elk have huge antlers rather than wings and their spittle isn't acidic. It's just disgusting. Their meat is delicious fried with blossoms and herbs straight from the meadow." He stopped moving and looked keenly at Annie. "You seem quite fixated on the prospect of *real* dragons," he continued. "Do you get many real dragons in your world?"

Annie smiled broadly at Finwe. *OK, so now perhaps I'm in on the joke, rather than the butt of it.*

"No," she answered. "Not many."

A brief look of sadness washed across Finwe's face.

"That is a great shame. We used to have many and see them all the time." There was something in Finwe's expression and tone that made Annie think that the elven realms having real dragons, probably wasn't a big joke after all. Her golden fleck began twitching in the hope of Annie getting the chance to see one.

"The real dragons themselves, were greatly sort after, but are never seen these days," Varis explained over his shoulder.

"Because of the dying realms?" Annie asked.

"Ah, no," replied Varis awkwardly, the same flash of sadness now sweeping across his face. "Since the ancient days, way before even Lucan was a youngling, the real dragons were hunted by Shadow Elves and far more so, by royal Sun Elves. The body parts were used by the Shadow Elf king in his dark magic. As for the Sun Elven kings, it was a keen sport for them and their households. The more dragon slaying, the better. The meat from the dragons was completely inedible and their skins were too tough to be of any use. Only the dragon heads were kept and hung as trophies that would be displayed to signify the strength and power of the monarchy."

Even Lucan looked sickened now. Annie, also appalled at animals being killed purely for sporting prowess, looked at Varis expectantly, urging him to go on.

"At the slaughter of their queen, the few remaining dragons, lead by their king, retreated to new lands beyond the Shadow Realm, up in the Layaimash Mountains."

Annie felt a little guilty at having assumed the elves were taking the fun out of her earlier. All four of them fell into a respectful and reflective silence.

"All this chatter of food and dragons must cease," said Lucan, raising his head from his moment of reverie. "And breakfast will have to wait. With every passing moment, Carric is growing weaker, and more pained. If we do not hurry back with the ingredients for Elva, Carric will, most likely, die."

An intense, gnawing pain in her chest made Annie realise just how much she couldn't bear the thought of losing Carric. She was just beginning to dare to care, to dare to love even, and was now being faced with the possibility of losing it all. It hurt. It hurt a lot.

Lucan and Varis began searching the hollows of tree trunks and near the dried-up riverbed. While Finwe had told them exactly where to look for the sturdy Cinnaflower, it no longer grew in such great abundance as it once had. The Woodland Realm literally ached for the return of the plentiful growth of their wonderful, natural remedies to heal their pains, diseases and injuries. The Cinnaflower was a trumpet-shaped flower of violet with a strong blue stem and lime green, veined leaves wrapped around it.

Described to Annie as a small, pink-stemmed flower with bright blue petals, she scoured the earth for the Lasyel. Her eyes methodically scanned the ground in search of the ingredient.

Finwe knew that the Lasyel plant used to be found easily, but only grew sparsely now, between the cracks of the wet bedrock in the near-empty streams, within the forest. He stood in one such stream, which once flowed quickly and easily, running clear with fresh, babbling waters. Now, it sat stagnant and brown, merely trickling over the slick rocks that stuck up out of the mud, made smooth and rounded over centuries of rushing water pressure. Without hesitation, he dove his hands into the pungent mud, scooping it up and away from the rocks. A plant, bravely facing its new, decaying climate, emerged victorious in its determination to grow. Once uprooted, Finwe murmured a whispered Elvish saying of thanks and appreciation for what nature in his realm always provided. Then, he pocketed the plant.

As Annie was just beginning to worry there was not going to be enough Lasyel left in that part of the woods, she suddenly heard a quiet giggle. Although muffled, it was clearly coming from within what looked like a large weeping willow tree on the other side of the stream. It was Finwe who cautioned the stranger, who was intruding on their search, to come out.

"Show yourself!" he demanded, in an unusually serious and commanding tone. Annie was both surprised and impressed.

Slowly, peeking through the long, wide tendrils of the tree, there emerged a small, heart-shaped face. Annie let out a light exhale of relief. It was a young Woodland Elf girl, no older than nine in Annie's human world. Her big brown eyes stared out at Annie in particular curiosity. Annie smiled at her warmly. She looked like a typical little girl, if a bit wild — not unlike Annie had been herself at that age.

"Have you lost your way?" Annie asked, casually pushing her hair behind her ears. The girl nodded solemnly. Then her mouth dropped agape and she gasped in wonder as she spotted Annie's ears.

Round ears.

Human ears.

For a second, Annie couldn't figure out what this young elf found so interesting. But then the girl stepped forward, emerging fully from the shade of the tree and boldly hopped, and skipped across the trickle of a stream to join Annie, and Finwe. She tentatively reached up her hand. Going onto her bare tiptoes, she touched Annie's left ear and then her right, gently rubbing the tops of them between her fingers.

Well, yet again, I'm the odd one out, the wierdo, Annie thought, as she stood there amused by this youngster who was intently inspecting her ears, in this stranger-than-strange world, that she had stumbled into. Annie straightened up and announced to the girl with a playful shrug,

"Yup, I'm a human."

The child gasped and was so excited, and giddy, that she squeezed her fists so tightly to her chest, and her whole body shivered.

"The elders in the village told me about *humans*," she said. "They told all sorts of stories, but I thought they were just tales to frighten younglings with!"

Annie laughed and shook her head. "No, no, I'm real, I promise. And, I'm really not that frightening. Not unless I have to be."

As silly as it would seem to the little girl, Annie wasn't frightened of her, either. She wasn't hastily pulling her hood up over her head to hide her human status or pretending to be like everyone else. She could tell there was no judgement from this youngling. There was only wonderment and awe.

With a shy smile, the young elf reached deep into her a large pocket in the fold of her long, woollen skirt. Very carefully, she pulled out her little fistful and showed that it was full of bright blue flower petals.

"Is this what you were looking for?" she asked, holding them up to Annie in an outstretched palm. The petals slowly sprung open like tightly creased, limp pages of an old book. With a gasp of delight, Annie gestured to Finwe.

"Finwe!" she whispered excitedly. Finwe hurried over, holding open the leather satchel hanging across his chest.

Turning back to the girl, she smiled gratefully.

"Thank you," she said. "This is exactly what we're looking for. Where are you from?"

The little Woodland Elf was looking extremely pleased with herself.

"I am from the village over there," she replied confidently, but looked a little uncertain of where 'over there' was at that moment. Her eyes glanced around the forest, unsure of which identical line of trees to follow next. Annie smiled reassuringly and held out her hand for the girl to take.

"I think we'll be heading through there in a little while. Would you like to come with us while we help our friend? I'm Annie and this is Finwe. What's your name?"

In a loud, proud voice, placing her hands on her hips in a burst of confidence, the young one announced, "I am Lilyfire, Foundling of the Woodland Realm."

Annie's eyebrows raised and she looked back at Finwe, who only chuckled in agreed amusement.

"How very nice to meet you, Lilyfire, Foundling of the Woodland Realm," said Annie, holding her right hand out in a formal greeting.

With a giggle, Lilyfire grabbed on to Annie's hand and shook it with both of hers, while nodding her head vigorously.

"Okay," Annie replied, extracting her hand from Lilyfire's surprisingly tight grip. "Now, we need to go and help our friend."

"And catch a couple cottontails to cook up," added Finwe, his stomach growling in agreement.

At that moment, Lucan and Varis emerged from the trees. Varis waved. In his other hand, he held the limp body of a large bird-looking creature. "We've taken care of it," he announced.

"Wonderful, Varis, wonderful! What a team!" Finwe jumped up, clapped and, were it not for his catlike reflexes, would have fallen directly on his rump. Instead, in one sweeping dance-like maneuver, he caught himself up on his tip-toes, leaped over a fallen tree branch that was sticking up precariously close to his ankle, and ended up leaning against a tree as if it was what he'd meant to do all along. In delight, Lilyfire burst out in fits of laughter and Annie stifled a snort. Finwe, a good sport as always, picked up a dripping hunk of mud from the earth and slung it at

Annie's feet. She shrieked with laughter, jumping out of his line of fire just in time. Lilyfire mimicked her, jumping away and giggling.

"Prince Carric awaits," announced Lucan, abruptly ending the very brief moment of lighthearted play, and Annie immediately felt terrible. Thinking of him in pain, his life possilby ebbing away, she turned to Lucan.

"We'd better hurry back to him," she said, and he nodded curtly.

After Finwe straightened himself and dusted off the shoulders of his leather vest, the expanded group set off in the direction of the impromptu camp. Lilyfire tightly held Annie's hand and began skipping. She didn't stop talking the entire way.

<><><><><><><><>

Elva and Carric were sat together in the small clearing, waiting for their companions to return. Elva was sat back on her heels as she carefully tended to Carric's wound. She unwrapped another blood-soaked bandage from around Carric's hand. It was now visibly pulsating. The toxic black goo, like slick, crude oil, oozed from his hand at a steady rate now. The skin around the cut was a bright, angry red. The redness, threaded through with the ominous black, had spread across his hand and was slowly making its way up his forearm. This was no ordinary cut.

"Ouch, don't touch it!" Carric winced, but Elva yanked his arm forward, firmly holding on to his elbow.

"Hold still or you'll be dripping blood and goo all over your princely trousers," she demanded, clearly annoyed. Narrowing her eyes, Elva placed a clean bandage across his palm and, maybe a little too tightly, began wrapping it around his hand, and up his arm.

"It hurts like dragons' fire!" spat Carric in protest.

With a deal of self-restraint, Elva exhaled the smallest snort of amusement as possible, through her nose. "I can assure you that dragon's fire hurts far worse than that."

The Sun Elven prince and Elva, Young Healer of the Woodland Realm, had never really got on that well. Carric often demanded obedience and blind affection, and perfection. He had grown up as a high-ranking royal and could afford to be that way. However, Elva found him to be wholly uninteresting and egotistical. Still, she made an attempt at goodwill with him for her brother's sake, who had, for reasons Elva couldn't fathom, forged a friendship with Carric.

Elva was also concerned about Annie's wellbeing. Her concern for this young human woman, who she had only just met was surprisingly acute, even to Elva. With the arrival of Annie, she could see how this band of young elven adults was gelling. She could only hope that Carric would respect and cherish Annie's heart. While she had a captive audience with Carric, Elva seized the opportunity to give him a clear warning.

"You've grown close with Annie, have you not?" she asked, already knowing the answer.

Carric raised an eyebrow a little at this and cleared his throat, shifting uncomfortably — and not just because of his hand.

"You know me, Elva," he said, in his most amiable tones that he knew never fooled her. "I'm always hospitable."

"When it suits you Prince Carric," she shot back. "My brother befriends you, like he befriends everyone, but I *see* you. You have your father's vitriol."

"My father —" Carric started to protest.

Elva instantly cut him off, staring into his eyes now with admonition in hers, as she spoke very precisely and concisely.

"You would do well to heed my warning, prince," she said leaning farther towards him. "Annie is an innocent. I have vowed, as have you, to your father, to protect her. I take my vow extremely seriously and as such, I am loyal to the human. In fact, I believe that we are becoming friends. However, I have absolutely *no* loyalty to *anyone* who toys with another's emotions — and I mean *anyone*, prince or no prince."

Carric wrestled with his facial muscles to hold back a sneer, and stay quiet. He eyed Elva, studying her, sizing her up. He could see that she was completely serious and, as he knew, dangerous. Just as he was leaning forward, about to hiss something into her face, their collective elven ears pricked up at the sound of twigs snapping under foot.

As one, they whipped their heads in the direction of the intrusion. Carric had pulled a concealed knife from his boot. Elva had her bow with an arrow already drawn.

"Announce yourself," she demanded, her eyes narrowing. Suddenly, there was another sound and Elva shifted towards this second noise, still holding her stance.

From behind a smooth rock, came a little elven girl. Lilyfire, with her grubby little youngling feet, took as large a step as she could into the clearing. She eyed Elva nervously and looked alarmed at Carric with his short-handled knife. Elva immediately lowered her bow, her shoulders relaxing in relief. Carric returned his knife to down the inside of his boot. Annie and Finwe emerged behind the young elf with Lucan and Varis at their heels.

"Fool!" Elva reprimanded. "I could have killed you!" To underline her frustration, Elva threw her bow to the ground out of anger. Lilyfire giggled nervously at Elva's ferociousness.

"And who is this?" she demanded, pointing at the young elf.

"Why, it's Lilyfire of the Woodland Realm," answered Annie with a cheesy grin, in the hopes of lightening the mood.

"You are becoming more and more like my brother every day, Annie," said Elva flatly, her amber eyes rolling skywards.

"Ah, you mean unbelievably hilarious and undeniably good looking, sister of mine," stated Finwe brightly. He walked over to Carric.

"How is the wound, my friend?"

"Revolting and, despite your sister claiming to the contrary, it hurts like dragon's fire," grimaced Carric, then with a glance at Elva, he corrected himself. "*Almost* like dragon's fire."

Finwe tugged the loop of his satchel up and over his head and handed it to Elva, who quickly emptied the contents directly into a wooden bowl in front of her. She then took the Cinnaflower that Lucan and Varis had found. With a heavy rock that she had found in the clearing, she began to mash both the plants into a wet paste. Elva then turned to Annie and beckoned her over.

Annie was at her side at once, kneeling down with her in front of Carric. Catching his eye, she smiled reassuringly while Elva scooped the paste out of the small bowl and carefully, began spreading a thick layer of it over Carric's open wound. He sucked air in through his teeth, cringing in pain.

"So, I am guessing that probably does hurt like dragon's fire," grinned Finwe. Carric attempted a grin in reply, but the pain was too much and he could only achieve a tight-lipped grimace.

"Annie, it is your turn now," Elva said, holding out her hand for Annie's. Not knowing what Elva meant by 'your turn', she silently gave her hands to her. Elva placed them both to hover just above Carric's wound.

"Now, use your intention," she said.

Use my intention? Annie thought. *What the hell does that mean?* Her golden fleck swished encouragement. *Oh well, in for a penny and all that jazz.*

Annie was surprised that Elva had requested her help. She had been made aware of the incredible healing abilities of one of the Woodland Realm's finest practitioners of first aid. Annie saw the clear yet quiet confidence she had too. Now Elva was showing that confidence in both Annie and in her abilities, to save Carric's life. It was clear that Elva's knowledge of what mother nature had to offer went beyond making herbal teas and healing pastes made of crushed flowers. Elva continued to encourage Annie to focus her 'intention' on healing Carric's wound.

Her golden fleck created a physical jolt within her. *Now get focused on healing Carric*, it said.

Without arguing or really knowing what she was doing, Annie did as she was told.

Suddenly, she felt a sharp pain being gradually pulled through her. It was as if Carric's agony was seeping through her own skin. It travelled across and down her body, finally leaking out through the soles of her feet, and into the ground. She realised her eyes had been closed and wondered for how long. When she opened them she saw Elva smiling at her. She was still holding Annie's hands.

Everyone now leaned in and looked down at Carric's wound. They watched Elva slowly and expertly scrape away the paste she had smeared over it, to reveal... absolutely nothing. There was no deep gaping cut, no oozing blood, no black threading spreading poisonous goo up his forearm. Nothing. There was just the remnant of a thin, white scar to remember it by.

"Beautiful work as ever, dear sister," piped up Finwe, adding, "and your skill with your magic seems to be improving, Annie."

Annie, with a shy smile, replied,

"I think I'm just learning to control it a little more, thanks to Elva."

Elva squeezed Annie hands and looked at her earnestly.

"I could not have saved Carric without you, Annie. It looks like you have learned to gain some control over your magic just in the nick of time for Carric's sake. You are developing skills with your magic for healing." She added with a quirky smile, "You had better not replace me here in my realm."

Laughing, Annie turned to Carric who was rubbing his palm and staring at it from every angle before deciding he was satisfied that he was healed.

"You two have done an outstanding job," he declared. "I believe that healing magic is not easy." For a moment, there was an air of gratitude about Carric, even towards Elva, but it was quickly replaced with his stomach growling across the clearing. It was both loud and demanding.

With another laugh, Annie patted Carric reassuringly on the arm.

"We've brought breakfast, too," she said.

"Now that is music to my ears," replied Carric, his usually ebullient character restored. "If I had not died from the crystal poison in the wound, I would have surely died from hunger!"

Chapter Thirteen

Skipping most of the way, having regained her bearings, Lilyfire was the one to lead the way into the village. Lucan and Varis, like always, walked in step, side by side, chatting with ease about the various ways in which to hunt the lakes for fish and droobtàr — whatever that was. As she skipped along, Lilyfire would hold one finger of Lucan's large hand, much to his awkward surprise and everyone else's amusement. When not doing that, she would run back to the rest of the group, where Annie walked alongside Carric. In this instant, she would slip her hand into Annie's and swing their arms rhythmically to and fro. In the next moment Lilyfire would turn and run up to the front, and grab onto the finger of Lucan's hand again.

She is quite like an eager spaniel, thought Annie, smiling fondly at their new companion, her hand not designated for Lillyfire firmly enveloped in Carric's.

As they followed a winding, narrow dirt path, that wove between the trees, they saw a village. Once within it's outer perimeter, they saw the village square, ahead. It was full of life, its energy apparent in the chattering between younglings playing tag and 'snag the gringlesnap'. They ran between elderly male and female elves who were working together to, what Annie guessed was crocheting, a large blanket, and between different huddles of elves playing cards or some version of pétanque. There was also a buzz of chatter coming from the elves going in and out of an inn on the east side of the marketplace, called The Silkworm. Light from within spilled out onto the street and as the day began to surrender to the darkness, a peaceful, warm glow lightly touched every inch of the village, and its community. These were clearly not the Woodland Elves that lived in the trees like Elva and Finwe.

On Carric's suggestion, the group of comrades opted to head into The Silkworm.

The inn was almost writhing with life and merriment. There were elves singing or dancing, or drinking, and some were doing a combination of two or even all three. A warm, affable glow permeated throughout. The Woodland Elves were the happy-go-luckiest in all the elven realms. The Sun Elven Elves had instantly struggled with even the prospect of the their realm dying. However, the Woodland Elves, while finding it significantly challenging, continued to use every part of what the nature still managed to offer them. They were flexible in their approach and even found joy in the effort it took to get by. Their pelts made of Elora Bears' skin kept them warm and dead tree branches, whittled to create flutelike instruments, created taverns full of merriment across their realm. They had also discovered that even the hitherto-never-entertained crushed, dried leaves of a Moss Mud Ragsnortle plant could be brewed into a surprisingly palatable beer.

It was all a most welcome sight, sound, and smell from the harshness they had been enduring of late. The group of six hurried into the belly of the inn, practically salivating over the idea of a hot meal, several frothy beers, and a warm, comfortable bed. A large fireplace roared and sprawling flames licked at the edges of its soot-covered brick housing. They suddenly realised how tired they were and made a beeline for the empty seats around the hearth. Their hair and robes, made damp by the thick mist of earlier that day, would quickly begin to dry in the toasty atmosphere.

Finwe was the first to plop down into a deep, high-backed sofa by the fire. Almost the very instant that his backside touched the leather of the seat, a gravelly voice, shrill with panic, snapped them all to attention.

"Get off the rug! Get *off* of the rug! You lot are making an absolute *mess!*"

The source of the grating voice was an extremely short, waif of a Woodland Elf — the only short adult elf that Annie had seen. She gripped Finwe's mud-streaked arm with surprisingly strong and bony fingers. Wrenching him away, she pulled him out of his seat and made him stumble off the fur rug and over to where Elva stood. Elva rolled her eyes in sisterly embarrassment. Annie shot him a coy, teasing grin, to which he promptly stuck out his tongue.

With absolute authority, Carric stepped forward.

"I will handle this," he whispered quickly to Annie with a wink. Turning to this short Woodland Elf, who had just nearly pulled his friend's arm out of its socket, he swept his cape back and placed his hands firmly upon his hips. To the surprise of the others, the elf squared up to Carric and pulled herself up to her full four foot, eight inches.

"I am Prince Carric of the Sun Elven Realm," he announced louder than one would need when addressing just one person. The others cringed a little. "My dear innkeeper —"

"I am not the innkeeper, you flopsquib," she interrupted him. "I am the barmaid."

"It matters not," Carric continued, unabashed. "My followers and I would like room and board for the night."

Elva tightly pressed her lips together before tersely muttering under her breath, "Followers? Really?"

Her brother ignored her and instead, watched as the barmaid studied Carric with shrewd, and mildly amused curiosity.

Finally, she walked, in not the least bit of a hurry or impressed by the prince being a prince, to behind the bar. She rummaged around underneath it and, standing on a roughly carved stool so she could see and be seen, popped her head above the bar with one key clutched in her fist.

"This is the last one left," she said in her flat and gravelly voice. "You can use the extra bedding in the closet for a pallet. Now, move along, I am much too busy for all this 'I am a prince' nonsense."

Deciding to completely ignore the rudeness and disbelief of the barmaid, Carric nodded triumphantly, and swept up the key in his large mitt.

"Well," he said, holding it up to the light, "now that we have a room for later, let us find some food right now, shall we?"

The aromas tantalisingly wafting through the kitchen's open door and directly into the bar *did* smell delicious. And

Annie's stomach grumbled loudly at the hint of pot roast with crushed garlic with a generous garnish of rosemary in the air. It was all mixed with the enticing smell of woodsmoke from a cooktop that sat over an open flame atop a pile of logs.

The group made their way back to the seats by the fire and sat down — diligently avoiding the rug. Annie lounged back amid the oh-so-comfortable cushions and looked up to see a somewhat crumbling, lofty roof. From the night sky, the stars twinkled their way through missing tiles and glinted down on the room of near-drunk and totally drunk elves. The froth of their beers sloshed over the sides of tall horn mugs and they laughed, and sang together, tapping their feet along to the band of lutes, yartings, songhorns, and vihuelas that played together in near perfection, each note matching the other in an equally pleasing sound that resonated throughout the inn.

Lilyfire had slipped away in search of her friends and Annie, worried, searched for her. She saw some of herself in Lilyfire and, in the very short space of knowing her, had grown fond of the innocent, waif-like youngling. Annie reflected on just how much she had begun to keep a close eye on the girl. As chaotically hyperactive and as fascinated with Annie being human as she was, Annie was just as fascinated with the elves around her, every single one she had met, not the least of them being Lilyfire.

The crowd was large and lively. Predictably, Lucan and Varis had sat down side by side. They had sighed in unison with great contentment, the both of them relieved to finally, not only sit down, but settled into a safe, warm place with good people, good food, and surprisingly good beer. However, being soldiers through and through, they couldn't help but also keep a protective eye on their prince, who had already beckoned over a different and very comely barmaid, and was now ordering a fifth round of beer, and most of the menu.

"A rack of bambly, my fine woman, and how many gobblefousters do you keep on hand?" he was saying, as Annie was tucking into a warm, crusty roll from the basket on the table, that had been set up before the fire.

Elva, as satisfied with their surroundings as Lucan and Varis, was more than ready to relax. She shoved her brother so firmly that she slid him along the bench. They sat together, but Finwe couldn't stop moving and jiggling in his seat in time with the music. As he stuffed his face with warm bread rolls, he spun in his fingers, a bread knife he'd found on the floor. Without warning, after Elva had so unceremoniously relocated him, he stabbed it into the wood of the tabletop.

"Come on, sister," he said with a big laugh. He looked at Annie, grinning that wide, near-glimmering grin of his. "We have got to celebrate our homecoming, do we not?"

With an amused smirk, Annie shrugged and replied, "You should at least enjoy the evening, I'd say."

"That's the spirit!" Carric chimed in. He turned back to the barmaid, who still stood there taking his order, wholly unamused. Guffawing, he announced, "A round of moss mead for everyone here!"

The patrons of the bar all cheered uproariously, the band played louder, and the merriment increased tenfold.

Suddenly, Lilyfire appeared next to Annie, who was pleasantly surprised to see her and, from her seat, gave her a quick hug around the shoulders.

"Lilyfire. Where did you run off to?" asked Annie.

"I was sampling the warm pastries," she said happily. And before Annie could respond, a young elven woman came into focus behind Lilyfire. The woman was tall and beautiful.

Like all the elves I've seen so far, thought Annie. *As far as I can tell, with the exception of the grumpy barmaid, there really are no uglies here. Not even Tathlyn and his cronies.*

This elf had skin like pure gold and eyes that matched the woods Annie had spent countless hours trudging through to make it to where she now sat with her friends.

"She's an orphan here," the woman said simply, smiling at Annie, who quickly brushed her hair forward, covering her ears so as not to alert any attention to them. As it was, she had already had to firmly catch hold of Lilyfire's hands several times, to prevent her from stroking them. Now, for what felt like the millionth time, she was having to keep Lillyfire from reaching up and exposing her human ears for those around to stare at, and potentially be horrified by. This was the first time Annie realised that Lilyfire had no parents. She thought they were keeping Lilyfire with them on their travels until they came upon her family or she remembered where her home was.

But Lilyfire had only the people at the Inn

"My name is Meara. I am the innkeeper here at The Silkworm. Thank you for guiding Lillyfire back to us. We all look after each other here in the Woodland Realm." Her voice was breathy and calm. "She typically sleeps upstairs in the attic among the sacks of flour, under blankets croqueted by our elders. But she is always running off into the woods.

Sometimes she is away for days and we do worry about her so. Somehow, she always comes back to us a little grubbier, but safe, often with a braggart of breckle for the pot."

That's far more than anyone ever did for me, thought Annie, a little bitterly. Stepping forward, Meara placed a kind hand on Annie's arm and smiled warmly.

"You are most welcome in our realm," she said reverently, and Annie, unsure of what to do, nodded her head, and returned to her a slight, and what she hoped was, a respectful smile.

Annie glanced down now at Lilyfire with some sorrow and much empathy in her eyes. She felt that in another time and place, she, and Lilyfire would have most likely been kin. Increasingly, she could see much of herself in the little elf youngster. She could relate to the struggles she most likely went through every single day, having to find her own bed, her own food, and her own way through life. Rather than having a family to give her a sense of identity, Lilyfire had, in a sense, adopted the inn and the adults within it. Unlike Annie, Lilyfire had been blessed with adults who, despite not being her biological family, had shown her consistent kindness.

Despite having only just met the girl, Annie had a driving instinct in her gut, an urgent wanting from deep within, to protect her. Her thoughts and musings on just *how* she would protect and even nurture Lilyfire, were abruptly hijacked by the knowledge that she was being hunted down by Tathlyn and his Shadow Elves. How could she possibly be of any real use to the likes of Lilyfire when she herself was being preyed upon? And furthermore, how could she protect Lillyfire from something like that?

"We're not staying for long, my group and I," Annie explained to Meara. "My companions and I are headed back to the Sun Elven Realm to…" She faltered and quickly decided to keep things simple. "We're headed back to the Sun Elven Realm on urgent business. Lilyfire has been a delightful distraction from our serious business."

Meara and Annie both smiled warmly, and once they had exchanged thank yous, and well wishes, Lilyfire danced away, around the table and back to Annie. Once she was sat down, Annie wrapped an arm around the girl's small shoulders again and squeezed, making Lilyfire giggle in delight. She, in turn threw her arms around Annie's neck, and Annie felt a sense of warmth, and contentment knowing that at least one lone youngster was safe, at least for now. However, Annie thought that she would always feel a twinge of pain when remembering her own childhood, and the little girl she never really got the chance to be.

Actively brushing this negative feeling off, Annie focused on the large tray of drinks that had been carefully placed down in the centre of their table. Lilyfire's eyes grew large and ravenous when she was presented with a rather large bowl of wild berries and cream, and she poured all of her focus into. It was a little treat that Finwe had thoughtfully requested for her. Everyone else at the table reached for their flagon of moss mead and smiled at one another in anticipation of the most welcomed nectar. Annie could feel the positive glow in the air — the realisation that they'd successfully crossed the Shadow Realm and were embarking on the remainder of their journey through friendly territory. While there was still so much ahead of them to accomplish, this night was for them to enjoy.

The tavern was full of hearty song that drowned out much of the drunken chatter and many stood up for yet another dance. Annie looked around her, chuckling at how lively the Woodland Elves could be, even when they were surrounded by decay and death in their own realm.

The cumly barmaid almost sloshed a large jug full of mead all over Annie's head, as an elvish couple slipped past her, intent on getting to the dance floor. Hand in hand they hurried to join the circle of dancers. Annie was watching them go with a broad smile on her face, when she realised Finwe was speaking to her.

"Come and dance, Annie!" he shouted, his face dominated by his usual, huge smile. Infected by the good mood that saturated the room, Annie smiled, nodded, and jumped up with him. She had no idea what she would have to do and she knew it really didn't matter. They moved to the middle of the floor. She saw that there was no formal series of moves in this dance. What seemed to matter was that, when you moved, you moved with joy.

The local patrons began stomping and clapping in unison as Finwe did a sort of tap dance. He moved incredibly lightly, as if he were dancing across clouds. Everyone stepped in time to the yartings, songhorns, and vihuelas. Annie laughed in delight. As she twirled herself in tight circles, first one way and then the other, she was caught by the hands of Carric, who deftly guided her into his sphere. He smiled easily at her, spinning her out before pulling her back in, close to him.

Really close.

Annie gasped at the speed he spun her and let out an exhilarated laugh. They locked eyes. His deep hazels connecting with her blues, the small, golden fleck in her eye twinkling in the candlelight from around the room.

With a coy smile, she took the pin from her hair, letting it fall in loose waves around her shoulders and down her back. She had never felt such freedom to simply embrace and dwell in joy. Still with their eyes locked, she stepped back, shrugged her old, cracked leather jacket down off her shoulders, and tossed it aside to Elva, who caught it in one hand, and rolled her eyes.

Annie stepped up to Carric, who pulled her back in to him. They moved closely in unison. Carric effortlessly lifted her off the ground, holding her high and close. Everyone began cheering. The room was bursting with jubilation.

A feeling of exhilaration came over her. Her golden fleck performed rhythmic figures of eight, languishing in delight. Annie laughed and danced without care or worry for any of the realms. In that moment, with Carric, she felt completely safe and even maybe treasured. For the first time in her eighteen years, she really felt she was a part of a real family. A family forged in friendship rather than bloodlines. She even dared to admit to herself that she may also be loved by this particular elf.

No, that's just ridiculous! she chided herself. *This isn't some dumb fairytale where the lowly maiden wins the heart of the prince — and an elven one to boot.*

Isn't it though? she parried herself. *Perhaps that's exactly what's going on here. I'm not some hapless female who can't make it by on my own. I've proved that already. But there was my birthday wish to —*

She cut herself off, quickly and firmly deciding that this was no time to be overthinking things. This was a moment of merriment and there was much of it to be enjoyed.

When even more elven folk took to the dance floor, Annie danced her way through the crowd. She shifted around, in between, and in, and out of bodies, until she exploded out of the ebbing, and flowing sea of dancers, gasping for a breath of fresh, cool air. The fresh, cool air hit her like fiercest of air conditioning. She briefly thought back to the hottest summers in the Human Realm, where she would seek some relief from the stifling heat by ambling around the supermarkets with their second-to-none air conditioning. She used to smile to herself at the shoppers in their skimpy tops, who would come inside and put on a fleece to survive the cold of such places.

Annie stood there, outside the tavern, under the inky cloak of the night. The blinking stars speckled the sky, like rhinestones sewn into the cloak, and a few swaying lanterns, hung brightly from long poles along the dirt road, leading around the outskirts of the village. Following this trail of lanterns took Annie on a short walk up a steep hill which led to a barn. Exhilarated, full of energy, and enjoying this new feeling of not having a care in the various realms, Annie jumped straight into a pile of hay that was neatly stacked against one inner wall. It was no where near as soft as she had imagined. With a groan and a laugh at herself, she turned over. With hay sticking out of her loose, tangled hair, she jumped out of her skinn as she met the intensely bright gaze of Carric.

He stood nonchalantly, with a shoulder leaned against the wooden door frame. He wore a cocked, half-smile on his face as he watched her with curiosity.

"I see you have made your way up to the horses' barn," he said, teasing her. "Did you fancy your chances at another ride on the back of a stallion?"

Sitting up, Annie giggled, blushed at the innuendo, and did a half hiccough, half belch.

That'll be the moss mead then, she thought. *Very attractive, I'm sure. Contrary to popular belief, it seems that some things are better in than out!*

"Not in the slightest," she retorted, and couldn't believe her own boldness as she patted a patch of hay next to her, beckoning Carric to come sit down. Without a moment's hesitation, he did so. He almost glided over in a manner that made Annie's heart beat quicken. Flopping down into the hay with a soft chuckle, Carric and Annie's eyes met once again.

"So, how's your hand?" Annie asked Carric, a little frantic to find something to say to fill the silence that was fast becoming awkward. She smirked at him nervously, trying to play it cool and failing. He didn't answer. He didn't need to.

Their gazing at each other carried on. Carric smirked back at her for what felt like a millennium before she broke away and turned her attention instead to the stars that she could see through gaping holes in the barn's roof.

Everything around them was wilted and dying, the trees were drooping sadly and the earthen floor was thick with dust to the touch. The feeble sprouts of grass only grew around the few trickling brooks to be found throughout the realms. And yet, the sky was crystal clear almost every night and was always full of dazzling stars, untouched by the loss of the Labradorite Amulet. The air remained cool and crisp, creating a breeze that ruffled Carric's hair. It brushed his sandy locks away from his face, intermittently allowing a few locks to fall against his cheek and outline his sculpted jaw.

"My mother would look at the stars with me," Annie announced suddenly, eyes still fixated on the glittering sky above. She was too afraid to look at Carric. She felt that if she were to look in his eyes any more, she would never ever want to look away. Inhaling sharply, she continued.

"When I was a little girl, she'd wake me in the middle of the night and we'd take a large, scratchy blanket outside. We'd lay in our tiny garden together, looking at the stars and finding the constellations. She'd tell me that the stars were the same in every realm... I always thought she just meant around the world, but now, I think... I don't know... maybe... maybe she knew more than she was letting on."

As her voice petered out, Carric turned to look at her and saw in her eyes, the small, subtle golden fleck glittering brightly now behind her welling tears.

Slowly, he propped himself up on his elbow and gently reached for her hand. She silently let him take hers into his own. Her tears slowly trickled and fell onto his fingers. His huge, warm hand enveloped hers entirely and when she looked back up, he was gazing into her eyes more intensely than before. It was as if he was searching them for something.

"Annie" he murmured, softly and her heart skipped a beat. His gaze drifted from her eyes, downwards to her lips and back up again. "You have the most beautiful eyes in which I have ever been lost."

Without another word between them, their lips touched, tentatively at first, searching and exploring. This then served to open the emotional flood gates that had been held so tightly shut within Annie. Their kisses became increasingly intense, ebbing and flowing like a wave against its shore, rumbling, rolling, and roaring in a sea storm. Annie felt his arm wrap around her and she clung onto him, giddy from this never-before-felt, rush of passion. She'd never felt more safe, more wanted, more loved, or more desired. The longer she was in this elven world, day by day, Annie felt more confident in her abilities, and even more like she truly belonged. For the first time, she was starting to feel accepted. Looking back on her life in the Human Realm, she recalled always feeling incredibly alone and like a square peg trying and failing, to fit into a round hole. Maybe the elven realm was where she could fit in. Maybe this was her place.

Maybe Carric was her person.

Forgetting all about the dying realms and the pursuit by Tathlyn's Shadow Elves, they spent the night together in the barn and Annie finally fell asleep contented, in Carric's arms.

Chapter Fourteen

Ribbons of a delicate and rosy pink teasingly rippled across her mouth, kissing soft lips as they entwined. They coiled their way down across her stomach, and around her thighs. They fluttered against her bare skin, snaking around her ankles and reaching up to brush against the curve of her breast that was so very hot to the touch.

And right before it slipped around her neck, aching to wrap around and squeeze to the rhythm of her breathing, it released, and the ribbons fell, leaving blush-red traces of desire where it had tightened against her supple flesh.

From above, she saw herself lying there in tall grass. Swooping lower, Annie saw sheer bliss in her eyes and the glint of her golden fleck as she blinked up into the bright suns.

"If Elva was here, right now," Varis whispered very softly, his head tilted ever-so-slightly towards Lucan, still side-eyeing the couple sprawled in the hay, "she would most likely reopen that wound of his and create a few new, and possibly much deeper ones."

Shocked out of her sensual dream by Varis's voice, Annie sat bolt upright with a jolt and frantically wrestled to gather her clothes to cover her modesty.

Hell's teeth, she shouted wryly at herself, in her own head. *It's a bit late for that!*

She felt the familiar buzz rush through her, like a head rush that exhilarates and vibrates every nerve before either turning in on oneself, or blasting outwards. She couldn't tell if it was her magic or the complete and utter embarrassment that was now crashing down on her.

Nausea engulfed her.

Snorting a hot breath of amused air through his nose at Varis's comment, Lucan reassured Annie, unfolding his arms and putting his palms out in a stopping gesture. His body language expressed truthfulness, but his facial expression remained hugely amused at the situation.

"Fear not. We will not tell her," he smiled, exchanging a rather secretive look with Varis, who said nothing and simply smiled back, knowingly.

"Right... right," said Annie awkwardly, scrambling to her feet and trying to navigate her way into her clothing while at least leaving something to the imagination. She kicked at Carric's foot as she had got up. Irritably, she was questioning how he did not wake up this entire time. Carric finally did awaken and sat up with a start, unleashing the concealed dagger he always kept in his boot, and brandishing it at no one in particular.

Swiftly leaning out of reach of his knife arm, Annie gingerly pushed his hand and the dagger down. Clearly confused, Carric shook his head to become fully awake before looking at the three who stood before him. Realising they were of no threat to him, he held the dagger in a looser grip without so much as an apology for nearly stabbing one of them.

"Ah," he said, seemingly utterly unfazed. "Good morning to you both. I would say that hay is quite good for a bed. They should stuff mattresses with it." He laughed loudly and croakily as his throat also struggled to wake. He'd made a brilliant joke, at least, in his own mind. No one else laughed and he seemed not to notice. Brushing himself off and casually, almost languidly, shrugging on his clothes, Carric stood, sheathed his knife back into his boot, and placed his hands on his hips before asking,

"Breakfast, anyone?"

<><><><><><><><>

The bar couldn't have been more of an antithesis to the night before. It was like a ghost town. Various patrons slept, slumped over their chairs and tables, snoring into their empty drinks, and bowls of congealed meat stew that was last night's dinner. There was no band playing merry music. The snoring, snuffling, groaning, and farting of those present was the only accompaniment. As customers began to stir, barmaids unceremoniously pushed them out of chairs, scolding them and spitting to 'clean' where they had lain drooling, only moments before.

Annie sat at a long wooden table, slouching over it and feeling the effects of the previous night's merriment, and pleasure. Lucan and Varis appeared superbly wide awake, and utterly relaxed in each other's company, without headaches or nausea to show for their copious drinking. Annie envied them.

Carric, who seemed similarly untouched by drink, or even by the few moments of sleep he and Annie had snatched across the night, waved over a barmaid who held a large, metal pot of turut tea. He told her in the least words possible to leave it on the table. Brushing Annie's arm tenderly, he reached for the pot and her teacup, pouring her a cup first. Gratefully, she reached for it and took a small sip. She enjoyed the burn of it going down her throat and the way that it both warmed, and reinvigorated her from the inside out.

To her left, Finwe had appeared as if out of thin air. Expertly, he spun a chair on its wooden legs to face backwards and plopped down astride it in one fluid movement. He placed his elbows over the back and rocked it from side to side until he finished on one of its legs, in a precarious balance. Moments later, Elva ruined his antics when she lightly pushed him, forcing him to sit down with all six legs flat on the floor again.

Annie studied her Woodland comrades. Like Carric, Lucan, and Varis, neither looked the least bit worse for wear from the previous evening's drinking. Finwe looked spritely and awake while Elva was relaxed, and graceful. She sat with her back straight, pouring herself a mug of tea and blew on it for a moment before bringing it to her lips. She moved as if she were a goddess sipping from a chalice. Annie mused at how Elva looked elegant, mysterious, and seemingly harmless until you caught a glimpse of the curved dagger she always kept menacingly sheathed at her side.

The only other slightly groggy one of the group, beside herself, was Lilyfire. But the little one's grogginess was not to be blamed on drink. She had been up with the adults until almost two in the morning — way past her bedtime, according to Meara. Elva had draped a fur-embellished blanket over Lilyfire where she had fallen asleep in the corner of the room, long passed out from too many sweets and far too much dancing. She had pouted as only a youngster can, when Lucan had firmly, yet kindly said no to her tagging along with them on the remainder of their journey. He had explained that their mission to get back to the portal and retrieve the amulet was far too important to have a youngling with them. It was also too dangerous. Not one to easily give up, Lilyfire had not succumbed to sleep until she had first secured the promise of a visit to the Sun Elven Realm with Annie once the Labradorite Amulet had been restored.

Having gratefully consumed a breakfast of a hearty bean and cheese soup, lembas bread, and another pot of hot tea, the group of six set out once more, accompanied by the well wishes of the villagers. Annie noticed that Lilyfire was nowhere to be seen and was a little concerned. She spotted Meara in the crowd and made her way over.

"Knowing Lilyfire," laughed Meara, over the noise of the crowd. "She will be hollering her displeasure at Commander Lucan's decision, to the four corners of the boar sty. Once she calms down adequately, I will reassure her that you will return for her."

"Please do," said Annie. And with that she rejoined her friends and crossed the village boundary into the woods.

Elva and Finwe left with some sorrow, as they'd had a reminder of the nature and nurture of their kinsfolk. Experiencing the kindness and jovial merriment of the village's people and having the opportunity to relax, and to connect with others in chatter, song, and dance, had reminded them of what they loved about their Woodland Realm. Finwe had announced to the bar that he would return and that the Woodland Realm would be restored to its former glory very soon. At this point, Elva had yanked him from the top of the bar hissing that,

"You should not go promising our people things that you cannot be certain you can fulfil." Finwe just smiled at her and shrugged.

As they journeyed back into the Sun Elven Realm, the Woodland Realm would mourn the twins' departure, in return. Finwe and Elva were well-known and well-loved in their kingdom, both having dutifully served their own versions of King and Queen — their most senior elders.

Many, many moons ago, when Finwe was a much younger elf, he was the principal guard for the youngest granddaughter of such an elder. Much to the desperate grief of the realm, as not much more than a youngling, she had cruelly perished at the hands of a posse of Shadow Elves. It was a time that Finwe never spoke of, no matter how much his sister encouraged him. She could see and feel just how much it haunted him, but he remained stoically silent on the matter.

The group waved their last goodbyes to the villagers and went on their way.

Chapter Fifteen

Both suns were now at their highest for the day, and the group had not yet stopped for a break. The elves could have maintained a swift run and covered twice the ground, but Annie, fit as she was, could not have kept up.

"This is all taking far too long," Lucan barked into the sky in an uncharacteristic display of frustration. "Every moment that the amulet is missing is a moment closer to the realms being unable to recover, even if it were to be returned."

Annie began to apologise and was abruptly stopped by Carric.

"No Annie," he said, glaring at Lucan. "You have nothing to apologise for. Firstly, you cannot help being slower than us elves across this foreign terrain. Secondly, if it was not for you, our elven realms would not have the slightest chance of recovery."

"Perhaps we would be best not going over land at all," Finwe suggested, breaking the tension between the two elves who were now glowering at each other in a tacit standoff.

"What does that mean?" asked Annie.

"Well," Finwe continued. "We can commandeer a ship and sail across the ocean to the Sun Elven Realm. This would take significant time off our trip even if we were to ride."

"Assuming we could even find any horses," Varis interjected, showing his approval of Finwe's plan by the nodding of his head.

"And days," Finwe continued. "If we were to continue walking with a human in our midst. No offence, Annie, " he added with an apologetic upwards turn of his palms.

"None taken," she replied. *Although I am a little offended*, she thought. Finwe suggested that chartering a ship was the best option.

No further debate could be had as Elva suddenly readied an arrow to let fly at what ever had just created a disturbance in the fern-like plants to their left. Within a second the other elves had adopted fighting stances with their weapons drawn. To flush out the intruder, Finwe let loose and embedded an arrow into the trunk of a tree barely millimetres above the now trembling ferns. Looks of confusion passed between all six of them as high-pitched squeak was emitted from among the ferns.

This was no Shadow Elf.

"Step out slowly and show yourself," Lucan ordered, not letting his guard down for a moment. "Now!" he insisted as the ferns continued to tremble. But, initially, no one emerged.

Then a small foot tentatively stepped out. Annie burst through the group, reached into the ferns, and took hold of a small hand.

"Lilyfire!" she exclaimed, pulling the youngling through the vegetation to stand before them. The others relaxed and sheathed their weapons. Lucan groaned, loudly.

"You were, in no uncertain terms, specifically ordered to stay in the village," he rumbled. "I specifically told you that the mission is too dangerous to have a youngling with us. You will simply have to go back to the village."

"But I have managed to keep up with you for hours, with not much trouble at all, and there has been no danger" Lilyfire insisted.

"Now," he growled turning away and venting his anger with his fist on an unsuspecting tree trunk.

"You cannot make me go back," she shouted at Lucan's back. Lucan whirled round and, with fury in his eyes, picked the girl up under one arm.

"Oh I cannot, can I?" he seethed and started to march off in the direction from which they had come. Lilyfire wriggled and kicked all the while. She too was seething.

"I will run and track you again, and again, and again," she squealed while beating her tiny fists on Lucan's arm. She turned to pleading and bargaining.

"Please, please let me come with you. I want to see the Sun Elven Realm palace. I want to be with Annie. I can be a useful lookout. Please, please, pleeeease."

The others looked dumbfounded at Varis.

"Leave this with me," he assured them and hared off after them. He caught up with his commander and stepped ahead of him, placing a hand on his chest to halt his progress.

"Commander," he reasoned, firmly. "As you rightly pointed out, we cannot waste time. We certainly cannot waste time taking this sneaky snippet back to her village."

Reluctantly, Lucan grunted in agreement. Varis pressed on, while he had the upper hand.

"We cannot, in all good conscience, leave her here, where she will, most likely, be attacked by Shadow Elves or navarlops. And, as she has stated with absolute clarity, she would still try to follow us." Lucan seemed completely impervious to Lilyfire's continued thrashing and kicking. Almost imperceptibly, his chest sagged beneath Varis's hand.

"And so," he said, dumping her into the arms of Varis, "this irritating little varmbat makes us a company of seven." And with that, he about-faced and marched back to where Annie, Carrie, Elva, and Flowe were still waiting.

"The varmbat comes with us," he announced without looking at any of them. "But know this. We shall not slow our pace to accommodate her or risk our own lives to save hers if we are attacked. We are on the most important mission there has ever been and it will take all of us if we are to have a chance of succeeding in it. If she falls behind, she is to take her chances in the woods, *on her own.*"

The others, including Lilyfire, nodded in agreement — not that it was actually up for discussion. Without another word, Lucan marched on and the others followed in silence.

There was not much talk as they continued. That is except for Lilyfire, who, holding Annie's hand, skipped along and chit-chatted away. Two hours farther along, and she had held all but Lucan's hand.

She's not exactly struggling to keep up, thought Annie, smiling as she watched Lilyfire taking three skipping steps to each of Finwe's strides.

When they finally come to a fork in the road, Elva insisted they cut through the woods as the more obvious roads would most likely be watched by Shadow Elf spies out on the hunt for them. She felt it was only sheer luck that they hadn't met any already. While Finwe, Varis, and Lucan had stopped to discuss the tactic with Elva, Carric had already veered off the path, and off mission.

He'd heard the inviting sounds of a waterfall nearby. Weaving between the tall, twisted trees, he could see it clearly. With no foliage, the trees weren't in a position to give the waterfall any amount of its customary privacy. While the waterfall wasn't as strong as it once was, before the realms began to die, it was a steady, flowing stream and the large pool beneath was full, and expansive, surrounded on one arc, by a cliff with a high drop-off.

Without hesitation, Carric made a beeline for it. He pulled off his boots and shirt, which billowed away in a breeze and snagged on a tree branch. He looked back towards the others.

"I am in need of some respite," Carric exclaimed, interrupting discussions as he changed course and started heading towards the water.

"Let us go swimming and refresh ourselves!"

Elva rolled her eyes but remained unsurprised that the prince needed a break after only walking for half a day. She had always felt that, while his body was more than strong enough, his mental grit was weak.

"We should have brought the horses, to avoid this nonsense," muttered Elva to her twin brother. "It is a pity that we could not transport them through the Shadow Elf's portal." Finwe just smirked in sympathetic amusement and nudged her elbow gently with his arm.

"Come on, sister. It is going to be a good while before we return to our realm again. They do not have pools like this in the Sun Elven Realm any more. It is now far too hot and dry."

With a reluctant grin that said just how annoyed she was, and how easily Finwe could make her laugh, she said,

"Fine, then. The water does look very inviting. Try not to scare the fish and maybe we can catch some for supper."

Carric had already jumped into the pool first, leaping from a large, granit-like boulder in a single fluid and graceful movement. Annie noticed his muscles ripple beneath his skin as his body stretched out with arms poised overhead in perfect formation. Effortlessly, he dived into the pool, barely making a sound or a ripple as he broke the water's surface.

Varis opted out, choosing instead the comfort of a shady weeping willow-like tree. Lucan paced back and forth, ever mindful of the need to press on.

"They are not soldiers of the Sun Elven Realm, Lucan," Varis soothed, with one eye resting and the other alert. "Unlike us, they need to regroup, refresh, and re-energise." Lucan wasn't the least bit pleased.

"Hmmm," he grumbled. "Carric has been trained as a Sun Elven soldier and yet he is the one to claim he needed to regroup, refresh, and re-energise." Varis smiled and gestured for Lucan to join him in the shade of the tree.

"He has been trained," smirked Varis. "And yet, he is first and foremost a prince." Lucan sighed and nodded, admitting defeat.

"We shall give them until the two suns are aligned," he said and he too closed one eye.

<><><><><><><><>

Elva had removed her leather waistcoat, boots, and breeches, and slid under the water for several beats before she popped back up. She broke through the water's surface and pushed her hands through her hair, sleeking it back as cool, clear water dripped down her nose and off her eyelashes. She took in a deep, restorative breath, and submerged beneath the surface once more.

Stripped to the waist, Finwe was thigh-deep in the water and poised with an arrow in his left hand. His eyes scanned the water to catch sight of a fish. He reminded Annie of the human statues that frequented the touristy cities in her Human Realm. She had always been fascinated and admiring of how such street artists made themselves so still for so long.

I've always been quite the fidget bum, she thought and she could feel her golden fleck wiggle as if in agreement.

She walked leisurely upwards to a higher edge of the cliff near the waterfall and removed her own jacket, and combat boots. From nowhere, as she tugged at a particularly fussy knotted bootlace, Lilyfire came up behind her. The youngling slipped her skinny arms around Annie's waist and hugged her tightly. With a quick, surprised laugh, Annie reached around with one arm to awkwardly hug her back. A moment later, Lilyfire had let go and was dancing, and singing an ancient Elvish younglings' song.

It was high pitched with each note a trill like that of an exotic bird. The sharp sounds of the Elvish language blended harmoniously with her small, sweet voice.

As she listened, Annie was still wrestling with her defiant boots and imagining what sort of boat would hopefully take them across the seas, and into the Sun Elven Realm. She had no idea that Lilyfire was precariously close to the edge of the cliff, skipping over small rocks and paying little attention to her surroundings.

Finally, with a satisfied grunt, Annie managed to free herself from her boots and tossed them to the side. It was at that moment that Lilyfire slipped, disappeared from view, and plummeted into the water below.

In an instant, Annie felt a deep dread encase and grip her entire body, drenching her and crystallising into ice crystals. Echoing her feelings, just for a moment, the entire forest felt the same thing. All of the various plant life and the wildlife hiding within it was covered crystals of ice, including the pool of water itself — including her friends.

It only lasted the briefest blink of an eye, but it was felt across the entire immediate area and Annie knew this was her magic. Her inner emotions were screaming at her so loudly that they made her head pound and her magic wreak havoc. Had she not been a complete novice, still at the beginnings of her magical powers, and had young Lilyfire not been the most important thing to her in that moment, she might have iced over the entire realm — permanently.

Annie heard Lilyfire scream and turned, immediately searching for where the scream had come from. Her internal alarm bells were ringing in her ears. She hadn't even noticed that she was creating the hard frost, and barely remembered feeling the chill. Racing to where the scream originated, Annie frantically scanned the water. Far below, she saw a terrified Lilyfire breach the surface close to the waterfall, only to be immediately sucked back down again. Although the water's current was weaker these days, it was too strong for the small, featherweight girl. Annie saw her little hands desperately reaching out of the water, struggling to resurface.

"Lily!" Annie shouted, looking back to her comrades for assistance, but she was too far away and they were all already busy finding the best spot to jump off from into the water. They were chatting and laughing amongst themselves. Lucan and Varis were nowhere to be seen. Shocked and frantic with worry, Annie peered over the cliff once more and hesitated.

Like an intense electric shock, flashbacks hit Annie, one after the other. Images of her younger self, underwater, struggling for air, lungs burning. She had mostly blocked out the memory of nearly drowning as a child. Her mother had been too drunk to notice her, never mind jump in and save her. Recalling images of her younger self, round-cheeked with bubbles of air slipping like clear glass marbles from her mouth as she lay still under the water, Annie could feel her magic building up pressure again. But she didn't bring on a hard frost this time. This time, an icy shiver ran down the length of her spine like a melting ice cube trickling down the back of her neck and beyond. It felt so real that she ran a hand through her dry hair. This was not just her magic. This was an everyday, ordinary, human panic attack.

Beginning to shake with fear, Annie's knees buckled under her and she fell to the dirt, panic rising in her throat, tightening it so that she couldn't scream for help again. With a Herculean effort, she hauled herself to her feet. She swayed a little, but she was determined and her decision was made. Before she could change her mind, Annie pulled her shirt off, clumsily summoned some magic within her for courage, and jumped in after Lilyfire.

After what felt like hours rather than milliseconds, Annie hit the water hard, crashing through the surface, shoulder and arm first. Searing pain shot through her right side at once, but she ignored it. Piercing through Annie's instinct to panic, her magic snapped her eyes open in order to search for Lilyfire underwater. She felt her before she saw her. Right below her, Lilyfire's little hands were floating above her head. Her hair stood on end and swayed like seaweed in a lazy current. She was unconscious and blood clouded Annie's vision as she reached for her. Through the murkiness, she managed to grab Lilyfire under both arms and tug, again and again.

Her vision now entirely obscured, Annie could not see what was keeping the two of them down. Pushing through her pain and fear, Annie's golden fleck, now thrashing wildly, enabled her to illuminate her surroundings, as if her eyes had inbuilt torches. Horrified, she could see that Lilyfire's skirt was caught on a large, thick tree branch that had long since fallen into the depths of the pool. Now, one of its long, spidery branches struck through Lilyfire's skirt material and held it there, snagged. Letting go of Lilyfire, Annie dove down further, her heart pounding and her lungs burning intensely. A surprising calm swept over her as her magic eased the burning sensation, miraculously filling Annie's lungs with more air. She pulled with everything she had in her. She ripped the skirt and, hooking her arms back under Lilyfire, she pushed off the large branch to kick-start their ascent to the surface.

What felt like an eternity, was merely moments before they breached the surface. Lilyfire was limp in Annie's arms. She weighed next to nothing and Annie held onto her with one arm, keeping Lilyfire's head above water as she doggy-paddled to a low edge where the shore met with the water. The water rippled and frothed at its sudden intrusion of movement, crashing against the muddy ground as Annie hauled them both out, and landed in the grass with a resounding, squelching thud.

Annie's chest was heaving so greatly and her heart was pounding so hard, that she feared she might never breathe normally again. She felt completely drained of all strength. Coughing and spitting out water, she once again mustered some of her magic to create the strength to pump her hands against Lilyfire's torso, using what she had retained of the free CPR lesson she had attended at her local college. Annie would often escape to the college for a warm building to pass the time in, sneaking into various courses unnoticed. Never in a million years would she have imagined that that particular lesson would come in useful in an elven realm.

Annie didn't even hear the others shouting in the distance. They must have noticed her in the water, heard her scream, or seen her clumsy launch into the pool. She couldn't focus on them. All her focus was on the slight youngling lying splayed out across the wet earth, her hair soaked with blood from a large, seeping wound on her head.

Lilyfire's chest wasn't moving.

She was blue.

Cold. Wet. Still.

Chapter Sixteen

She must have hit her head when she reached the bottom, was all Annie could think while desperately trying to stem the bleeding from Lilyfire's wound. She must have hit her head, she must have hit her head!

Annie had swiftly removed her wet jeans and was holding them tight against Lilyfire's head. In truth, there was no more pumping of blood. There was just a thin streak of crimson down Lilyfire's now blue and lifeless face. Lips parted, eyes closed, and chest unmoving, Annie could see that the little life in front of her was forever lost.

Emense energy surged through her. Her magic rapidly, relentlessly pulsed every nerve, stirring up inside her, fighting and searching for a way out — any way out. Annie cried out in anguish, howling like a baying wolf into an uncaring skies. Lightning shot from her fingers and into the ground. The tremors knocked her companions off their feet and the inhabitants of several nearby villages, ignorant of what was happening, hung onto their possessions as their houses violently shook, and shivered.

Scrambling to their feet, her companions sprinted to the source of the violent tremors, to find Annie cradling the lifeless Lilyfire in her arms and carefully wiping the blood away from her cheeks with the end of a jeans leg.

Through angry, despairing moans, she was slowly rocking Lilyfire back and forth, soothing, and reassuring the little waif in her leaving of the living realms. Annie did this despite knowing deep down, that her Lily had already gone, only moments before.

"Annie."

The soft voice of Elva unleashed tears that ran like the nearby waterfall, pouring down Annie's cheeks. She lowered her head. Her wet, stringy hair fell across both her and Lilyfire's faces.

Elva's warm, assured hand on her cold, aching shoulder was the only thing to bring Annie out of her shock. She looked up at Elva with a start, tears welling in her red, wide eyes, her golden fleck twisting, and arching in emotional anguish. Elva looked down at Lilyfire, assessing quickly that this was far past anything that her healing powers could accomplish.

"My magic can fix her, right? Can my magic fix her?" Annie asked over and over while looking back down at Lilyfire's inanimate face.

"No," answered Elva simply, with deep compassion. "There is no magic for this and it would be wrong to even try. Any such efforts would torture Lilyfire's soul and end in the same result."

Annie let out a choking sob. Glancing up, through her bleary vision, she saw Lucan, Varis, Finwe, and Carric standing there powerless. Their heads were lowered, their hands clasped, and each of them looked solemnly at the scene before them. Finwe wanted to say something but didn't know what. Carric and Varis also had no words, and even Lucan, who hadn't wanted the youngling with them in the first place, was clearly heartsick.

Carefully, lovingly, Annie lowered Lilyfire's body down with Elva's help. Annie kept her head supported as if she were a fragile newborn baby, lowering it gently down onto the brown grass.

Annie didn't speak for what felt like a decade in anyone's realm. The group allowed her time to at least start processing what had just happened. Elva gently murmured in her ear that they couldn't take the little one's body with them and that, as a Woodland Elf, Lilyfire's body belonged to the forest, now.

Annie looked on with unseeing eyes as Elva finished carefully cleaning up Lilyfire's bloodstained face. Finwe and Carric surrounded Lilyfire's body with petals. Finwe had even found lilies sprouting near the top of the waterfall. Their colour had faded, the malnourished earth giving only what little it could these days, but Annie still placed one in Lilyfire's hair. She tucked it behind one of her long, delicately, pointed ears. Annie gently touched her ears in the same way Lilyfire had admired Annie's ears only a day before.

Before slowly walking away, the male elves quietly said their farewells in old Elvish, to the fragile, yet feisty youngling that they had known for only the shortest time. But Annie didn't budge. She sat close to Lilyfire's body, her gentle little face now clean and her hair draped over one small shoulder. Annie sat back on her heels and watched Elva, who had stayed with her, gently tuck another faded flower behind Lilyfire's other ear. Together they had plucked dozens of small blue flowers and then covered her body with them.

They sat together in silent contemplation. Annie wondered why such tragic things happened and why they always seemed to happen around her.

But then, maybe everyone, every human and elf, thinks like that about their lot, she thought.

Annie noticed that Elva was looking at her closely and that her expression had darkened.

"Are you all right?" she asked, sniffling quietly.

Elva carefully gathered her innermost thoughts and looked directly at Annie. With a small sigh, she placed a long, slender, yet strong hand on Annie's smaller, squarish one .

"I think it would be best if you see the whole picture," she said, matter-of-factly.

Confused, Annie stood and brushed the dried grass off her knees. Self-consciously, she muttered the few words of the Lord's prayer that she could remember and slowly walked away from Lilyfire's body, over to a twisted, lop-sided tree. She leaned against it. Her eyes were red, small, and puffy, and she squinted at Elva, whom she increasingly thought of as her trusted friend. Elva also stood and followed Annie over to the tree. Both of them looked and felt emotionally exhausted.

"What are you talking about, Elva?" Annie asked to break the mournful silence.

"Keep your eyes wide open," Elva warned, earnestly. "It is just... I have seen how he looks at you, and I do not find him to be safe, and true. There is something... something different about him. I do not know quite what it is, but I am sure of it."

Annie screwed up her face in distaste and disbelief.

"Carric? You're worried about Carric at a time like this? Elva, I'm sure his intentions for me are good, or even better than good."

"And what if his intentions are purely for his own good?" replied Elva sharply.

Annie took pause at this. She stood and turned to squarely face Elva. She looked up at her closely, putting Elva under acute scrutiny, like a Detective Inspector with a suspect. She couldn't figure out where this was all coming from.

"Elva, I've been taking care of myself for as long as I can remember. I can look out for myself and if Carric's intentions were nefarious, trust me, I'd be able to see it. I need you as my friend, not as my nanny."

Unsure as to what a nanny was, but getting the general gist, Elva felt somewhat defeated, for now. She decided that she had no choice but to concede to her friend's wishes. She hoped she was wrong, but feared that she was right.

It was true. They had known each other for only a short while, but Elva knew that Woodland Elves, in fact all elves, lived for an exceedingly long time, and their friendships often lasted for as long. She wasn't sure that this was the case for humans. To think she may have only a relatively short amount of time to have Annie in her life, bothered Elva immensely. She felt that, in Annie, she had discovered a kindred spirit. She knew her time with Annie was precious, and despite Annie's insistence that she was totally capable of looking after herself, Elva resolved to always keep an eye out for her. She let out a heartfelt sigh.

"Well, dear friend, I am glad to see that you are so perceptive," she conceded, far from wholeheartedly. "But if ever you need anyone watchful to be at your side, to act in support of your interests, I am your elf."

Through her tear-stained face, Annie managed a smile of gratitude, that broke the tension between them. Following a big hug, they turned back to face their immediate and pressing mission. It was time to move on and to sadly leave what had been lost behind.

So there, in a patch of grass under a weeping tasar tree, where the suns' beams streamed through at just the right angle to cast light on her face, they left Lilyfire to be at peace and to be reclaimed by her Woodland Realm.

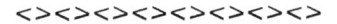

<><><><><><><><>

Having found her voice again during her talk with Elva, Annie decided to let the group in on a very private part of who she was. It was as they walked that Annie, without prompting, addressed everyone in the group. She knew that while she had only met them so very recently, these strangers had cemented themselves as her friends — and she'd never really had any of those. She could feel her magic welling up inside her, welling up tears and creating gentle, sorrowful rain. It fell in sporadic drips that were big and loud as they hit the treetops.

"I nearly drowned," she announced, quite matter-of-factly. Rather than feeling ashamed about it, for the first time, she felt relief and somehow lighter at having said it out loud. The rain reduced to a light mist. She shook her head to clear her thoughts, and rubbed an itchy eye, as if its golden fleck was bothering her. Did it want her to carry on or keep quiet? She couldn't tell.

She pressed on.

"It happened when I was eight years old and it has stayed with me. I've been scared of the water ever since." Carric squeezed her hand, urging her to continue. "Once, I was perfectly happy swimming. I was a strong swimmer for my age, but I had never jumped in. I didn't like the thought of it and I didn't see the need to when I could simply get in using the ladder at the side of the pool. One time, an adult came up to me and said that such a good swimmer should be happy to jump in. I was just explaining how jumping in and having a good swimming stroke were not necessarily linked together, when she started to turn away and then, without even looking back, shoved me in! I hadn't taken a breath. My lungs were empty of air and felt full of water. I was terrified. I felt I was dying."

No one uttered a word. They silently urged Annie to go on with her story.

"After what felt like an eternity, I burst through the water's surface, coughing, spluttering, gasping for air, and flaying my limbs in an effort to reach the safety of the pool's edge."

Annie's breath, gasping and rasping, echoed the experience of her eight-year-old self.

"I distanced myself from water after that. At fifteen, before I headed out of my home for good, I tried to get back into the water at the local indoor pool." Annie sighed while shaking her head. "I had a panic attack in the shallow end. I've just felt so ashamed. Such a failure about it ever since."

Everyone remained respectfully silent.

Carric was the first to speak, characteristically devoid of sensitivity.

"What is an indoor pool?"

And while the others unceremoniously shot him down with their looks, Annie burst out laughing. Falling into step with Carric, she wrapped an arm around his waist and gave him a quick squeeze. He reciprocated with an arm around her shoulders. She needed the laughter and with hers came a chorus from the rest. They walked through the forest, laughing together, relieving the tension and sadness of what had just happened. The realms were dying and they couldn't afford the luxury of grief at this time.

Chapter Seventeen

As the group made their way towards the harbour of the nearest Shoreland settlement, Elva and Finwe quietly sang old Woodland Elvish songs that they'd grown up with. Together, they taught Annie some of the tunes and lyrics. Carric frequently took Annie's hand, squeezing it gently, showing unabashed affection by bringing it to his lips and smiling at her with his almond-shaped eyes.

Finwe and Varis had caught a couple of jackhàres, and a làgomorph to cook for dinner. By the time mid-afternoon had arrived, the group was at the edge of the forest, at the edge of the Woodland Realm and within sight of the harbour.

Annie ogled the impressive ships that lined the harbour wall. The huge, silvery wooden hulls bobbed up and down in the gentle waves. Each ship had its own, unique figurehead with an additional carvings at the stern. Unlike the female characters common to human ships in the Human Realm of old, these ships had different sea creatures' heads. The carvings at their stern were that of the the sea creatures' tails. Some reached high into the sky while others curled around the side of the ship, coming to rest on the port side of their decks. Annie recognised only a few of the carvings and many were alien to her.

Lucan resumed command of the situation.

"Finwe and I shall head to the harbour, and charter a ship. It is best if the Shoreland Elves do not see you, Carric and it is absolutely essential that they do not see you, Annie."

Seeing Annie's confused and a little offended expression, Varis ventured to explain, while Lucan, and Finwe left camp to charter a ship.

"The Shoreland Elves have a strong affinity with the seas and, since they spend much of their time at the mercy of the those seas, they are a naturally suspicious nation."

"What does that have to do with me?" Annie asked, unable to see what this suspicious nature had to do with her.

"They are watchful and wary of bad omens," Varis explained. "And I am sad to say that having a human on board their ship would be viewed as a very bad omen indeed — possibly one of the worst."

Annie understood. These sea faring elves were similar to sailors of old in her own world. Anything could be a bad omen if you looked hard enough and the elves wouldn't need to look very hard at Annie to spot that she was 'bad news'.

"But what about Carric?" she asked. "He's not a bad omen. He's an elf and a prince at that."

Varis pursed his lips and took in a sharp in breath. Annie could see that he was taking pause to corral his thoughts and selectively pick the right, most tactful words.

"Indeed, Carric is a prince and a Sun Elven prince at that. However, our prince has not... *endeared* himself to the Shoreland Elves. Many moons ago, Carric and the Shoreland Elves' leader, Lord Arel had a... an... altercation."

Annie was really curious now.

"Do go on," she said, conspiratorially. Varis looked over his shoulder to make sure Carric was out of earshot.

"Please bear in mind that this all happened before his highness met you," Varis pleaded. This only served to further pique Annie's curiosity and she urged him further, to go on.

"The prince had a close relationship with Lord Arel's daughter, Firana. Their relationship was far too close for Lord Arel's liking, especially since Firana was not that many moons beyond being a youngling. Carric was told by Lord Arel, in no uncertain terms, to back off. Carric was a young royal buck and unaccustomed to being told what he could, and could not do. And so, he continued to see Firana behind her father's back. Lord Arel found out and insisted that Carric should marry his daughter in order to keep her honour intact. Carric simply laughed and flatly refused. Firana's heart was broken and Lord Arel was, and probably still is, furious."

Annie nodded in understanding.

"So a request from Carric for a boat would be flatly turned down by these Shoreland Elves out of respect for their Lord Arel," she said.

"At the very least," Varis replied. "As I say," he continued, "this was all many moons ago and long before Carric met you."

Annie couldn't help but glow a little at the thought that Varis acknowledged Carric's feelings towards her. They broke camp and before long, Lucan, and Finwe returned with the news that they would be setting sail at nightfall.

Elva had helped both Annie and Carric to disguise themselves. She had combed Carric's hair through with lampas mud to darken his locks and had fixed it to the nape of his neck to give him more of a Woodland Elf look. His disguise was completed by swapping out his Sun Elven finery for Finwe's more rustic tunic and belted waistcoat of the Woodland Realm. While Finwe put on Carric's embroidered, fine wool and silk mix shirt and heavy buckled belt, he declined his princely waistcoat that was embellished with embroidery in gold and silver thread.

Elva platted Annie's hair in a typically Woodland Elf style. She took particular care to ensure that her ears were covered and would remain so. The addition of Elva's velvety cloak around her shoulders and a light smearing of lampas mud to make her face more weathered, completed the look. Elva stood back to look at the pair, taking in her handiwork.

She was satisfied.

They were ready.

"It is time," said Finwe, and the comrades made their way down to the quayside. Annie and Carric shrouded themselves in the dark, and velvety Woodland Elf cloaks, their roomy hoods pulled down to shadow their faces. The suns had all but set and the early evening had grown unusually cold and dark. It was as if the evening knew that the comrades were about to embark on the dangerous task of smuggling two of their number, and Annie was incredibly grateful for the warm fabric. She hugged it around her as she stepped over fallen branch after fallen branch, that soon gave way to a steep sand bank.

Everyone followed Finwe. With limber, precise movements, like that of a cat, he progressed up, over, and down the extensive dunes. Carefully he kept his feet dug into the sand so as to control his descent. The others followed suit, kicking up light puffs of sand as they went. Finally, they came out onto the cobbled surface of the quayside itself.

The sea lapped against the harbour wall in frothy, rhythmic waves. Close up, it was clear to see from their pock marks that these ships had been involved in age-old elven battles. They were massive. So massive, that as Annie peered upwards, she could not see the rail around the deck. She had only seen ships similar to these in movies on the TV.

Now that she was close up, she could see that the entirety of their hulls above the water were beautiful pieces of art. Every inch was carved to make plants, sea creatures, and elves. It reminded her of the vaulted ceilings that were found in the great cathedrals in her realm. Despite the darkness, Annie could make out the smaller, intricate carvings, all etched in between the figurines and flora . However confusing and unreadable they were to Annie, their beauty moved her. She reached out and touched the wooden wall that was the hull of the ship nearest to her. Instantly, she could feel and even smell the reek of the long history of the vessel — the blood, sweat, and tears of elves from over many thousands of moons past.

The ships were dimly illuminated by lanterns hanging from tall poles that swung in unison with the waves. The lanterns' glow alighted on the dock workers as they performed their nightly maintenance duties. They looked strong and wiry like Woodland Elves, but their skin was an electric blue and wind-worn from being brought up around the water rather than in the woods.

Lucan gave the group one last reminder before they ventured out into the open of the broad stone jetty that would lead them to their ship. Here, with no shadows or ships for cover, they would be exposed.

"Be quiet. Be calm. Be vigilant," he said. "Keep a lookout for Shadow Elves and, if you see any, kill them quickly and swiftly, and with no noise. We cannot afford to spook the Shoreland Elves. "

His words chilled Annie to her core, surrounding her heart in ice. Having to kill was something that Annie knew might happen. Worried, she wondered if she was capable of this last instruction. Was her heart capable? Was her magic? Was it strong enough? Was *she* strong enough? Annie forced herself to focus back to remaining quiet, calm, and vigilant.

On a word from Varis, everyone unsheathed their weapons. Annie had been given a short, double-edged dagger by Carric. Beside her, he had gently held her face, while holding his sword in the other.

"You are one of us," he whispered. "You are mine."

Annie experienced an unprecedented flush of her cheeks, throat, and chest. Effortlessly, she quelled the swell of her magic and the quiver of her fleck.

Bracing against a quick, cold breeze that brushed past her already-rosy cheeks, Annie was not sure she was fully prepared to deceive an entire ship's crew and slip past them undetected. Back in her own world, her own realm, she'd done more than her fair share of deceitful behaviours. She wasn't particularly proud of it. In principle, it went against her deep seam of integrity.

However, Annie had grown up surviving mostly on her own wits. While she'd had a mother present, her mother was rarely, if ever present. On the regular occasions when Annie's mother was too inebriated, high — or both — to care for her, Annie would take coins from her mother's purse to the corner store to buy whatever was on final reduction. To supplement this, she had learned how to snaffle extra items, unaware that even at that tender age, her magic enabled cloaking to literally hide the evidence. Annie never questioned how she'd come away with such big hoards. She was a child. She thought it was perfectly normal. She thought that anyone could do it.

Annie peered through the dark, lit only by the bright stars scattered across the sky and a few hanging lanterns at the dockside. She took a deep breath, understanding completely that she was not merely risking being caught with an unpaid for loaf of bread, or carton of milk. This was *so much* bigger and *far* more serious than anything she'd done before or dreamed of.

She was especially glad to have Finwe on her side. She watched him and waited on his every move. Lucan had placed him in charge of getting Carric and Annie on board without incident, as it was Finwe who knew how to be perpetually stealthy. His hunting skills had given him years of experience in being ultra quiet, stiff-still, and unfailingly patient. He could slip past and sneak up on virtually anything undetected.

Finwe had placed Elva behind Annie. He trusted his graceful sister to practically pirouette her way onto the boat with the ease of a principal dancer at the ballet. She had demonstrated her poise and stealth many times while they were growing up, and often, by his side in combat.

Carric wasn't known for cat-like poise and he felt Annie was an unknown quantity. Sandwiched between himself and Elva, provided Carric and Annie mimicked his moves, he felt the four of them could pass as a group of Woodland Elves. Elva was tasked with picking off any assailing elves at their backs should Carric's and Annie's identities be discovered. Under her cloak, Elva had her bow drawn with an arrow at the ready. She was looking all around, her elf eyes seeing through the darkness with relative ease.

Moments after stepping onto the jetty, Annie heard the soft rustle of Elva's cloak moving with her body and the barely-audible *zip* of one of her arrows releasing from her bow. It made Annie flinch. She knew someone had just taken their last breath.

"Shadow Elf," she whispered from behind Annie, her warm breath touching Annie's ear. "He came out from behind the fish barrels behind us, on our left. There was only one to pick off. A spy monitoring activity at the harbour for Tathlyn. We'll be gone before he is discovered."

Those words of reassurance didn't particularly have their desired effect of settling Annie down, but she nodded along anyway, knowing there was truly no other way to ensure their safety.

<><><><><><><><>

Lucan and Varis confidently strode up the gang plank, and shook hands with the Shoreland Elf captain who was awaiting their arrival up on deck. The captain looked beyond Varis's shoulder and Finwe gave him a jovial wave.

"Annie," Finwe whispered loudly without looking back at her, his deep voice unusually steady and commanding. "We are going to need you. Any elven enemies we may face, the rest of us can handle. But there may be unforeseen forces and needs that will never be in our control, but they are in yours."

Annie nodded that she understood. For the first time, she knew that she would and possibly could, do whatever it took to keep her friends, and herself, from the dangers ahead. She realised that at least some of these possible dangers were things that she couldn't imagine. She had only ever had to live off her drive for self-preservation, but this had been transformed by her experience in these elven realms. Here, among these elves, for the first time, she was living off her drive for the group's preservation. It was no longer *me and I*, it was *us and we*.

"I suspect that the first thing we are going to need is a wind to set sail by," he continued. "Right now, there is nowhere near enough breeze and we cannot afford to delay, and wait until tomorrow."

The refreshing, salty-sweet smell of the ocean that took up the entire horizon, and the stars that stretched like a glittering blanket across the pitch-black night sky, filled the senses, and were a vision to behold. It was, by anyone's standards, a beautiful night. In the Human Realm it would have been the kind of night to be enjoyed, but the reality for these friends left no room for pleasure. They had been refreshed at the village and now there was no letup in urgency.

Annie's pulse had quickened and ahead, more forceful waves collided with the land, warning land-dwellers from entering its vast, chilling, and secretive otherworld. The sea had started to crash and froth against the wall of the quayside, and the ships bobbed more vigorously.

Finwe led his fellow 'Woodland Elves' up the remainder of the gang plank. Using a thick rope that formed part of the rigging he swung through the gap in the rail, leapt onto the deck, and landed silently. Carric and Annie followed suit, but rather than landing silently, they each landed with a conspicuous thud. The captain eyed them with some suspicion before Elva distracted his attention by performing a perfectly executed backflip and landing on the deck rail with obvious ease. As Annie's boots had touched down on the sturdy wood deck of the ship, she stopped dead — fear suddenly striking her immobile.

Carric stood behind her, making sure she didn't stagger with the seesawing of the ship, and stepped up closer to her, whispering in her ear,

"What is wrong, Annie? Did you look over the rail? Do you have a fear of heights?"

She shook her head while screwing her eyes shut. She tried to take a deep breath but found her lungs were tight and preventing her from filling them completely.

"Like an utter idiot, I've just realised I'm about to be surrounded by water again. And not just a pool. I'm not at all looking forward to this part of our journey, Carric. This *entire* part." There was panic in her voice now, and the rope that she had grabbed hold of, was beginning to shake from her hand, and on up into the rigging.

Carric, knowing that this could mean Annie's magic may dramatically unleash itself at any moment, took hold of her. Gently, he placed both hands on her shoulders and said softly, but with complete certainty,

"You will not be taken by these waters, Annie. I solemnly promise to protect you from such a fate."

His words and touch certainly helped, and while her hands still felt numb from the cold, and shaky from nerves, Annie loosened her grip on the rope. It ceased its tremors and she let it fall limp onto the deck. To move them away from the captain's continued gaze, Finwe patted Carric on his back and gave Annie a reassuring wink.

An elf winking, she thought. *I don't know why, but I assumed I'd never see such a thing.* She felt her golden fleck do a sarcastic zigzag. *Yes, I know,* she admitted to herself while smiling a small, half-mouth grin. *As if an elf winking is the thing that smacks me as strange after everything else I've seen.*

Annie couldn't help but stop and look around in awe at her current surroundings. She had never been on even a rowboat, let alone a ship of this magnitude and grandeur.

"It's beautiful," she whispered to Varis, who had come to stand right beside her and was brushing an imagined speck of dust from his sleeve.

"It's imbued with the sweat, toil, and blood of Shoreland Elves from thousands of moons ago. It's carved into every surface of the ship including the decking," Varis whispered back. He was always one for imparting nuggets of his vast knowledge. It was something for which Lucan often teased him, but secretly admired. Looking closely, Annie could make out further intricate carvings etched into the under-side of the hand-smoothed, wooden railings. Such beauty had obviously required the skilled hands of master craftsmen — or, rather crafts-elves.

She was still in awe of the enormity of it all as Finwe led the way and the rest of the group made their way to seating where they could see what was gong on without getting in the Shoreland sailors' way. With just one word from the captain, the ship became a hive of activity. Elves that Annie had not noticed were there, suddenly came forward out of the shadows as one and sprang into action.

Once the ship had been successfully pushed away from the quayside, Finwe and Elva exchanged a concerned look. The captain started to shake his head.

"As I warned you, when you chartered my ship, there is not enough wind to take us out of the harbour and into the open sea," he announced to his passengers. "We will have to bide our time here and set sail tomorrow."

Lucan sprang to his feet and flailed his arms in extreme frustration.

"We cannot wait," he exclaimed, but the captain simply shrugged his shoulders.

"We *really* cannot wait, brother," Elva whispered urgently to Finwe. "The body of the Shadow Elf will be discovered at dawn and there will be all manner of héllè to pay."

"Will the Shoreland Elves not be pleased that there is one less Shadow Elf among them?" Annie asked from Elva's other side. Elva shook her head.

"The Shoreland Elves like to remain as neutral as possible," she explained. "While they do not help the Shadow Elves, they do not get in their way either. A dead Shadow Elf on their quayside will attract trouble."

At this, Finwe took two strides to stand before Annie. She looked at him with wide, ready-to-jump-into-action eyes.

"Annie," Finwe said, looking deep into those eyes with full confidence. "We need the wind to pick up to move the ship. I had hoped that the drop in temperature tonight would create the wind we need, but it has not. This lightest of breezes will not lift the sails. We need you, Annie."

We need you, Annie. It was a sentence she had never heard before but it now made her heart swell in tune with the seas. She had dreamed of being truly needed — being part of something — and now she was. She answered with a firmly confident nod and her rhythmically twisting golden fleck signified that a silent plan of action was at the ready.

Annie took a deep, readying breath — not sure quite what she was readying herself for. She felt her arms begin to rise and her hands turn skywards. She sensed that she was placing all of her intention into the air around her, persuading it to move faster, to push against her with all of its might. Like an acquaintance she was befriending, a light breeze grazed her fingertips at first, then quickly firmed up until there was a steady, strong breeze blowing back her hood and plats, and causing the beams of the rigging to strain against their anchoring hooks, and ropes.

Astonished at the instant change in weather, the captain barked orders to his crew. They did as commanded, tugging at the sails they had been busy untying. Finally the sails unfurled. They dropped from great heights with a massive ripple of cloth and a sound that reverberated off the waters themselves. Within seconds, they had snapped back with a crack, having reached their full length. The wind immediately pushed against the thick, yet silky fabric of the sails. They billowed out to their fullest tension, like great, smooth clouds that pulled, and slowly eased them from the harbour.

As the enormous, heavy lurch of the ship moved them farther out from the protection of the harbour and out into the ocean, Annie was surprised that her full weight pulled forward with it, but a beat behind. Although she regained her balance quickly, on looking out to the sea, she knew that she may well feel, at the very least, uneasy and queasy for the entire trip. She half-seriously wondered if Elva had any restorative elixir to turn her stomach into a turgid blancmange rather than the swishing, watery consistency she was currently experiencing.

She didn't, sadly, but she did have a pouch full of ginger-mint leaves that were known to give at least some relief. Elva took a few of them, pressed them between her hands while uttering some old Elvish, and handed them to Annie.

"Chew them slowly," she instructed. "No... slower. Much slower than that."

It helped, certainly, but Annie still feared that her wobbly legs would never again resume their strong, lithe gate and that her stomach would churn until it was butter. The farther they sailed out to sea, the sicker Annie felt. Being surrounded by water, the thing she feared most and that had taken Lilyfire, was a nightmare made real.

She could feel her veins start to bubble up with something powerful and quite possibly destructive, so she forced herself to focus on something, anything else. She chewed another ginger-mint leaf and focused solely on the way it tasted — sweet, a little spicy, a little bit... like grass.

Just chew, she told herself. *Chew slower... slower.*

Only opening her eyes to find where the railing was, Annie launched herself towards it and puked over the side, retching up a bright green, acidic vomit that was, thankfully taken away by the wind that she had created.

Chapter Eighteen

The deep moans coming from his throat were like animal noises, pained and guttural. His body thrashed in the bed. His silken sheets were being twisted and tossed, pulled and wrapped around his flailing arms, and legs.

"Meredith," he croaked aloud, to no one in his large, empty bedchamber. He was alone, all alone, always alone. "My love, my Meredith. Please... why did you forsake me? Return to me, return to me, return..."

Each sob he choked out was answered with a cruel silence. Cold and indifferent to him, even his own dreamscape despised him and wished him emptiness, bitterness, and loneliness.

Still asleep, Tathlyn felt like he was rising from bed like a mummy from its sarcophagus — lurching, moaning, and wrestling to free itself from its bindings, half-alive, half-dead. But suddenly his eyes, sharp and catlike, took in his real surroundings, alerted to his own body's stress as he was jerked out of his anguish and out of his nightmare.

His bare, skeletal feet touched down gently onto the icy, stone floor of his bedchamber. Inside this cavernous austere room, besides himself, King Tathlyn kept a numerous assortment of oddities. There was a desk of tortured, dark wood that leaned against the far wall. Its tabletop was scratched by a manic hand with a sharp tool, and carved with old Elvish inscriptions. Birdcages of various sizes hung throughout the room. Some held fion, haro, and other birds of prey that dared not squawk in his presence. They knew why some of the many cages hung empty and they were fearful. Several skulls from winged wilin, maiwë, and tuilindo were randomly scattered across most surfaces. The prodigious skull of an endangered elke hung above a roaring fire. In the uplighting of the flame this most noble of creatures look sinister and possessed.

Despite the cold, Tathlyn left his one window uncovered. The tall, narrow glass was plain and had a spidery crack that began in the bottom left-hand corner. It looked out into the night sky and down upon his realm.

I am Tathlyn, King of the Shadow Elves, King of the Shadow Realm, King of... more, he thought. He had always desired more, for as long as he could remember.

Since before his time, this realm had been colder, darker, and more devoid of life than any of the other realms. The Shadow Elves had always had to survive rather than thrive. While there was plenty of water, food was not a given. Shadow Elves had evolved into a race with wiry, hardened strength and constitution. A natural hatred of the Woodland and Sun Elven Realms virtually ran through their DNA. Young Shadow Elves were raised on stories that sowed, watered, and fed the seed of hatred of the other elven races. They particularly scoffed at the self-aggrandising they witnessed in the palaces, gardens, sports, fashions, dances, attitudes, and mindsets of the Sun Elves.

They saw the Woodland Elves as the pathetic, tree-hugging lapdogs of the Sun Elven Realm. And, the Shoreland Elves? Well, they were just flaccid and gutless.

Tathlyn could think of nothing better than to bring down these other wretched realms and then to spread his net of power even wider, into the Human Realm as well. At least, with all this hatred and plotting on his mind, he had little time in his waking hours to think of *her*.

Meredith only came to him in his dreams, or nightmares, depending on how he chose to look at it upon waking. Each night, when he was completely alone in his foreboding tower, with only his birds and skulls as company, King Tathlyn could hear Meredith's sweet, melodic voice filling his ears. He could see her sparkling image that appeared to him, standing in front of him in soft, smudged pastel hues, like a sensitively executed watercolour painting. She both haunted and taunted him.

He groaned and grunted as he gingerly levered himself out of bed. While he nor anyone in any realm would admit it, the king was visibly older and weaker than during his time with Meredith. While it was never spoken of, mainly because his followers dared not to, it was the reason why he sent out armies of spies in search of her and, more often than not, stayed in his tower. Still, what strength he lacked in body, he made up for in mental agility that was fuelled by pure hatred, anguish, and devious plotting for his own self aggrandisement. As a catalyst for his passionate hatred for the humans and his desire to conquer all, he need only think of Meredith.

She had scorned him, denied him, rejected his undying love for her, and now, as far as he was concerned, everything around him — even Tathlyn, himself — was bitter and dying because of her. For that, given the chance, he would reject her far more than she could ever reject him. Because she had stolen his bitter heart, he would steal the hearts of everyone and everything — across the Sun Elven Realm, across the Woodland Realm, across the Shoreland Realm, and across the Human Realm — especially the Human Realm.

He would rule over them all.

He would make them all suffer.

You could have been my queen, Meredith, he thought. *We would have ruled together. We would have been magnificent and gloriously terrifying in equal measure.*

As it often did when he awoke late at night from one of his vivid dreams, his mind wandered to the last time he saw her — to her soft, supple skin, and her beautiful face with sharp features outlining large, beautiful blue eyes — one of which contained a single golden fleck — and all of her heart's warmth for him.

Were he not used to the bitter, leaden ache in his heart and the burning in his throat, King Tathlyn might have thrown a chair, splintering its wood into the stone wall, or cursed aloud and taken his anger out on his birds, or his own realm. More than a few Shadow Elf soldiers and spies had met their untimely demise when standing in front of King Tathlyn's ferocious anger and pent-up anguish. He recalled throwing several out of the very window through which he now gazed. The night sky, even through a slight haze, shone bright with stars that blanketed the realm. As peaceful and as calm as the night was, the Shadow Elf king could feel in his bitter bones that something, or someone, was afoot.

He could almost hear Meredith whispering in his long, thinly pointed ears, and for a moment, he let his eyes close tightly shut. They only fluttered back open when the sounds of one of his loyal follower's shouting roused him from his miserable reverie. He turned to the door with a whirl, his long black robe following him in ruffles across the cold, stone floor.

"Announce yourself!" he demanded.

"My lord, it is your loyal servant, Rennyn," he called from behind the heavy wooden door. "I've come with news that I am sure will be of great interest to you, my king."

From across the room, with a flick of his wrist, Tathlyn flung the door open wide. Rennyn almost tiptoed in, his glance humbly cast downwards and with his head hung low. Tathlyn smirked at how his spies always felt so obviously uneasy with his magic. He like them being this way. He liked the way it made them twitch and squirm.

"What *interesting* news have you brought me?" the king asked, unable to hold back a sneer as Rennyn and another shuffled in. *They are all so much smaller than me and so much weaker than I,* he thought. His nostrils pulled back and his lips curled meanly, in their presence. "This had better be about my escaped Meredith."

"My king," said a Shadow Elf spy, standing timidly at Rennyn's shoulder. "We have heard from our spies to the west, who have travelled long and far to find the human, Meredith." He winced slightly at the mention her name and held his breath. No one could ever be quite sure how King Tathlyn might react to hearing it.

"They gave word of sighting her," he pressed on. "Her comrades, too. They are helping her cross the seas on a ship they chartered from the Shoreland Elves. We believe they are planning to get back to the Sun Elven Realm without having to cross the rest of the Woodland Realm."

Slowly and deliberately, King Tathlyn's body grew. His chest rose and his shoulders lifted as he inhaled an enormous, deep breath of air. Just as slowly, his eyes fluttered closed and back open, into mere catlike slits. A wicked, disparaging smile crept over his face and he responded with words heavily laced in contempt. He knew that now, if his spies were quick enough, he could catch his Meredith and through her, retrieve the Labradorite Amulet for himself.

"Bring me a bird," he said in a low voice. The birds in cages around him immediately erupted into terrified squawking and frantic flapping of wings attempting flight. The birds were fully aware of what this would mean one for their number's fate.

The Shadow Elf spy approached a lone hanging cage directly behind the king. Tathlyn waited as his follower opened the cage and struggled to grip onto the bird, pulling it from its enclosure, and bringing it over to his king. King Tathlyn took it into his hands more gently than a Woodland Elf cradling an infant morco. He took great care of his animals — that is until they had a specific purpose and had served it.

The hawk now looked with trepidation, into his eyes as Tathlyn took a small, sharp blade, the handle of which was encrusted in rubies, and sliced directly through the hawk's throat, killing it instantly. The bird fell limp into his hand — silent and spilling blood. The king used the bird's blood to smear across his face, lining under his eyes and across his sharp cheekbones. As a finishing flourish, he drew three small circles with his thumb across his forehead.

Without a care or a speck of guilt, he dropped the bird's body and it landed on the ground with a sickening thud. With the remaining blood, King Tathlyn pressed his palms together, red and slick. Pulling them apart, he reached out to the moons. Only his hands and arms protruded out of the open window, directly into the moons' light.

Gently closing his lids and rolling his eyes backwards, Tathlyn chanted in old, dark magic Elvish. The blood on his hands began to move, splitting and crawling over him like red ants, stretching in regimented lines up his arms, and pooling on the centre of his chest. From there, fewer, thicker lines crawled up his neck, across his face, and into his eyes. He snapped them open. They were completely crimson.

In an eerily calm voice, he turned only his head, like a door creaking open, to look down at the now quivering spy. He spoke barely above a whisper.

"In order to succeed, we must be able to reach them through the waters, undetected."

Then, gripping the spy's shoulder with one long-fingered hand and the other taking hold of his ruby encrusted dagger once more, he said, with sheer menace in his eyes,

"Come closer."

Chapter Nineteen

It took the full moons glowing softly orange in the vast midnight black-blue sky, the regular, repetitive sounds of the sea waves lapping against the sides of the ship, and a cool, wet muslin-type cloth draped over her forehead, before Annie was feeling anything remotely like herself again.

She had passed out for a while after Elva suggested she sit down and rest. Once the ship had gotten underway, Finwe had brought a small bucket of fresh water, and the muslin square. He even let her squeeze his hand and curse the waters, even though this made Finwe and those of the crew that overheard, incredibly nervous. Finwe knew that cursing anything was never to be taken lightly in the crew members' minds.

Being a creature of land himself, Finwe was highly suspicious of the high seas but had spent plenty of time on the water with his father — a elf of great honour, fine-tuned skills, and honest humility. After first teaching both of his children how to carve their own bows and arrows for hunting, he had raised them on ships during the summer months. He felt that having a greater understanding of another's culture was important. He first taught them how to build the boats and then how to sail them.

"He was well-known throughout all the elven realms and not just ours," said Finwe as he sat next to Annie for a while during her slow recovery. With his back against a large pile of coiled rope, watching her slumped over, covered in a blanket, and groaning miserably, he took several satisfied puffs of a simple clay pipe, and recited tales of his childhood to her.

It was a very welcome distraction from her unending nausea.

Before too long, he had leapt up and was acting out all the players in a story about his mother fighting an aëron uluun on a voyage they had taken across the expansive En Nén lake when he was a young elf boy, on the very ship his father had built.

Finwe's animated, intense, and passionate way of storytelling distracted Annie to the point where she suddenly realised she was rather enjoying the smell of the sea. Its sandy, sharp, and seaweedy scent, and the crisp, fresh feeling of the ocean breeze against her skin was now refreshing, rather than sickening her. Feeling more and more revitalised, she stood up and slowly turned to face the water. She gripped onto the rail as the sea rushed past her and she watched as what looked like dolphins repeatedly emerged from the water. Except, upon further inspection, Annie noted that they absolutely were not dolphins. Able to make out just enough in the soft light of the moons, she saw the shape of a fin covered in sharp, taloned spikes. Reeling back, she suddenly felt a quite ill again.

"How are you feeling now, Annie?" asked Carric, who had brought over three mugs of wine for them, much to Annie's brow-raising. She would have preferred tea, or more ginger-mint, but took the mug graciously anyway. It wasn't like anything she drank could maker her any sicker than she had just been.

"This is, by far, the longest trip of my life on water," she admitted with a slight groan. Her memory served up a long forgotten memory of the only other time she had been on water. It was one of the few school trips she had engaged in and before she'd become fearful of the water. They had been bused up to the Lake District and had a boat trip on the impressive Lake Windermere. Carric nodded as he took a long slug of his drink, careful not to leave any foam across his upper lip.

"That is quite the understatement, I am sure," said Lucan, making Annie jump and spill some of her wine. Both Lucan and Varls had a knack of appearing soundlessly. Annie supposed it was something to do with their elven soldier training.

And they're both bloody good at it, she thought wryly. *They are quite the ninjas.*

Lucan was casually leaning against the ship's railing, gazing out at the horizon. There was nothing but sea for miles in every direction.

"This voyage will be a long one and, if we are fortunate enough, possibly quite peaceful, and without danger."

"Possibly?" repeated Annie, giving him a worried look.

"Hopefully," he corrected himself, which didn't make her feel any better.

With a big sigh, exhaling her breath into the cold night air, Annie gazed up at the stars. Upon Lucan's suggestion, she decided to take a walk to the other end of the ship, where a small lit lantern swung from a hook above the railing. Not trusting her sea legs, she held the railing all the way, like a novice and petrified skater at an ice rink. She stood there in the warmth of its light, taking deep gulps of the fresh air and feeling the sea-spray splash up from the side of the ship, and mist her skin in a salty dew. She felt quite peaceful, like Lucan had promised, and the longer she stood there, the more she could feel the synchronised sway of her body with the ship, as it moved swiftly through the waters.

<><><><><><><><>

It felt like the middle of the night, or at least nearing it, and everyone else in her group was asleep in the belly of the ship, cosy and safe from the elements of the sea, and weather. Even Carric had respected her request for some space to get accustomed to her improving relationship with the water, and the skeleton crew on deck were high up in the rigging. For the first time in the last few days, she was completely alone.

Being alone was something Annie had long since become accustomed to. It was her default setting, her go-to safe place. She could survive on her own and adjusting to being surrounded by not just people, but elves of all things, for days on end was, quite honestly, exhausting.

She reflected on her time growing up.

As a little girl, she had always longed for a friend. A best friend to be her partner in crime, as it were. But, instead she ended up on her own, literally committing petty crimes. She had thieved from the corner store and nabbed clothes from charity shops. She had spent most of her life alone and, mostly through necessity, had decided to like it that way, despite the never-ending aching that she always pushed down. This ache was her longing for a family and a permanent place to call home. Somewhere safe, somewhere accepting, somewhere loving.

Despite all the need for caution that her eighteen years had taught her, Annie realised that she had quickly grown to love her newfound friends. She trusted them more than she had ever trusted her own mother, and was even beginning to see a sisterlike figure in Elva.

I would love for Elva to see the same in me, she admitted to herself as she hugged her jacket closer.

Her contemplation and alone time was cut short, but not un-welcomingly so, by Carric. The handsome prince came bearing something more fitting to Annie's tastes this time. He held it carefully as he came up next to her and turned her into him, wrapping his arms warmly around the front of her waist.

"Can't sleep, either?" asked Annie quietly with a little laugh.

Carric shrugged and sighed, nodding as he replied,

"I do not sleep well most nights. It comes with the territory of being a prince, I suppose. One always has to be on the lookout for someone who might want to kill you. Thankfully for me, I am the second born to the crown. Things are not anywhere near as constraining for me as they are for my brother, Adran. He is the heir. He is the important one. "

Annie completely missed the edge of bitterness in his tone.

Carric handed the package he was holding over to Annie, who took it and inspected the gift curiously. It was soft and squishy, and wrapped in a pale pink parchment. It crinkled quietly as she unwrapped it to reveal a square of what looked to be sponge cake.

"I thought you would like something sweet, after all that... jackhare and mead, and... well, the wine... and the... complete loss of your stomach's contents." Carric trailed off, uncertain and awkward. He clearly wasn't well versed in giving kind gestures or giving anyone anything. He was very much more accustomed to receiving the gifts and thoughtful acts.

His effort was not lost on Annie. She found his awkwardness in this instance, endearing. Carefully, she folded the parchment paper back over the treat and smiled. She turned to face him. She reached up to him and, lifting up onto her tiptoes as she wrapped one arm around his neck in a hug, she planted a soft kiss on his cheek and corner of his mouth .

Clearly pleased, he looked down at her as she pulled away and smiled a half-smile, the corner of his mouth twitching up where she had kissed him. Annie could see that he could feel his heart swell and further warm to her.

Clearing his throat to break the slight and teasing tension in the air, Carric turned to face the sea, gesturing to the waters ahead.

"Have your fears eased any, then?" he asked her, and Annie shrugged. She couldn't say no, but then she wouldn't be going swimming anytime soon either. She decided that she was neutral and reservedly pleased at her progress.

"At least I can feel fairly confident that I can stand up without going green around the gills and puking," she joked.

Carric moved closer to her and, for a moment, Annie felt a crescendoing surge. She couldn't quite tell if it was her magic welling up, or the fact that Carric was standing so close to her, or both. His arm, muscular and lean, brushed up against hers and it felt like static electricity crackling through and between them.

She attempted to ignore the feeling. They hadn't spoken about their night in the barn and now it felt too awkward to introduce as a topic of conversation. Annie leaned over the railing and looked out at the water rushing around them, frothing at the edges of the ship as it rolled up in soft, quick waves. She fished around her mind for a new topic of conversation.

"Have you ever been fishing?" she asked Carric suddenly, looking over to him.

Carric looked back with some surprise at the choice of topic, but shrugged and nodded slightly, the corners of his mouth turning down in a thoughtful expression.

"I believe I have, my love. When I was a young elf, my older brother, Adran, used to take me out to a little pond. It was a short distance away, behind the palace. It was like our own secret place. He would take us there with a pail for the worms. We would spend half the day digging for them. And we each had a pole that he had made from silkworm hair and the twigs of the great white Aspenian trees."

My love! Annie's thoughts shouted. *He just called you 'My love'!*

Not wanting to tear up this special moment, she fought down giggle bubbles of excitement.

Annie watched Carric closely as he spoke, getting more and more lost in his story the longer he told it. She could see that he, too, was lost in this beautifully preserved memory.

"We caught plenty of fish, but he insisted on never taking more than our fair share. He can be annoying like that," Carric finished, wrinkling his narrow nose up in a sniffle and exhaling a cloud of cold breath into the chilly night air.

Raising her eyebrows, Annie wondered, as she pressed her lips together, how Carric's eldest brother, heir to the throne of the kingdom of the Sun Elven Realm, had managed to keep control of someone as pugnacious and ready to defend his own honour as Carric. The parts of him she loved shone brightly through the cracks in his virtual armour — the armour where she saw how quick Carric was to fend off emotions as if they were an enemy attacking him. Clearly, she thought to herself, the prince had more scarred-over wounds than just his hand.

"Well, personally, I've never been fishing even once. I tried to catch a turbot with my bare hands when I was living in the forest once, but it didn't turn out well. I fell into the stream. I swear, it was only a foot deep, but I got stuck in the muddy stream bed!" Annie started laughing. Carric joined in and their guffaws echoed over the water.

"I cannot believe you have lived in the forest. Did you, really?" asked Carric, in bewilderment.

"Well, it was more like the wooded area outside the city, but it felt like a deep forest most of the time, when I didn't hear car horns honking."

"What is this car beast whose horns honk?" Carric asked, earnestly.

She giggled and explained with a coy shrug, laughing again as Carric was clearly paying her explanation no attention. He had other things on his mind. He tugged her towards him, wrapping his arms around her to keep her warm, and lightly kissed her neck.

Lost in the pleasure of Carric's tender embrace, Annie didn't, at first, hear the way the water below was now whipping about, sloshing, foaming, and moving in all different directions, as if there were something right underneath the surface, aggressively swimming back and forth.

"Carric..." Annie started slowly, half distracted by the movement under the water that was growing more rapid by the second. "Are there... sharks here, or something? Maybe really big kipper?"

"We do indeed have millions of creatures in our waters. Some say we have dragons that have gills, whose wings fold and transform into fins, and who can breathe fire underwater," he told her with such enthusiasm in his voice that Annie had only heard accompany him talking about food, or during their sexual liaison in the hay.

Carric's face was beautiful in the moonlight. The subdued light reflected off the water casting perfect shadows over his face, which was all hard angles and high peaks. His jawline glittered with a five o'clock shadow, scruff that none of the male elves had been able to take care of since they left the inn and Lilyfire. A sob caught in Annie's throat at the thought of that spirited little elf.

She noted that he looked rugged. Not simply the handsomely groomed, clean prince she'd been presented with at the start of their relationship.

She chastised herself. *Just how terribly superficial am I? I'm grieving for Lilyfire while also admiring Carric's good looks. Get some perspective!*

Hang on. Relationship? she thought again. *Is that what this is, a relationship?*

She remembered back to her wish over the birthday candle in the Necropolis. She didn't dare allow herself to think that the wish might actually be coming true. She was fearful that merely thinking it would risk it being snuffed out.

She looked at him in Finwe's shirt and waistcoat that formed part of their ruse for getting the prince onto the Shoreland ship. He looked so very different from when he wore his leather and metal armour for the tournament, with its family crest emblazoned across the chest plate. He looked more relaxed, more kind. Despite being royalty, he had travelled far and fought hard just like the rest of them, and Annie registered how much she appreciated him for it.

"Thank you," she said suddenly, turning to look into his eyes, which almost glowed. "I've ever had anyone take care of me so much before, let alone so many people... er, I mean... elves."

They looked at each other for a long, lingering moment with only the moons, stars, and the small lantern to illuminate them. As Carric began to lean towards her for a kiss and Annie's heart fluttered in a welcoming response, they felt something slam into the side of the ship. Annie stumbled forward, into Carric's arms, as he staggered backwards. They caught on to each other and then hurried to look over the side railing. Below, the water stirred violently and they both heard a high-pitched note that struck through the air.

As if in an enormous cave, the whistling note echoed, reverberating off the water and piercing their ears. Annie winced, grabbing at her head and Carric, who seemed unfazed, put his arms tighter around her, asking,

"Annie, are you all right? We have to get you below deck, right now."

Annie groaned and cried out as a vicious, stabbing pain seared through her head.

"Ugh, why? What was that?" she asked, her voice beginning to slur from the pain. She felt woozy and limp, and had Carric not caught her once more, she would've fallen overboard into the cold seawater below.

Suddenly, they heard another shrill whistle and this time, something emerged from the water. As if with no effort at all, swimming in rapid pace with their ship, the head of a woman emerged, breaking through the sea's surface. Beads of water streamed down her hair and skin. They formed perfect shining pearls that sat pimpled across her body, as if her sleek skin was water repellant. Her eyes, a pale yellow, shone in the moonlight. The moons had become fuller and brighter, and Annie could now clearly see that something was splashing a few feet behind the the woman. She seemed oblivious to it and almost enticingly, gazed at Annie, running her hands through her hair, ruffling it and pulling it over one shoulder, seductively. Amidst the splashing, a large fin was visible, covered in bright scales that shimmered and shifted colour from purple to green, and back again.

From their spot at the deck railing, both Annie and Carric saw her, and stared in disbelief. Annie watched as the sea woman swam inches closer, her eyes locked onto her own. Annie felt oddly attracted to this strangely alluring creature, as if she were both a beautiful piece of moving art and the warmest, safest place Annie could be at any time, in any realm. Pushing away from Carric, Annie wanted to be held close by this woman, who was now holding her arms out, beckoning for Annie to jump in the water and join her. Her golden fleck swayed wistfully to and fro, yearning.

It was as if they'd entered their own little intimate world together, there at sea — Annie aboard her Shoreland Elf ship, and this mysterious siren-like sea creature restricted to the foaming waters. The woman began to sing. She sang a most beautiful tune, lilting and clear. It rang out into the open night air and Annie felt her magic surge from deep within. She was filled with light and warmth, and a sense of happiness so strong, so all encompassing, that it made her want to weep joyful tears.

Suddenly, Annie felt supremely loved. Far more so than the love she'd received from Carric. It was the kind of love she had never felt before and most likely would never feel again. It felt titanium-strong, utterly and tenderly caring, and like it would never once wane, for all eternity. Tears freely spilled down her cheeks. Her golden fleck shimmered behind the saltwater that filled her eyes as she wept. Her skin buzzed as her magic surged over and over, and row upon row of goosebumps raised the hair on her arms as she began to climb over the railing.

Robotically, she kicked off her boots and brought a leg high and over the railing, hoisting herself up. As she listened to the beautiful song swirling in her head, the notes began to distort into dazzling colours and sweet scents. It was as if each melodic line had taste, smell and touch, as well as sound. With her leg nearly entirely over the edge, she stopped to adjust her footing. As she stepped down, she felt a slickness under her bare foot and completely lost balance. In such a trance that she did not utter a sound, never mind a scream, Annie was unaware of Carric catching her by the arm and, unceremoniously, hoisting her back over the railing to relative safety.

Neither did she remember how they fell and landed hard onto the unforgiving wooden deck of the ship. Annie landed on top of Carric as they went down. She barely noticed. As she scrambled to get back up, Carric held onto her, tightly. His strong arms wrapped around her waist, holding onto her much smaller frame, as she tried to pry his forearm off of her with her nimble fingers. Failing to prise him away, she dug into his flesh with her short, yet sharp, nails.

"Ow! Annie, cease now! Trust me, you do not want to go out there!" But Carric's desperate plea fell on deaf, human ears as she simply continued her efforts to join the woman of the sea.

"Let me go, Carric," she ordered. Her voice was eerily calm and stilted, and there was a soft, melodic echo behind it now. Above the ship, heavy clouds began to form.

"Annie, look," shouted Carric, above the sea creature's song and gesturing to the sky. "Look at what you are doing. Ignore her, Annie! It is just a siren, she is just singing whatever will get you into her clutches. No magic you do will get me to release you to that fiend." And Carric hugged her so tightly to him that he thought her ribs might break. "You are safe with me. You are mine."

Hefty spots of rain began to patter against his skin and clothes, and as a storm began raining down on them in earnest, the two of them were sopping wet in seconds.

It was then that the siren, her spiked fin flashing violently in the water, let out a long, ear-piercing shriek, and the water around her became tinted with red. She lashed out at what struck her, and from the lower part of her fin, hidden in the water, she pulled a long, jagged knife. With a scream of pure anger, she threw it back in the direction of Finwe.

It whizzed past Carric's head, barely nicking him on the highest crest of his cheekbone, and he craned his neck, bewildered, to see Finwe standing there, also drenched by the rain, his eyes wild.

"Get Annie down below deck, highness. I shall handle this fish-faced tröllöpk."

Nodding agreement, Carric hoisted the thrashing Annie over his shoulder as if she were a mere sack of potatoes and turned to hurry down to the cabin below deck. But before they could reach the steps, Carric heard Finwe's panicked shout behind him.

"Elva. Do not. No!"

Elva had jumped into the foamy waves.

Chapter Twenty

Finwe was readying to launch himself off the deck and jump in after to save his twin, but instead, he felt the strong hands of Lucan hold him back. Whipping around to face the Sun Elf commander, Finwe couldn't hold back his angry exasperation. He spat out his words as he tried to free himself.

"How dare you prevent me from saving my precious sister! Oh but of course, *you* have no love in you. Your heart is made of the hardest nellon. You just have your soldiers. No, you just have *Varis*."

Lucan arched an eyebrow and wore an expression that Finwe couldn't read.

"More could show up," Finwe continued, desperately looking back over his shoulder to the waters below, while still trying to free himself from Lucan's grip.

"Which," Lucan replied in his typically commanding tones, "is why we must keep our heads clear and our wits about us."

Elva was swimming towards the siren and quickly gaining speed. Lucan relaxed his brow and refocused on the immediate task in hand.

"Finwe, your sister's collection of knives, her satchel, do you know where she has left them?"

Finwe's eyes brightened as he thought, his head moving from side to side as he looked around, as if his thoughts were cats and he was trying to herd them. Suddenly, his thoughts were all marshalled into the same litter tray. He nodded vigorously.

"Oh, she will be furious at me when she snaps out of this and discovers I have used her precious knives," he said, trying to rally his usually easy-going manner and failing.

"If she snaps out of it," warned Lucan. "Which she will not if you do not retrieve the satchel, now! We need every weapon that we can lay our hands on, to throw."

The shrieks and the shouting had spooked the skeleton crew on deck and they, as one, backed away from the commotion and held the narbuck tooth charms that they wore around their necks to ward off bad omens and monsters of the sea. The shrieks and shouting had also woken Varis and, moments later, he was right at Lucan's side, with his long, slim dagger drawn, prepared to defend his companions and himself. He needed only to see Elva in the water and Annie pushing, and scratching away at Carric's arms around her, to understand what was going on.

"Sirens," he said without hesitation, looking in Lucan's deep-set, concerned eyes. "How many?"

"Just one, for now."

Varis tilted his head quizzically.

"Strange, they usually appear in groups."

"Exactly," replied Lucan, flatly.

Human eyes would have seen nothing while peering out into the vast, unending darkness, with the only light coming from the moons and their reflection off the salty water. However Varis's eyes, as with all elf eyes, adapted well to the dark, and he watched now as Elva single-mindedly continued to swim towards the siren. She was gaining speed and quickly closing the gap between herself and this tantalising woman-creature of the water. The temptress stretched her arms out to Elva. She had almost reached her when something from behind Elva whizzed past her ear, nicking her left lobe. Elva's trance instantly broke and she watched as the beautiful creature hissed and snarled at the elven spear that had hit her directly in the chest. Her face, which had now turned ugly, bared its rows of sharp teeth at Elva. In response, Elva yelped and pushed this speared body as far away as she could through the waves, which were growing in size and ferocity.

The singing siren had abruptly stopped her song. With apparent ease, she snapped the substantial shaft of the spear like a twig and launched herself through the water. She grabbed hold with both webbed, clawed hands that drove like spikes into Elva's shoulders and head. As she climbed up and over her, she used Elva as a springboard from which to leap. Clinging onto the side of the ship, the siren's elf-like arms became multiple tentacles and she scaled the hull in no time. The salty water around Elva began to turn red and she whimpered in pain, trying her best to remain stoically silent.

As Elva struggled to swim, rivulets of blood dripped into her eyes. Unable to heed Lucan's instructions any longer, Finwe had pulled away and jumped into the sea. He caught her just before her head went under the water for the final time and she clung tightly on to his broad back.

"You are all right sister. I have got you!" he shouted over the sound of the swirling waves that he now struggled to swim through. But, ever the determined Woodland Elf, Finwe forged ahead, dragging Elva with him as he swam in strong, sure strokes, back towards the ship. There, Varis had found, unravelled, and tossed over the rail a sturdy rope ladder for them. Finwe began his ascent with Elva limply hanging off him like a sodden woollen cloak.

Meanwhile, the siren had crawled up the side of the ship and was now, on unsure, fish-scaled legs, steadily making her way over to Annie. Annie was still there, fighting with Carric. As he'd tried to get her below deck to safety, he'd been struggling to pry Annie's hands away from the doorframe. Her grip was stronger under the influence of the siren, and Annie herself could feel her magic igniting, and coursing through her veins, enabling her to effectively fight against Carric's usually iron grip. Had he had time to reflect at this moment, he would surely have felt rather emasculated. Carric freed a hand and outstretched his arm.

"Lucan! Varis! Sword! Now!" Carric called to them, as his tussle with Annie continued. Allowing no chance for his commander to be unarmed, Varis unsheathed his sword at once. With great might, he tossed his sword through the air. For a terrible moment, it looked like it would slice clean through Carric's hand but, with the deftness of a lifetime of training, Carric caught it by the hilt in one swift move. It felt reassuringly heavy and solid in his hand. And, with a renewed sense of urgency and surge of energy, he smirked, and bellowed above the raging waters and the struggling Annie,

"Have a taste of a Sun Elven blade, you scaly, guileful nasto!"

Undeterred, the siren remained on course, quickening her unsteady pace to reach Annie, who, at the very last moment, Carric tossed aside. Annie hit the deck with all the grace of a newly birthed giraffe and rolled a couple times. Unfazed and unharmed, she sprang up, ever steadfast in her attempt to reach the siren again.

Carric lunged for the siren, but surprisingly, she deftly swerved away. He swung his sword, missing again by barely a hair's breadth. Stunned at his inability to connect with this temptress, he lost his footing and fell, hard. The force of his swing sent the sword clattering out of his hand.

With a gasp, Annie was swept forward into the siren's sweet embrace. She smelled of saltwater and millions of Annie's own memories, some real and many others mutated into how Annie would have liked them to have been. She could smell the cookies she had burned on her mother's birthday. She had forgotten them in the oven because she had been too busy holding her mother's hair back as she wretched into the toilet following a night of monumental drink binging. She smelled the acrid, herby firewood lit by Elva for the last several nights, and the fresh-cut grass in Glasgow's Linn Park. Even the smell of a particular perfume, a bottle her mother owned, grabbed onto Annie like a heavy nostalgic vice, and she felt the siren's tentacled embrace tightening.

Tightening... tightening... tightening. The siren's embrace progressively tightened.

Suddenly, Annie felt acute distress. She felt suffocated, literally. Unable to breathe, she started pulling at the siren's tentacles that had coiled further and further around her. Annie felt herself begin to black out, her lungs and ribs slowly being crushed.

And then she heard it.

A voice.

It was familiar and entered her head as if it were her own thoughts speaking out loud. But this voice was cold, sinister, dark. This voice relayed bitter anger and spite, hideous betrayal, and painful despair. The sudden abject loneliness she felt from hearing the voice made her cry out, involuntarily.

"Now you have seen what I can do," the disembodied voice whispered, and Annie gasped. The single siren meant for her, that had lured and attacked Elva, he was controlling it. Annie now saw the same dead eyes she had stared into, inside his dark and murky tower. Even in the shadows, his catlike eyes were unmistakable.

Tathlyn had found her.

And now, he was somehow telepathically communicating to her. She spat her reply in a defiant whisper,

"Screw you, you total dräbssta."

An angry, shrill scream pierced her ears and reverberated throughout her entire body. Annie lurched forward, rolling her head in pain. The voice buzzed through her, ricocheting off the insides of her skull as it hissed at her with nothing but contempt,

"Vile, putrid female human. Deceiver! Now that I am inside your head, it is crystal clear that you are not she. How could I have ever thought you were my Meredith?"

Each word stabbed like a barb into her brain, and there was that name again. Annie, desperate, cried out for Carric.

Carric had regained his bearings and was running to her. He was shouting something to Lucan and Varis, who were helping Finwe to carry a bleeding, thrashing Elva away from the sea and away from the siren.

Tathlyn's voice persisted in Annie's ears, now with an intensifying cruel and sneering tone.

"Oh, I see. You love him... You. Love. Him. How utterly foolish!"

He mocked her now, his tone childish, almost silly, as if he were dancing about like a jester right in front of her.

"You stupid girl. Do you not know what love gets you? It gets you nothing but misery and anguish. It makes you weak and vulnerable. This Carric is nothing. He is simply a pawn in my way."

Then, almost as an afterthought, he added,

"I wonder just how far you'll go for him."

Annie shook her head, frustration and magic growing inside of her as she could not avoid listening to the confusing and invasive, voice. Originating from deep in her belly, Annie let out a terrific roar in fury, trying her hardest to use her magic to shake him, and failing.

King Tathlyn would not budge.

While the siren he embodied raged on, the frothing, angry waves intensyfied, Annie called out for Carric once more.

This time, he reached her. She shut her eyes tightly and held her breath as Carric lifted his sword high above his head, and swung the blade down, beheading the siren in one clean slice.

Annie hit the deck, hard.

As suddenly as the voice had entered her head, it disappeared.

Instantly, Annie felt an enormous weight lifted off her. As Carric wrenched the siren's lifeless body away, she found that she could use the fullness of her lungs to breathe again. After a couple of preparatory breaths, Annie pushed herself up onto her elbows. She stared with somewhat wild and frenzied eyes at the headless sea creature now spilling black-blue blood in front of her.

Carric rushed to her side, pulling her away from the pool of blood which now oozed in her direction, almost touching the tip of her toes. Disgusted to the point of retching, Annie made no protest as Carric swept her off her feet and into the safety of his arms. Once out of the sight of the siren's bloody corpse, Carric gently placed Annie back onto the deck.

"Are you all right, my love?" asked Carric, checking her over. She had several small cuts and scrapes, and surely a bruise or three would appear later but, for the most part, she seemed fine, though shaken — very shaken.

Emotionally, she felt far from fine. The idea of Tathlyn somehow being in her head and knowing her location, had left her feeling completely freaked out, and vulnerable. But, being in the habit of fighting her own battles and disguising her emotions where possible, she nodded, slowly, not letting on what had just happened inside her head.

And what has just happened? she wondered. *Did it even happen? Was he here with me? Did I simply imagine it? Was that singing sea woman thing simply getting off on messing with my head?*

Her golden fleck quivered and twitched nervously as if supplying her with the answer. One which she wished wasn't true.

So, he really was inside my head, she concluded.

The terrifying thought sent an ice-cold shiver down her spine that was only warmed by the large, yet elegant hand of Carric's, resting on the small of her back as he helped Annie to her feet. She was so glad to have him there, a steady and protective presence. She almost told him of the voice, of Tathlyn's voice, in her head, but instead she stayed quiet. Still feeling incredibly weak from the attack, she was grateful that he was holding her up.

"We must be more diligent and never be off our guard," demanded Lucan, who walked over with Varis, his hands and arms covered in Elva's blood.

Annie's eyes went wide in alarm.

"Is that... is that Elva's blood? Is she okay? Please tell me she's okay."

"She is not okay, but she will be," assured Varis. "She is an experienced healer, and Finwe is not as versed as she in creating the medicines Elva needs to treat her wounds, but he is not unskilled. The wounds are not so deep that their damage is irreversible."

With determination in her eyes, Annie pulled out of Carric's embrace and walked unsteadily towards the cabin stairs, down which Elva had been carried. Slowly, she wobbled her way down the steps. Groping her way down the dark corridor, she appeared in the doorframe to see Finwe pressing a cold, wet cloth over Elva's forehead. It had been soaked in a blue-green liquid that Annie assumed was some sort of a healing balm. There was a long, thin gash that ran across from the hairline at the right of her forehead to the outer edge of her eyebrow on the left. While Varis had tried to reassure Annie that the damage wasn't irreversible, she found it hard to believe.

Annie gingerly knelt beside Elva where she lay on the wooden floor. She noticed that the floor was almost shiny, worn glassy smooth by the tread of a thousand elven feet over hundreds of years. Elva's facial features were drawn tight from the shock. A small porthole channelled the sunbeams of the waking dawn to dance across Elva's face, and she squinted as Finwe continued to cool and salve her wounds. Elva did not wince, nor groan. Annie admired how tough she was. She didn't tote ample flashy weaponry or leap first into fight mode in a skirmish, but she was tough — really tough.

She was quietly, determinedly stoic and brave.

Annie couldn't help but feel guilty.

Chapter Twenty-One

After what she thought had been a very much-needed and good few hours sleep, Annie awoke cradled in Carric's arms. She was exhausted following the siren attack from the night before and had barely been aware of passing from weary wakefulness into the heavy, enveloping dream-state sleep.

She could feel and hear Carric's strong heartbeat pounding with rhythmic assurance. The depth and speed of his breathing told her that he was still asleep. She took this opportunity to simply breathe, relax, and recharge. She didn't know when she'd be afforded such an opportunity again.

Admit it, she told herself, her fleck gently swishing back and forth in coy satisfaction, *you love being held in this way.*

But it feels so alien, she replied. *Not so much because this man isn't human. More because this elf is kind, caring, heroic...*

And... she pressed.

And... She dared not think it for fear of losing it. *And loving.*

Carric's fingers played with a lock of her hair that had fallen across his chest.

"You had a fitful sleep, my love," he said and yawned. "You were shouting at and trying to fight something you thought was in the corner of the room. It took me almost all my might to restrain and reassure you."

At this, her mind served up a flashback into her dreams of the early hours. It had been so vivid, real, and so frightening. In these dreams, Elva was stood at the end of her bed. She was soaking wet, her skin grey and drained of life. Behind her, from the corner of the room, there emerged a shape of darkness that swirled to take on first, the form of the sea siren and then Tathlyn. As Annie had screamed for her to move and lunged forward to defend her from it, Elva was consumed by the darkness. And then there was nothing.

Rising out of this heartbreaking memory, Annie realised that her cheeks were damp from her tears of anguish and frustration. Carric listened to Annie's recount of her dream without interruption.

"And, none of that actually happened," he reassured her, while stroking her hair. "Elva is much recovered and Finwe assured us that she will be fully healed shortly."

There was a gentle rap at the door and Carric bade whomever it belonged to, to enter. Finwe's head appeared around the door. He momentarily pulled up short at the sight of Annie and Carric entwined beneath the blankets, but almost instantly recovered himself, and rearranged his face into a warm grin.

"Annie," he announced. "I have someone who wants to see you." He stood to one side to allow the someone to enter.

Elva walked in with only the merest hint of pain or restricted movement. Annie leapt out of bed, not caring about her complete lack of clothing, and ran over to envelope Elva in a heartfelt embrace.

While Carric clearly appeared to be enjoying the view, Finwe blushed, reached for a silk sheet and quickly draped it around Annie's shoulders, while averting his eyes.

"I remember little to nothing of what happened," Elva told Annie, their foreheads touching. "I just knew that I wanted to be with that siren, no matter what."

"Me too," said Annie. "Nothing in this realm, or any other realm mattered, but her."

There was another rap at the door and in walked Lucan.

"Ye gods!" Carric exclaimed. "Will the entire crew be joining us, Commander?"

"I am sorry, Your Highness," Lucan replied, missing Carric's sarcasm completely. "Although I understand the need for any royal personages to rest after yesterday's events, I am sure you will agree that we all need to be up and on the alert as soon as possible."

While Carric would have gladly, in no uncertain terms, told Lucan exactly what he could do with being "up and alert," he conceded that, with the current situation as it was, Lucan had a good point.

<><><><><><><><>

Up on deck, the sea was pleasantly undulating in a steady rhythm. The crew were going about their business, but Annie noted that they were giving the two females a wide berth. The sky was a brilliant clear blue and she noticed that there were no birds.

"That is because we are too far out for any bird except the alberster, which only heads for land every sixteen moons," one of the crew explained, in humble tones. "And you are only like to see an alberster once, maybe twice in your life."

Catching a harsh look from the other crew members that were nearest to him, he skedaddled up the rigging and disappeared behind a sail.

Annie liked the sea like this. Its consistent, gently undulating rhythm gave a sense of assurance, of steadiness, and security. She knew that this could all change within a second, but for now, she simply lapped up these moments of calm and pleasure.

Throughout the day, each of the group joined forces with members of the crew to patrol the deck, keeping watch for anything that was heading their way to do them harm. Secretly, Annie was also hoping that nothing would appear that Tathlyn could use to mess with her head again. Thankfully, the rest of the day was uneventful. Despite this, the members of the crew and Annie's friends remained vigilant throughout, and soon night fell once more.

<><><><><><><><>

In the dead of night, Annie's dreaming woke her and she sat bolt upright, in a cold sweat. Carric's breathing was deep and even. Her sudden burst into wakefulness hadn't disturbed his sleep. She thought she could hear something unusual. Or was it a remnant left over from her dream?

Pulling her clothes on, Annie stealthily moved across the cabin and through the door, being careful not to wake Carric. Making her way up the steep staircase and onto the deck, she opened her eyes fully. Her vision was fuzzy for a moment from the leftover sleep sand sticking her eyelids together. When she rubbed them and restored her sight, she was sure that she could see the outline of something large. Unable to make it out, she reached for a lantern and held it up, squinting.

In the distance, with sails blacker than the night, was a ship. It was notably smaller than theirs and heading their way, fast. It made no wake and could only be seen in Annie's peripheral vision. If she looked at it directly, it disappeared.

How the hell are you doing that? she wondered.

The ship was long, narrow, and jammed tightly with cargo — living cargo — that now silently slithered into the waters, one by one, as if snakes hypnotised to swim in formation. They slipped completely under the surface, barely breaking the water's tension. Like smooth mako sharks, they swam swiftly towards her ship, undetected by all but Annie.

Not again, she groaned, as she turned on her heel and headed to alert those on guard, and raise those who were wrapped in slumber.

Chapter Twenty-Two

"Really?" she asked. "Can you really not see them coming?"

There was a desperate shrillness in Annie's voice that she was struggling to keep at bay.

Sounding panicked, even though you are, isn't the way to go, right now, she told herself.

"Baring in mind what we have encountered thus far on our journey," said Varis. "I am very much inclined to trust what Annie is saying she sees."

"Agreed," asserted Carric, unsheathing his sword and standing at the ready — for what, he didn't know.

As a commander, Lucan quite literally commanded and had all members of his group, and the crew stationed at strategic posts around the ship.

They waited...

waited...

and waited.

Nothing happened.

Nothing.

Nothing at all.

Annie was beside herself with the embarrassment of having created a huge call to arms over what had turned out to be absolutely non-event.

Just as Lucan was giving the call to stand down, there was a sudden, towering tsunami of water that shoved their hefty ship to port and scattered those on board like bowling pins.

As the wave was about to engulf everyone and send the ship the bottom of the sea, it dissipated, and reformed as easily more than a hundred Shadow Elves. They all spat out what looked to Annie like a kind of kelp, and rained down on them.

"Where the héllè did these lot come from?" shouted Carric to Lucan, while piercing a Shadow Elf on his sword.

"I expect these are what Annie saw coming at us through the water, Your Highness," Lucan replied, while swiping his sword, causing a Shadow Elf to part company with her head. "We must ensure that they cannot take Annie!"

The Shadow Elves swarmed over the deck, sure footed and intent on causing all manner of havoc.

Finwe and Elva were releasing their arrows at an impressive rate and hitting their mark every time. They, with Lucan and Varis backed up to form a protective circle around Annie. The rest of the crew used their daggers, swords, ropes, and weights to fend off as many Shadow Elves as they could.

Annie wasn't content with remaining a passive 'protectee'. She discovered that, if she corralled her magic and focused it through the palms of her hands, she was able to discharge an electrified pulse that sent those who would do her harm flying while clutching their chests in agony.

Nice, she thought as she gained some mastery through repeated, honed practice. Her fleck, while agitated, also swished its 'tail', gratified as she hit her mark, time and time, and time again.

The crew, though primarily sailors, still put up a good show and thwarted Shadow Elves both left, and right.

Carric headed to join the elven shield around Annie. Just as he turned to run towards them, a Shadow Elf, prostrate on the deck having been mortally injured by him moments before, grabbed hold of Carric's ankle and sent him sprawling to the ground. Carric hit his head and lay unconscious.

Several Shadow Elves mobbed him.

"If we cannot grab that brükling Meredith woman, we shall grab the precious prince instead," a Shadow Elf female hissed.

Instantly, Annie burst through her protective elven wall, intent on saving Carric. Lucan tried to stop her, but she was too nimble, too hellbent. She ran towards Carric firing off her newly discovered 'palm bombs' as she went. Finwe was one step behind her — something Annie only discovered as one of his arrows whistled past her ear into the eye of an assailing Shadow Elf to her left. Had she not been so single minded about the rescue of her Carric, she would had stopped to thank him.

As best they could the rest of her group maintained a protective perimeter around her. Now that they knew that Annie was the key to arresting the death of the realms and bringing them back to life, she was their primary concern. Although Carric was a prince, currently, Annie easily trumped him in terms of importance.

As more and more Shadow Elves were killed by Annie and Finwe, more still enveloped Carric, and gradually pulled him backwards to the far rail at the stern of the deck. Fewer Shadow Elves were advancing on Annie and, instead — finding her wall of protection too strong — they too, shifted their efforts to Carric. They inched the unconscious prince farther and farther away.

And then came the tipping point. The moment when Carric teetered between remaining on deck and plunging into the foamy waves, thirty feet below.

Two final Shadow Elves joined the throng and that was that.

Carric disappeared.

Letting out a foxlike howl-cum-scream of, "No!" Annie reached the rail just as Carric fell. As limp as a discarded puppet, he hit the waves surrounded by Shadow Elves. They pushed the kelp-like seaweed into his month before inserting their own, and then they pulled him under the waves.

Finwe grabbed Annie around her waist and held her tight as she attempted to scale the rail, and jump after her love. She wriggled and fought against Finwe's hold. She beat her fists on his arm, but to no avail. Her magic burst forth, stomach-punching Lucan, Varis, Elva, and the crew, and sending them backwards onto their arses. But still Finwe held on.

She went limp and sagged in his arms, letting out another fox-like howl. Bringing her gently to the deck, Finwe carefully handed Annie over to Elva's care, like a first-time dad transferring his newborn over to a smitten aunt. Elva cradled Annie. Annie wept, letting out gut-wrenching sobs. Elva said nothing. She wasn't about to insult Annie with useless platitudes and instead, she simply let Anna's head sink into her chest.

It rained, but only on the ship. It rained hard. It caused the skin of whomever it hit to sting and bounced six inches off the deck.

She had been wrenched from her own realm, kidnapped, rescued, discovered magical powers she didn't really know she had, fallen in love, overcome (almost) her fear of water, been attacked by a siren, killed elves, lost Lilyfire, and now this. Her newfound love had been cruelly wrenched away, right from under her nose.

They simply stayed there, their salty, sea-soaked skin washed clean by the rain. Many moments passed. Varis placed a gentle, yet fatherly hand on her shoulder. Annie slowly raised her head from the sanctuary of Elva's bosom.

"I am so sorry Annie." he said quietly. "You will understand that we cannot go after the prince. Our primary mission is *you*. You are the one who can retrieve our Labradorite Amulet and save our realms from certain death."

"But what if your *primary mission* decides to rescue Carric?" Annie blurted, angrily.

Elva attempted to keep Annie close within the safe harbour of her arms, but she was having none of it. She wriggled free and shot up, standing square in front of Varis, and Lucan.

"They put that kelp stuff into his month. They haven't killed him. They've taken him. We can get him back. We can save him!"

"Agreed," said Lucan, frankly. "But Varis is correct. Going after Prince Carric is not our immediate mission. We must first get you back to your portal so, together, we can retrieve the Labradorite Amulet."

Annie was incensed.

"I'm your primary mission and your primary mission orders you to come with me to rescue Carric, now!" The rain had turned to golf-ball-sized hail now and everyone dove into the safety of below deck to prevent themselves from being pelted to death.

Once inside, Lucan squared Annie up to face him, and spoke again.

"With all due respect," he said, through gritted teeth and clearly with no respect whatsoever, "the subject of the primary mission does *not* give orders."

The pair glowered at one another as the others looked on. Varis slowly removed Lucan's hands from Annie's shoulders.

"Once we reach the palace, King Peren will decide how Carric is to be rescued. He will not be left in the clutches of Tathlyn. Hard as it is, we really must place the needs of the Sun Elven, Woodland, and Shoreland Realms before the needs of one elf. Even if that elf is a prince and even if he means all the realms to you."

Annie exhaled long and hard, but didn't take her glowering stare away from Lucan. The hail stopped and they were left with only heavy clouds overhead. Lucan huffed a grunt of approval to Varis and went on deck to check on the crew.

Chapter Twenty-Three

"So why did the Shadow Elves not kill any of us or the crew?" Elva wondered out loud. "We were completely out-numbered. I mean, we are good, but not that good."

Varis offered up a possible explanation.

"Could it be that, while Annie retrieving the amulet would save our realms, Tathlyn has realised that having the Labradorite Amulet in the elven realms, gives him another chance to take it, destroy it, and finish us off completely?"

Elva's face blanched as her mind searched for other possibilities.

"Perhaps Tathlyn's plan is more sinister than we first thought. Perhaps he has further use for Annie, beyond and bigger than our realms perishing," she suggested.

"Well, they were not having any luck in taking Annie, so they must have taken the prince as leverage over King Peren." Finwe suggested.

"Whatever reasons there may be," said Varis looking over at Annie, who was sat staring blankly out over the waves, "we must keep our minds, hearts, and bodies locked onto our primary mission."

Annie was so lost in her thoughts that she didn't even hear Varis refer to her in a way, that would have riled her so.

She was remembering how Carric had saved her from being trampled, from the kidnapping by the Shadow Elf near The View, and from the singing siren. She touched her lips as she recalled their first kiss, the first kiss that she had ever actually wanted. With tears pricking her eyes, she laughed a little as she remembered Varis and Lucan waking them up after their night in the hay. She choked back a sob as she savoured each sumptuous moment of their lovemaking. Her fleck thrashed, aggravated, as she relived how she desperately fought to save Carric, using her palm bombs. And she gasped as she remembered Carric falling, falling, falling into the ocean.

It was too much for her to bare, so she buried her head in her hands and let the tears flow. After her tears ran dry, she curled up into a tight foetal position. Without a word, the others agreed to leave her be for a while.

Unexpectedly, there came the twittering of a bird. Thinking that she was imagining things, Annie looked up to confirm it was nothing. Her eyes, however, did no such thing, for there was a bird flying around *inside* the cabin.

I'm guessing you are one of those alberster bird things and I should be in awe and wonder about witnessing such a rare sight, but I'm not, she thought. *I absolutely, couldn't care less.*

"Well, I rather think that you should," said the bird.

Annie almost fell from her seat in surprise.

"What the —" she exclaimed. "Are you telling me that this place has talking birds now? And ones that can read minds?"

"Hardly," replied the bird. It coughed like a seventy-a-day smoker and then spoke again in a voice that sent ice down Annie's spine.

"There are no mind-reading, talking birds in this, or any other realm," said Tathlyn. "And it is not an alberster, it is a kystralla, which do not naturally fly this far out to sea."

"You dräbssta," Annie hissed as she lunged to catch the bird and missed. "What do you want? Have you come here to gloat?"

"Well there is that," Tathlyn agreed, smugly. "But do you think I would waste a complex, ancient spell and a perfectly good kystralla simply to gloat? I am offended that you would think me so petty-minded."

"What then?" Annie demanded. "What is it you want of me?"

"Ah," said Tathlyn preening. "Straight to the point, Annie. I admire that. It has occurred to me that you and your merry little band are most valuable alive, and focused upon the retrieval of the Labradorite Amulet."

Surprised, Annie tried to interrupt, but the kystralla put up a halting wing and Annie swallowed her words. Tathlyn went on.

"While I can enjoy the demise of the various elven realms — in particular, the brükling Sun Elven Realm — with the amulet hidden in the Human Realm, I am prevented from ensuring that my strategic plans come to their gloriously all-encompassing fruition."

"And what 'gloriously all-encompassing fruition' would that be?" Annie asked, finding her voice once more.

"Hmmm..." mused Tathlyn. "As if I would share my vision to the likes of you. No, for the time being, let us simply focus on the here and now."

The kystralla fluttered closer and came to rest on Annie's shoulder. They came eyeball to eyeball.

"While your flopsquib cronies are fixed on retrieving the amulet to save three of the elven realms, I want you to be wholly focused on Carric."

Annie angrily brushed the bird from her shoulder, stood in the centre of the room and let loose two palm bombs that simply bounced off the birds feathers like a light breeze.

Tathlyn went on.

"You can posture and bluster all you like, Annie, but at the end of the day —"

"It gets dark!" Annie spat, feeling that sarcasm was her only weapon right now.

"Oh, how very droll," he said, matching her sarcasm. "At the end of the day," he continued, his tone pressing home a point, "you will bring the Labarodite Amulet to me."

Annie laughed, harshly. "And why the *héllè* would I do that?"

"Because," said Tathlyn, with a mixture of smirk and menace in his voice, "it is the only way that you will get your precious Carric back alive. No amulet, no Carric."

And with that, the kystralla burst into a shower of feathers, like some macabre party popper.

Chapter Twenty-Four

Annie remained stock-still in the middle of the cabin.

She was dumbfounded. How could this have happened? In order to secure the life of the male elf whom she loved, Tathlyn had cornered her into choosing a behaviour that she detested, and that would bring about the loss of a value she prized above all other — namely, integrity.

Without integrity there could be no trust and without trust, there could be no positive relationship of any kind — not with friends, not with a lover, not with herself — none of it.

She crumpled to her knees as the thought of this pained her to the core and brought her to be violently sick. Her fleck thrashed angrily left and right, while her thoughts thrust and parried in her mind.

How can I not do as he demands?

I can't risk Carric being killed. I love him.

But how can I assist Tathlyn with destroying the Sun Elven, Woodland, and Shoreland Realms, and all those lives, to save one life.

But I can't risk Carric being killed. I love him.

How can I be the very thing that I detest? How can I be deceitful and untrustworthy?

But I can't risk Carric being killed. I love him.

And how can I lie to this group of newly found and true friends?

But I can't risk Carric being killed. I love him.

Annie's thoughts ricocheted back and forth, causing her intense anguish. And, much to the surprise and worry of the crew, the heavy clouds emptied their payload in the form of sleet and snow.

She was snookered — mentally, emotionally, literally.

Her fleck started doing rhythmic figures of eight and the sleet slowed.

What if I were to take the amulet to Tathlyn, free Carric, and then, I could swap the real thing for some sort of a fake at the last moment, and make off with both the amulet and Carric? That could work.

Could it though? She challenged herself. *I'd have to get from the Sun Elven Realm, through the Woodland Realm, and across the Shadow Realm, while avoiding being caught by Lucan, Varis, Finwe, and Elva, and quite possibly the entire Sun Elven Realm army.*

That's even before I do the sleight-of-hand business with Tathlyn to steal the amulet back. But hey, what do I know?

Look! she argued with herself. *I've got to try something. I can't allow Tathlyn to fulfil his diabolical and dastardly vision. And I can't let Carric die. And I can't completely betray my friends, and their elven realms.*

Completely betray eh? It looked like she wasn't going to let herself off the hook that easily. *So it's okay to betray them a bit? And how much is this bit, exactly? Twenty percent? Fifty percent? Eighty? I've either got integrity or I haven't. Can I live with that?*

But I can't risk Carric being killed. I love him, she responded, a tortured tone in her mind's voice. *I'm trying to navigate my way through the most difficult decision in my life here. And, let's face it, while I've never faced anything this big, I've certainly shouldered more than my fair share.*

Well, all I'm saying is, I'm going to have to face the consequences either way.

Annie's inner debate quieted down and she knelt for a while surrounded by vomit, and kystralla feathers, thinking nothing at all.

Eventually, she came to a decision.

Right, she asserted to herself. *I'm going to go big or go home, and by that I mean, die. I shall work with my friends to retrieve the Labradorite Amulet and somehow use my magic to manufacture a fake. I shall put the fake in the amulet's place and slip away to make my way to Tathlyn's tower. There, I shall give the amulet to Tathlyn, thereby freeing Carric. Together, Carric and I will steal the real amulet away from Tathlyn and get it back to the Sun Elven Realm. The real amulet will be in its rightful place, the realms will be saved, and Carric will be saved.

She was still riddled with concern. *Okay, that's a plan, but I fear it's too audacious and perforated with opportunities to fail. And, although I'm gaining more control over my magic, I'm way off having any morsel of mastery. And, while the realms and Carric will be saved, could I say the same for my relationships, and integrity?*

No, Annie replied in the smallest of voices. *I know it's overambitious and I will most likely lose my wonderful friends, and quite probably die.*

But I can't risk Carric being killed. I love him.

Chapter Twenty-Five

After attempting to mop up her vomit and the kystralla feathers with a silk pillow case, and tossing it out of the nearest porthole, Annie took a deep, steadying breath, and made her way up onto the deck.

In turn, Finwe, Elva, Varis, Lucan, and even a number of the ship's crew, paused to ask her how she was. Each kind word and compassionate look stabbed at her heart.

She said nothing of the visitation by Tathlyn.

Her deceit had already begun.

Varis and Lucan took her at her word when she answered that she was feeling well and rested, that she fully understood that the retrieval the amulet was the absolute priority, and that she was now completely comfortable with saving the many rather than the one.

However, Finwe and Elva were not so sure. There was something in Annie's movements, her words and the pallid quality of her skin that didn't quite ring true.

When either of them made further enquiries, Annie barked out a variation of her stock answers. Finwe was more satisfied than Elva, who insisted that Annie's words rang hollow.

"Sister," said Finwe as they shared each other's concerns. "I agree that she does not seem quite herself, but she has stopped insisting on us going to find and rescue Carric, and she does seem committed to getting through to the Human Realm, and retrieving the amulet for our realms."

"Of course" Elva conceded. "But she has lost her love."

Finwe gave an almost imperceptible wince at these words. He turned away from his sister slightly, in the hope that she wouldn't notice. Elva was too engrossed in thinking about Annie to take notice of Finwe's physical response.

<><><><><><><><>

The afternoon was tipping into evening when a member of the crew enthusiastically shouted, "Land ahoy!"

"Thank Gadr for that," announced Varis. "I for one will welcome some dry, solid ground beneath my feet and a guaranteed absence of sirens."

Everyone laughed. All except Annie. She was quiet and keeping herself to herself. Reducing interaction with the others made it easier for her to sustain the lies.

And it's not all lies, she thought, in an attempt to convince herself. *I am in complete agreement that we want to get the Labradorite Amulet. It's coping with* the lies once we return from the Human Realm that'll be the real test.

As the ship gracefully pulled into dock, the quayside filled with Sun Elves. Lucan and Varis looked at each other with bright smiles. They patted each other on the shoulder and indulged in a companionable hug as they stood next to each other, looking out over the rolling, vanilla hills of their Sun Elven Realm. Of course they longed for these hills to be awash with olive, artichoke, citron, fern, and deep forest green interspersed with splashes of cyclamen, alizarin, and buttery yellow, but this very much watered down view would have to do for now.

Annie felt such relief to be off the ship that she silently prayed she would never have to step foot off-land again. Her stomach agreed. Although she had overcome her abject fear, she knew she would never be a sea-dog.

"I'm definitely meant to walk on solid ground," she had said to Elva as they left their temporary, floating home. "All that swelling of the waves. It turns my stomach even thinking about them."

No, Annie would not miss it.

Elva vigorously agreed with regard to being off the ship, but for different reasons. Although Annie had been the main target of Tathlyn's siren, Elva had gone through the worst of it on the ship and in the sea. While most of her wounds were now merely thin, pale, golden scars across her copper skin, the large and angry gash across her shoulder, though healed on the surface, was still throbbing. The siren attack had clearly soured her experience of the sea. Being a bow-wielding, Woodland Elf through and through, she enjoyed the soft terrain of a mossy forest, as opposed to crashing waves. It had always been Finwe that had savoured the water excursions with their father. Annie put a light and compassionate hand on Elva's good shoulder.

Finwe was also happy to have completed the watery part of their journey. They were another stage nearer to saving their realms. Although, he was rather apprehensive as to what King Peren's response to the loss of his son, Carric, would be.

Elva shared Finwe's concern about Peren. He may agree that they needed to press on into the Human Realm with Annie. But he could just as well call for the rescue of Carric, putting the safety of his son above that of his subjects and all those beyond his direct rule. She hoped that, if that happened, Adran, Peren's first son and heir, would talk some sense into him. Peren was unpredictable and impulsive, and that, in the minds of the Woodland Realm twins, made him dangerous.

Annie stoically plastered a friendly, happy expression on her face and stepped onto to quayside to meet, and greet the elves who had gathered to welcome them back. She had found some peace in the thought that, at least for now, she and her companions' goals were completely aligned. In this moment and the moments more imminently to come, there could be trust, honesty, and integrity. There was no need to robotically go through the motions at this point. The tension in her shoulders eased a little and she was able to breathe, and move more freely. The group was all smiles, happiness, and anticipation, and Annie found that she could join in.

She was also pleasantly surprised by the warm welcome she received. In the minds and hearts of the elves, somehow, she had been promoted from being an accursed and loathsome human — someone 'other' and not at all to be trusted — to being hailed as a fully paid-up member of this group of respected, trusted, and well-liked elves.

"How's that happened?" she asked Varis, when they had a few moments to spare between exchanging respectful greeting traditions with local dignitaries and waving, and smiling to throngs of locals.

No handshakes here, I see, Annie had noted as various elves had crossed their left fist to the right of their chest and gave a crisp dip of the head.

Varis smiled.

"News of the progress on our journey will have been sent to the palace via craban birds from Lilyfire's village and the Shoreland Elves."

"Couldn't the Shadow Elves have intercepted those messages?" asked Annie, thinking back to reading about the World War II carrier pigeons that were used to transport messages back to their home coop from behind the enemy lines.

"Oh no," Varis assured her. "The messages are written in code and with the sap of the ooja tree, which renders it invisible. The Wise One created a solution that reveals the coded message to the elven eye. Only the palace has this solution."

Shielding her from the over enthusiastic back-patting of some of the crowd, Varis continued.

"It will have been noted, by powerful elves among the king's council, that you have fought hard alongside us and have worked your magic to save Carric's life against the poison from the crystals."

"I didn't succeed in saving Carric's life on the ship!" Annie blurted out bitterly and Varis sighed.

"You fought as hard for him as any one of us, perhaps harder. None of us succeeded in saving Carric, so we are all equally to blame."

Varis paused in quiet reflection before continuing.

"It will also have been noted that we trust you."

Annie winced at this. *If only you knew,* she thought.

"And if we trust you, others can trust you as well."

Inwardly, she was now screaming.

But you shouldn't be trusting me! I'm using you all. I'm lying to you all. I'm putting what I want before all of you, before those in the Sun Elven and Woodland realms. I'm lying to save Carric.

To save Carric, yes, but is it really just for his sake? her inner voice quizzed. *Be honest with yourself at least. You're also doing this for what you want, for your needs. You, who despises lies, dishonesty, betrayal. You should be ashamed of yourself!*

I am. You're right! Annie confessed to herself. *I should be ashamed. I'm ashamed and yet, also, I'm not. I love him. I love Carric. He would understand. He loves me.*

She was feeling utterly wretched.

Outwardly, she maintained an air of calm. Inwardly, her golden fleck sharply zigzagged in distress. Outwardly, the heavens suddenly opened, drenching all who had gathered. Everyone dashed for cover.

Lucan rounded the corner of the warehouse-like structure in which they were taking shelter.

"And now we saddle up," he announced and led the way to a sizeable pen with horses saddled, and ready to ride.

Annie groaned, loudly.

Chapter Twenty-Six

The journey back to the palace and to Annie's all-important portal, was still long. Despite the realm still looking a monochromatic palette of decaying browns, with the grass sun-bleached to white and crackling when stepped upon, the suns shone brightly and a warm breeze touched their skin.

Lucan, Varis, Finwe, and Elva maintained their horses in a close formation around Annie at all times. She had been given a trusted, gentle mare. She racked her brains.

What do the police say about horses that are utterly dependable in a panicked situation? Oh yeah. Bomb-proof.

This mare, Yavanna, really needed to be bomb-proof, as her rider was feeling more than a little panicked about being solo astride a horse. The last time she had sat in a saddle, Annie had been with Carric and hanging on to him for dear life.

Annie's bum hurt.

She had become accustomed to Yavanna's sauntering walk with the exaggerated swing of her hips from side to side. While Annie kept her seat reasonably well, considering the quick waltz rhythm of the canter, she was far less successful with Yavanna's trot. She found Yavanna's trotting motion far too frenetic and she painfully bobbled about in the saddle.

Her friends made it look so easy, transitioning from one gear to another with the slightest of indications to their rides. Their bodies and those of their horses were as one, in perfect sync.

They are playing the sweeping melodies of the romantic, Debussy, while I'm trying to perform syncopated jazz with a rusty saw and a nail, she thought as they pushed on through the woods at what Elva called a working trot. Annie's arse simply refused to stay in the saddle and insisted on jarring her sit bones against Yavanna's back every few seconds — relentlessly.

Taking pity on Annie, Lucan agreed to a brief period of rest before pressing on to the palace.

"We need to be at the palace before nightfall," he announced. "We cannot risk being out in the open when the inevitable Shadow Elf posses have a natural advantage. Once at the palace, we will need to gather provisions and rest up before heading through Annie's portal."

While the horses took this opportunity to graze on whatever brittle grasses they could find, Annie groaned in ecstasy as she sought, and found, blessed relief by laying beside a stream. The stream's bed showed evidence that it had once been a babbling brook, but now it was more of a leaky tap.

The moment he was out of his saddle, Finwe went off into the woods, bow in hand and his quiver across his back. Like all good Woodland Elves, he never missed an opportunity to acquire more food for the company he kept.

Likewise, Elva was off hunting. Rather than the grazing arasso, Elva's quarry was the roots of a particular plant that would form the base element in several kinds of healing potions and salves.

Varis plopped down beside the prostrate Annie. She had become particularly fond of Varis. He had always presented the more compassionate and considered face of the elven army. If she'd had a brother, she would have liked him to be like Varis. Without moving, Annie asked him,

"What did Lucan mean when he said he wants us to reach the palace before nightfall because we can't risk being out in the open when the Shadow Elves have a natural advantage? What advantage do they have, exactly?"

"Well now," Varis replied, settling himself into a more comfortable position. "Nobody knows quite how they do it, but the Shadow Elves have far superior sight at dusk and in the night, than either the Sun or the Woodland Elves. The Wise One has dissected many Shadow Elf eye balls and has observed no structural difference to that of either Sun or Woodland Elves." Varis sighed. "You will appreciate that having such a superior assist really does put us at a significant disadvantage in the dark."

Choosing not to dwell on the mental image of the Wise One surrounded by a sea of dissected eyeballs of all elf-kind persuasion, Annie was suddenly struck with an idea and hitched herself up on one elbow to face Varis.

"I've been thinking about the Shadow Elves that attacked our ship. When they swam underwater for all that time, they had some sort of seaweed in their mouths. I think Tathlyn may have used his magic to enable the Shadow Elves to breathe underwater using the seaweed." She added, somewhat sadly, "They even put the seaweed into Carric's mouth when they pulled him underwater."

Varis's face screwed up in thought as he considered Annie's theory. With a surge of enthusiasm that came to someone teetering on the edge of a revelation, Annie added,

"Could it be that Tathlyn somehow bestows this night vision ability upon his elves in much the same way as he enabled his troops to breathe underwater?" Annie was engrossed in the train of thought that she was riding.

"Rather than looking into the structure of their eyes, could it be that the Sun Elven Realm Wise One may determine just how these powers are bestowed by, instead, looking at the stomach contents of the Shadow Elf bodies?"

"The Shadow Elf cadavers? Oh my splendid elendil!" Varis exclaimed, clapping his hands together in newly discovered rapture. "I think, no, I know, that you are right! Nobody has considered what part Tathlyn's skills in ancient guldur magic plays in the abilities of his elves. That is, not until now."

His large hand clasped Annie's shoulder and gave her a congratulatory shake. Annie laughed as his display of appreciation and affection made her bones rattle from head to toe.

It was her first, genuine laugh since the Shadow Elves had attacked the ship and taken Carric. She suddenly felt guilty and abruptly stopped. Varis stopped shaking her and enveloped her small hands in one of his. With an unfathomable look in his eye and a voice barely above a whisper he said,

"Even when grieving the loss of someone dear to us, or annexing a part of ourselves that we dare not reveal, it is good to laugh. There is nothing, nothing for you to feel guilty about."

Annie looked up at him and gave a teary smile that silently said, "Thank you."

She wanted to explore Varis's mention of having to annex a part of one's life, but Lucan's call to action meant that there was no time to talk further.

"I fear that we have rested here for too long," Lucan announced. "I cannot guarantee that we will be at the palace before dusk."

Lucan, Varis, Finwe, and Elva deftly sprang into their saddles, instantly ready to set off. Annie quietly thanked the mare who patiently stood stock-still for Annie to climb aboard. She then, gingerly lowered herself into Yavanna's saddle.

<><><><><><><><>

Upping the pace in an effort to reach the palace before dusk, Annie continued to bobble about in her saddle. Often her downwards motion clashed with Yavanna's upwards one, that was accompanied by a painful judder up Annie's spine. It wasn't long before her bum was more pained than it had been before their brief pit stop.

The suns were certainly very low in the sky now and the threat of dusk was relentlessly breathing down the riders' necks. The palace emerged through the skyline, but was still only a silhouette in the distance.

Night fell.

They stopped again in order to re-group. Reluctantly, Lucan and Varis lit torches. They needed the light in order to see, but they didn't want the torches because they would easily be seen.

It's a Hobson's choice, thought Annie. *We're damned if we do and we're damned if we don't.*

But is it the only choice? She challenged herself. *Is there not another option?*

Adopting her childhood 'thinking position', Annie sat with her feet crossed, her knees up under her chin, and her arms wrapped around her shins. She rocked back and forth. Her fleck paced left and right, picking up speed as Annie's thoughts gradually fell into place like a complex Tetris puzzle. Without thinking, she was on her feet and addressing the group with conviction.

"Put out the torches," she instructed.

"We cannot do that Annie," Lucan said flatly. "While having a source of light makes us vulnerable to attack by Shadow Elf posses, having no light renders us even more vulnerable. We would not stand a chance in combat."

But Annie was adamant and pressed on with her idea.

"I can use my magic to infuse Elva's roots with my magic. I think I can make it possible for all of us to see as well as the Shadow Elves, in the dark."

"Do you think you can really do that?" Finwe asked. "I am not doubting your idea, Annie. It is just that your magic has quite the habit of becoming unfocused and unruly."

I'll give you unruly, she thought, but she said nothing, and simply glowered at Finwe — a tiny voice in her head agreeing that he had made a valid point.

"Annie has shown that her skills in harnessing her magical powers are improving," said Elva, strongly sensing Annie's animosity towards Finwe and standing between them. "Is there really any harm in giving it a try?"

Finwe spread his hands in a gesture of peace.

"I am sorry Annie," he said. "I am just thinking back to the huge blast that you created at the crystal caves. I do not like the idea of my guts exploding towards every point on the compass, having partaken in one of your magic-infused grothorf roots."

Once again, Elva stepped in between Annie and Finwe, the gap having become almost too narrow for her to squeeze into.

"I for one, think that it is worth a try," she said. "Let us continue with a vote. Varis, what say you?"

Stroking his chin thoughtfully, Varis came to a decision.

"I vote that Annie gives her idea a try. Right now we are simply sitting qüa."

It all came down to Lucan's vote. Annie couldn't help losing patience as the thought of a posse of Shadow Elves bearing down on them at any moment, filled her with dread.

"I can see merit in both sides of the argument," said Lucan.

Oh come on, you starchy elf, thought Annie. *There's no time for long, meandering speeches. Just say yes.*

"However..." Lucan continued, almost languidly. Annie was now fighting the urge to slap him. "We are far more vulnerable than we would usually be. There will be more Shadow Elf posses intent on absconding with Annie and we cannot, under any circumstances, allow that to happen."

Everyone was leaning towards Lucan now, all of them willing him to get on with casting his vote.

"And because of this," continued Lucan, seemingly oblivious to the rising impatience of the group, "I say we give Annie's idea a chance."

There was a collective exhale of breath in relief that a decision had been reached.

Elva immediately started to prepare the grothorf root that Annie was to infuse. Lucan and Varis remained on guard, looking outwards from the group with their weapons drawn. They squinted in an effort to increase their ability to spot any movement in the dark. Before joining them, Finwe stood awkwardly next to Annie. It was the first time she and Finwe had been at odds, and it felt incredibly uncomfortable.

"I am sorry," he offered, reaching a hesitant hand towards her, then thinking the better of it, letting it fall by his side. "It is not that I do not believe you could do this. It is just that I am unsure that you are ready to do it at this time. Controlling and using your magic is still all new to you. Gaining mastery takes time and effortful practice, that you have not yet had."

Annie's facial expression towards him softened.

"When you put it like that," she said, "I understand your concern Finwe. I've had to make my way around in the dark, metaphorically and literally, for most of my life. I really think I've got a good chance of nailing this one."

Finwe looked confused.

"You are going to put a nail into Elva's root vegetables?"

Annie laughed. Again there was that twinge of guilt.

"No," she said. "It's a human way of saying that I think I'll be able to get this right. As you voted against the idea, will you not take the potion once it's ready?"

Finwe stood to a mock attention.

"I am a member of this group. The group has spoken and I shall do as the group has decided."

With that, Finwe turned on his heel and joined Lucan, and Varis in keeping watch.

<><><><><><><><>

Shortly after, Elva told Annie that the grothorf-root stew was ready. Kneeling over the pot, Annie suddenly felt nervous.

What if Finwe is right? I know I've hardly practiced in order to control and use my magic. I know I haven't got — what did Finwe call it? — mastery. What if my desperation is getting the better of my logic? Who do I think I am to try such a thing? Annie's fleck danced a lazy figure of eight as if attempting to sooth Annie's unravelling nerves. To her surprise it did. Annie could feel a calmness and focus softly blanket her entire being.

Elva took Annie's hands and positioned them over the pot. Saying nothing, she moved away to join the others, leaving Annie space to work.

So what the hell do I do now? she thought.

Do like you've always done, she retorted. *Act as if you can already do it and blag it! We want a little less than your palm bombs and way less than that Mount Vesuvius impersonation at the crystal caves. Do like you did back then, but smaller and better.*

Smaller and better? Well that's really helpful. Annie laughed a little to herself. Did everyone have these kind of internal conversations, she wondered. Was everyone's inner voice so sarcastic?

"Well, here goes nothing," she muttered, placing both hands into the scalding steam that rose from the grothorf-root stew.

Chapter Twenty-Seven

At first, she flinched.

The rising steam burned and blistered her skin. But a moment later the burning sensation had gone, and so had the blisters.

Now her hands felt cool and alive with crackling electricity.

Initially, there came all manner of random and unhelpful meteorological expression, as her magic dispersed in all directions. It rained, hailed, sleeted, and snowed. Sometimes vertically and sometimes, whipped up by a squalling gale, horizontally.

"To say the very least," called Lucan above the howling winds. "This particular magic is not fit for the purpose!"

No shit, Sherlock, Annie thought glaring at him. Withering in the sharpness of her gaze, Lucan said no more and turned back to face outwards on the lookout for the enemy. Annie refocused her gaze on the stew and her hands.

What had Elva said? She asked herself. *"That's right... I need to use my 'intention' — I need to focus on the desired outcome.* Annie concentrated on her cool hands in the hundred-degree steam.

And here comes the magic again, she thought as the familiar feeling in the pit of her stomach bubbled and rose, and her fleck became increasingly, rhythmically agitated. Not wanting to waste any more of her power on any effect of a meteorological persuasion, Annie slowed her breathing and stared hard into the pot, to the absolute exclusion of all else.

Still not really knowing how to control her magic to do her bidding, Annie centred her imagination on the affect that she was trying to achieve. She saw Varis and Lucan moving around in the dark with catlike precision. They were moving as confidently as if it was a blue sky on a cloudless day. She saw Elva and Finwe readying, and firing their bows with keen accuracy, each arrow finding its mark in the chest of a Shadow Elf, their vision unimpeded by the dark.

Lost in her reverie, Annie didn't at first notice the changes that were happening to the stew. What was initially a squat, bubbling and plopping mixture was now a smooth, freely flowing liquid. The stew had been altered at an atomic level and those atoms were now moving in such a way as to create a figure of eight without the aid of a spoon. Her fleck lay still, curled up at the inner edge of her eye. It was as if performing this magic had been a significant effort, and now it was tired.

Typical, Annie thought. *I'd love to curl up and have a nap right now, but there's no rest for the wicked.*

And wicked is such an apt description, she sneered at herself. Annie chose to ignore herself as best she could.

"Chow's up," she stage whispered to the others, remembering that shouting while they were trying not to be attacked by Shadow Elves, would be a bad, bad move.

Not entirely sure what "chow" was or why it should be "up", the others came to her assuming that she had completed her magic. Whether she had succeeded remained to be seen.

With a confidence that seemed more than the situation warranted, Elva scooped up a ladle of the liquid stew and downed it in one. Each member of the group did likewise until the ladle was handed to Annie. She hesitated, but then, encouraged by the intense stares of the others she announced,

"Oh well. In for a penny, in for a pound," and downed it in one, like the others.

They all sat perfectly still, glancing at one another, saying nothing.

Moments passed.

Nothing happened.

More moments passed.

Still nothing happened.

"Well, at least the stew tasted good," joked Finwe, trying and failing, to deflect from Annie's failure and her look of disappointment.

Elva was just about to console Annie when, as one, two bolts of searing pain pierced the backs of their eyes. Squeezing their heads with their palms they made a concerted effort to ease the pain, and failed. Everything was too, too bright — so bright that they could see nothing but the light emitted from every atom of everything around them. They clamped their eyes shut in an attempt to shut out the light, but it kept on coming.

Suddenly, their eyes snapped open. Everything went dark.

No, not dark.

Black.

The rich, velvety light-absorbing black one saw on a newly brushed ebony stallion.

As instantaneously as it had come, the pain disappeared. Fluttering their eyes, as if to dislodge an irritating eyelash, the night in which they sat looked as clear as day.

Annie's magic had worked.

And not a moment too soon. Varis was about to congratulate Annie, when a Shadow Elf's arrow whooshed past the tip of Lucan's pointed ear and lodged itself in the empty pot of stew.

"Right," said Lucan looking at the quivering arrow, as the energy of forward motion reverberated and dissipated back up its shaft. "to work."

Without another word, the group set to, now fighting on an equal footing with their aggressors.

Lucan and Varis dispatched half a dozen Shadow Elves with either the deft parry and lunge of their swords, or with a controlled yet powerful swing of an axe. Finwe and Elva loosed one arrow after another with their usual and impressive accuracy. Their work-rate was fast, efficient, and sustained. Drawing an arrow from a quiver or a Shadow Elf's corpse, nocking it to the bow, and unleashing it, happened in one, slick motion. While Annie was the primary target for the Shadow Elves, she was now an equal member of the group, and no-one questioned her ability to hold her own against the enemy.

With increasing skill and accuracy, she released her palm bombs, with something approximating an 80 percent successful strike rate.

Is this really what I do now? she asked herself as she atomised a screaming, axe wielding, female Shadow Elf who was hell bent on cornering her, to be picked up, and whisked away by her comrades. A coarse netting was thrown over Annie. Without a conscious thought, Annie turned it to a hard frost and burst through its shackles to freedom.

I guess it is, she concluded, her lips crooked into a half smile.

Moments later, what remained of the Shadow Elf posse had retreated, melting into the cover of the trees, their shouted threats becoming whispers, the further away they ran.

Annie and her friends regrouped. Standing, their hands clamped to their knees, they were all breathing hard. At first no one spoke, the primary task being to simply breathe.

"So, I say we press on to the palace," Varis suggested between gasps.

"Agreed," the other four replied as one.

Finwe gathered their horses. They had been spooked and fled during the skirmish. Not listening to the groaning complaints of her buttocks and spine, Annie was grateful to be back in the saddle and heading, at speed, to the palace.

As the moons lazily and completely disappeared behind the mountains in the west, the group passed through the palace's outer gates.

Chapter Twenty-Eight

There was a mixture of celebration and concern as those in the palace first cheered the return of the group and then hushed to conspiratorial twittering, the instant that they saw Prince Carric was not among them.

As the grooms stepped forward to take the horses, Annie clumsily slithered out of her saddle and landed unsteadily on the cobbles. Her legs were like jelly. She wondered if she could ever become comfortable using a horse as her primary form of transport.

I suppose I won't need to once I'm back in the Human Realm for good, she thought. She noticed the sadness that accompanied this thought. Even if she secured the safety and rescue of Carric, and got his precious amulet back, it was highly unlikely that King Peren would allow her to stay as an honorary member of the elven realms.

Maybe Carric would fight for me to stay, she thought.

Would you want to stay? she asked herself. Without hesitation, her answer came.

Yes.

Elva's voice pierced Annie's internal dialogue.

"Annie, Annie did you hear me? We need to make haste to King Peren and tell him all that has taken place."

In a daze, Annie didn't resist Elva's hand at her elbow, guiding her along the high-ceilinged, marble corridors, and pillars carved with folds that perfectly mimicked delicate linen.

The royal gallery was just as intimidating as she remembered. Her long-practiced self-preservation kicked in and Annie's focus snapped back into a laser-like sharpness. She took in everything and everyone. She even saw details in the architecture and tapestries that had previously gone unnoticed. All the statues and figures depicted by the intricate thread-work served one purpose — that of glorifying Sun Elven royalty and more specifically, King Peren.

No surprise there, she thought and hoped no one noticed the roll of her eyes and the curl of her lip.

At the far end, large, heavy doors opened to reveal a banquet in the hall beyond.

Standing before the king and his council, each member of the group looked somewhat bedraggled. There was no time to be wasted on cleaning up and making oneself presentable. There was far too much at stake.

To no one's surprise, King Peren wasted no time on pleasantries.

"Where is my son?" he barked.

<><><><><><><><>

Lucan took a formal step forward to deliver the bad news. He bowed deeply, his right fist clamped to the left of his chest.

"Your Majesty, I am sorry to report that your son, Prince Carric, was taken by the Shadow Elves during our voyage across the ocean to our Sun Elven Realm."

"The stupid pellopë," snapped Peren, issuing a harsh laugh. "Hah! The stupid péllopé commandeers your services against my will, to save a human of all things, and promptly gets caught, and dragged away in the process. Brùkling typical!"

Annie seemed to be the only one in the king's royal court to be shocked by the king's cruel remarks. For everyone else, their king's vitriol seemed to be the norm.

Lucan, Varis, Elva, and Finwe looked dumbfounded. It was clear they had no idea that Carric's quest was against the king's wishes. Not giving the group time to digest the news that they had been duped into saving Annie, the king quizzed them further.

"Is the stupid pellopë dead?"

Annie flinched each time Peren referred to Carric in such derogatory terms.

"We think not, Your Majesty," Varis replied bowing in the same fashion as Lucan had done, moments before. "We saw the Shadow Elves place some sort of seaweed into his mouth before dragging him under the waves. They had used this seaweed in order to swim underwater and ambush us. It is our opinion that Carric...er... *Prince* Carric was taken hostage to be used as leverage by King Tathlyn."

It was dawning on Annie that it was Carric alone who had wanted to save her. Carric who had gone against his father's wishes, the king no less, in order to save her. Carric must have had strong feelings for her, right from the get-go. For a moment, Annie flushed in the glow of this knowledge. Her heart raced, her breath became shallow, her pupils dilated, and her fleck coiled around itself in pleasure. But the moment was fleeting and replaced by the guilt of having lost him to Tathlyn.

"I had *explicitly* told Carric to leave the human girl to the fate of Tathlyn's whim. Gone through the means of her portal, or gone through the savagery of Tathlyn was of no consequence to me. Either way, the human would have been gone!" Peren then spoke, half to himself. "And damned good riddance too."

In the awkward silence that followed the king's outburst, a quiet, yet confident voice came from somewhere behind him.

"Father." It was Adran, the king's first son and heir to the Sun Elven Realm throne. He came to stand beside his father. "I think you will agree, however begrudgingly, that not all humans are to be mistrusted and despised."

Peren's face flushed, pinched, and tightly screwed up.

Like someone's just guffed off a particularly odious fart under his very royal, upturned nose, thought Annie. She really didn't like this elf, king or not. There was nothing in his demeanour, voice, or beliefs that she could connect with or relate to. He was sour, bitter, selfish, and cruel.

Peren's eyes rolled in a silent, exaggerated performance of irritability and boredom.

"Not this again," he groaned and there erupted a smattering of animated whispering among members of the council.

"Yes, Father," Adran persisted in a measured tone. "This again. For the one who proved herself to be untrustworthy, deceitful —"

"And a thief," Peren interrupted with a sneer.

"Yes, Father, and a thief," Adran agreed patiently, his tone now changing to one of wistful nostalgia. "There was also the one that proved herself to be honest, warm, kind, trustworthy, and loving."

Again, there was the roll of eyes from Peren accompanied by a loud 'tut' that echoed off the gallery's walls.

There it is again, thought Annie. *Not just one, but two humans who have travelled through to the even realms. Everyone openly speaks about Meredith the Thief, but what of this other one? Am I ever going to get the complete story?*

"Well, this human has done nothing but waste the time of my two best soldiers and two revered allies from the Woodland Realm, and, on top of that, lose my son," Peren replied. He then hammered out each one of his next words with particular venom. "It was bad enough for me to almost lose my first son to a human. Now, this one before me has caused the actual loss of my second son! Péllopé or no péllopé, he is my son."

Adran blanched. The council continued to twitter, but louder now. Annie scrambled to understand the unspoken truths behind the king's words.

What's the story with Prince Adran and the second human, she thought. *What's with the wistful nostalgia of Adran? Had they? Surely not. Had they been... in love? Does he love her still? Yes... yes, he does. Where is she? Where is this second human whom Adran loves?*

The questions of Annie's thoughts piled up, one on top of another, over and over. She was all questions and no answers.

But this was no time to seek the answer to questions such as these.

Annoyed, King Peren smacked the end of his royal staff into the veined marble floor. Everyone abruptly clamped mouths shut, instantly giving way to silence.

"Enough," he bellowed. "As most of you here are well aware, the second human willingly returned to her realm some moons ago, having already bewitched Prince Adran."

Adran's pallor instantly changing from ashen grey to candy-apple red, he made to protest, but Peren brushed him aside with a flick of his hand and pressed on.

"While I had hoped that the heir to this throne would have pulled himself together once she could no longer directly influence him, it would seem that absence has not dimmed his affection... more's the pity."

Without a word and grim-faced, Prince Adran walked from the royal court with unhurried, dignified steps, looking at no one.

Wow, thought Annie. *That is one dignified and self-controlled guy.*

With a nod of agreement from his commander, Varis dared to take another step closer to the king.

"Sire, while the temporary — and I do believe it is temporary — loss of Prince Carric is devastating, we must, for now turn our attention to saving our elven realms."

The king was lost in his anger, but the Wise One, who seemed to have appeared out of thin air, placed a calming hand on his forearm. Without saying a word she managed to reduce him from a ten-out-of-ten to a five — enough, at least, to bring him back to consider the more pressing point at hand.

"As we have become accustomed to," she cooed, mildly, "the words of Varis are both wise and honest."

As per Annie's first encounter with the Wise One, she made absolutely no sign of deference to the king. If anything, it was the other way around.

For Annie, the most pressing point at hand was Carric. As Annie dared to step ahead of Varis, the courtiers took a collective step back, and gasped. Evidently, this was a significant courtly faux-pas. Even the unruffleable Wise One looked faintly alarmed.

To hell with all this dignity, deference, and pussy-footing around, boiled Annie. *Carric needs saving* and he needs saving now! If we do that first, there will be no need for any deceit around their precious amulet.

"Your Majesty, you must send your armies to unleash héllè upon Tathlyn and rescue Carric," she implored.

As one, the courtiers now leaned in, keen to catch Peren's response.

"Really," he replied in a dark, quiet voice that somehow still managed to resonate around the room. "I must, *must* I?"

Past caring about Peren's acidic nature and threatening tone, Annie pressed on. Carric needed to be saved.

"He's your son, he's a prince and —"

"And?" asked Peren.

"And I... I love him," she blurted, unintentionally.

In drama-loving anticipation, the courtiers leaned in still further. Unable to resist the unfolding drama, even the guards and servants did the same.

"You *love* him," Peren said with an extra lip-curling sneer. "Well, that makes all the difference. If you love him, we must put all our military might into rescuing the ridiculous pellopë."

The king was on a roll now. It was clear that he was thoroughly enjoying himself and the courtiers laughed at appropriate moments, lest his vicious tongue lashed out in their direction.

However, Annie's group of friends didn't join in with them. They remained silent, their stance square and their faces neutral.

"Thank you," replied Annie momentarily letting her guard down to make way for feelings of relief and hope. But Peren took a step towards her and laughed loudly in her face, slicing into her heart, and cutting down her hope.

"I care not one relyávë for what you like, love or loathe, *human*."

Annie's injured heart snapped shut and she stood cowed before the king.

"Even if I wanted to, which I do *not*, I could not send my army to take down Tathlyn and rescue my second son." With fists clenched, Peren swung round and strode back to his original place on the raised floor.

Once again placing a salving hand upon the king's arm, the Wise One offered an explanation.

"The removal of the Labradorite Amulet has weakened not just the Elven Realms, but the elves within them as well." She now looked a little chastened. "I too was duped by Carric's charming manner and used ancient magic potions to provide additional nourishment and strength to Carric's... rescue party. But this cannot be done for all the elves in the armies, as there aren't enough resources and it would take too long. In these conditions the Shadow Elf soldiers are stronger and have more stamina."

"If our armies were pitched against the Shadow Elves, there would be slaughter and one clear outcome. It would not be us that was victorious," Lucan explained to Annie.

Elva took Annie's elbow once again, and tried to lead her away. But Annie steadfastly remained in place.

"Carric still would not be rescued and, most likely, would be lost forever, along with countless swathes of our elves."

In the seemingly unending silence, Lucan spoke as the fine commander that he was,

"Sire, currently the most important quest is that of retrieving the Labradorite Amulet. We have learned that Tathlyn believed Annie to be The Thief, Meredith. We have come to theorise that Annie is some sort of relative to Meredith. We think that Annie could be instrumental in restoring the Sun Elven, Woodland, and Shoreland Realms to their former beauty, strength, and bounteous — "

Instantly and without warning the Wise One strode forward, making a bee-line for Annie and cutting Lucan off in his verbal tracks. Eyes fixed on looking into, rather than at, Annie, she placed a large yet elegant hand firmly on Annie's chest. She continued her unblinking stare while reciting some sort of elven incantation. Annie was so surprised that she made no attempt to dodge this latest intense inspection.

What now? Annie exclaimed internally.

This getting inside my head is becoming too much of a regular thing, she replied to herself. She hoped against hope that the Wise One couldn't see the contemptible deal that she had struck with Tathlyn. But the Wise One wasn't so much in Annie's head as in her very marrow and blood.

As suddenly as she had strode forward, the Wise One stood back, and looked skywards. Everyone could feel her mental cogs turning. Finally she announced dramatically,

"Yes, it is, indeed, clear."

She whirled around to face the king, her velvet, cloth snakes writhing and rearranging themselves on the floor behind her.

"This Annie *is* Meredith!"

Everyone in the royal court, including the servants and guards, gasped.

Annie was furious. The glittering chandeliers shook vigorously causing the courtiers to duck away for fear of shards of glass raining down upon them.

"I can assure you that I am *not!*" she shouted, determined that all present should hear her. Her fleck fizzed in disbelief.

Within a blink, the Wise One was behind her, holding her by the shoulders. Annie's attempts to wriggle free were futile. She flopped like a heavy cloak held in the Wise One's deceptively strong fingers.

"Annie is Meredith because she and The Thief do, indeed, share the same blood, but many, many moons apart," the Wise One continued, by way of explanation of her previous claim.

Out of the deep darkness of Annie's initial indignation, there came a glimmer of light. The chandeliers quietened.

"So, you are saying that you can confirm what we have thought — that Meredith is an aunt of mine?" Neuron by neuron, her mind was reforming into its more usual sharpness now. "You are saying that I am her because we share the same DNA... I mean... the same blood?"

"Not an aunt, no," said the Wise One. "I'm sensing that this is someone further back in your line. I am saying I can sense that Meredith the Thief is an ancestor of yours."

Annie felt her face warming in secondhand shame and embarrassment. A part of her had hoped that she and The Thief weren't related. She already hated to be related to her mum, with what she saw as such low morals and questionable values, and now it was confirmed that an ancestor in her family was no better.

But who am I to judge? she thought, reddening further still. *Isn't my deal with Tathlyn putting me on a par with Meredith?*

Then another thought struck her.

"Just how long ago was this sacred Labradorite Amulet taken?"

"Some twelve hundred moons ago," the Wise One answered calmly, without missing a beat. Annie's mind was wrestling, and failing, to comprehend.

"But, Carric, Lucan, and Varis all saw Meredith. How can they have seen an ancestor of mine? She was here, what, one thousand two hundred moons ago! That means that she would have been alive a hundred years ago. That's lifetimes ago, not that long after World War One."

She was really struggling with the notion that these elves could have seen a woman who came generations and lifetimes before her. It just wouldn't compute. It meant that this woman was basically her great-great-greandmother or some such.

"How can you have possibly seen her running around as a seriously old woman and also met me?"

Everyone present silently nodded an acknowledgement of the shrewdness of Annie's questions.

The Wise One was clearly pondering these questions.

"It will undoubtedly surprise you to hear that Meredith the Thief was not much older than yourself," she said, thinking some more. "Her style of dress was markedly different from your own too." She silently ruminated yet some more. "I have to conclude that both the passage of time and the life-span in our elven realms are very, very different to those of the Human Realm. Furthermore," she continued, before speculative chattering among the courtiers could ensue, "I strongly suspect that the time difference between our elven realms and the Human Realm is not consistent. I believe that it stretches and contracts, quite possibly at random."

Although Annie's brain was feeling somewhat fried at this theorising, she did manage to think about how well the Wise One and Einstein would have got along.

Another blink and, once again, the Wise One was at the king's side.

How does she do that? Annie thought.

"I believe that Lucan is right," she announced. "Annie is instrumental in the Labradorite Amulet being returned to us."

The courtiers chuntered among themselves, enthusiastically sharing baseless opinions and theories. The Wise One practically turned them to silent stone with a withering look that surpassed the look her friends had received from Elva outside the shallow cave, when she had effectively brought the male elves to heel.

"Remember that the Labradorite Amulet can only be held by the hand that took it," she continued. "I agree with Lucan, that we can safely assume that, being of the same bloodline, Annie's hand will be just as capable of touching our amulet and returning it, as the hand which belonged to Meredith. Annie is the key to opening the portal to the Human Realm and bringing the Labradorite Amulet back. Annie will be our salvation!"

Again, within a blink of an eye, the Wise One appeared at Annie's side and held her arm aloft as the courtiers, guards, and servants cheered, and shared a moment of triumph.

What is it with this woman? thought Annie as she danced like a limp rag in the Wise One's hand. *Why can't she just walk to where she's going?*

The Wise One just spoke with just Annie now.

"The blood that you and Meredith share is exceptional. I know that it is inter-threaded with magic, a powerful magic. I divined from the bronze bracelet left behind by Meredith, that she was a sorceress. A human sorceress, and one of the best in her time."

Annie's blood ran hot. Being related to a sorceress wasn't the sort of thing she'd expect to find on any search-your-ancestry website. She instinctively touched her own bronze bracelet — the bracelet her mother had given her. An antique bronze bracelet given to her as a baby. The only gift she received from her mother. And now she was wondering if the bracelet had originally been Meredith's.

Wait, she thought. *If my mother did give me Meredith's bracelet, maybe the same blood runs through her. Maybe my mother is a sorceress too.*

It may well explain at least some of her more erratic behaviours, she suggested.

There was no time to pursue her express train of thought, since Lucan had taken another firm step forward and was now almost nose to nose with his king. The tension was electric.

"Tathlyn knows that Meredith stole the Labradorite Amulet and spirited it away. We are all acutely aware that King Tathlyn wants to use the amulet to take over all the elven realms, if given the chance. Having Annie with us gives us a fantastic advantage over him. We must not allow him to take Annie back. It turns out that Prince Carric was right to go after her, after all."

"We both know that the wellbeing of the elven realms was not his motivation to save her," Peren hissed back. Lucan nodded agreement with his king and continued to explain his plan.

"I propose that the members of this group accompany Annie into the Human Realm to acquire the Labradorite Amulet. Once the Labradorite Amulet is returned to its rightful position, this same, strengthened group should set out to rescue Prince Carric. It will take time for our elven armies to regain their strength, time we cannot afford. As soon as Tathlyn hears that we have the amulet, he will use Carric as leverage in an attempt to trade. Our strong, nimble rescue party can liberate Prince Carric. And that strong, nimble rescue party includes Annie."

"The commander makes a compelling argument, Your Majesty," said the Wise One.

Now the rescue party and the Wise One joined the courtiers, guards, and servants in waiting with baited breath for the king to give his decision. The moments that passed felt like hours. Eyes glazed, the king was clearly ruminating on his options. Finally, he eyes snapped back into focus.

Peren was ready to give his commands.

"I have considered all the options that I have before me," he boomed slowly, allowing for the echo delay that could easily muddle his message. "The Labradorite Amulet is the absolute and only priority. Once it is restored to its rightful place, we can regain our strength and our armies will make all héllè rain down upon Tathlyn and his Shadow Elves. While we are preparing to do that, the rescue party put together by Carric, will go ahead with the objective of discovering the Shadow Elves' weak points. They will report back their findings to inform our fighting strategy. If an opportunity to rescue Prince Carric presents itself, they shall take it."

It? Annie seethed inside, her fleck glowing red and violet. If an opportunity to rescue Prince Carric presents itself? Well, you evil, bitter, and twisted old prune, I'll be making damned sure of Carric's rescue. I promise you that!

Chapter Twenty-Nine

With a flick of his wrist, Peren dismissed the courtiers, Annie, and her friends, leaving just himself and the Wise One alone in the cavernous courtroom.

The Wise One turned to squarely face the king.

"While I understand your distrust of humans, Your Highness, this particular human holds the vital key to saving the Sun Elven, Woodlands, and Shoreland Realms, together with all the elves that dwell within them. This human *is* the vital key. Without her we are lost. All is lost."

Peren nodded slowly.

"You, as ever, are right, my friend," he agreed, somehow managing to make the word 'friend' sound distasteful. "Although I despise the notion of a *human* rescuing the realms, I cannot deny that it is the truth. She is obviously a novice where her magic powers are concerned. I need you to assist her in recreating her portal. Just as you did with the other one."

The Wise One bowed in acceptance of this task and turned to leave. The king stopped her.

"Before you go," he said conspiratorially. "There is something else for you, and only you, to know. The human. She is somehow related to the other one."

"Yes, to Meredith," she answered. "We have established this."

"Yes, yes, I know that," he blustered. "I mean that second one," he said, his top lip curling in distaste.

"Lisa? Prince Adran's Lisa?" The Wise One asked.

The king nodded, annoyed at the mention of her name, and particularly in connection with Adran. The Wise One was surprised. She hadn't foreseen this.

"I noticed the bronze bangle on her left wrist when I first encountered her. It is the bangle that I placed on that other human... that Lisa." His mouth puckered as if the taste of her name was putrid.

It was clear that the Wise One was slotting pieces of information into a mental jigsaw puzzle and was coming up with a completed picture. With her eyes, looking skywards, it was clear that she was making some mental calculations.

"But, Your Highness," she said, unable to hide the eagerness in her voice. "taking into account the differing passage in time between the Human Realm and our own, the number of moons between Lisa's departure and Annie's arrival would make Annie Lisa's —"

"I know!" snapped the king, preventing the Wise One from completing her sentence. "And Adran must never know."

"But, Your Highness, if he knew, he could find out what had happened to Lisa. It would lighten his pained and heavy heart," the Wise One implored.

Peren shook his head vigorously. "If Adran knew, he would try to go through the portal to the Human Realm with the rescue party, in order to break away from them and find her. I cannot and will not risk losing Adran. He is my number one. He is the heir to my throne."

A hostile silence fell between Peren and The Wise One.

"No. Adran must never know," the king asserted and the Wise One knew that their discussion was over.

Chapter Thirty

Once outside the royal throneroom, Varis took the somewhat dazed Annie by the shoulders.

"Come Annie," he said, giving a slight smile. "We must prepare for our journey to your Human Realm."

Seeing her distress, he added,

"The sooner we retrieve the Labradorite Amulet, the sooner we can rescue Carric."

"But first," quipped Finwe, "we must eat!"

Reluctantly, Annie went with them.

After all, she thought. *What else can I do right now?* Her mind was scurrying about, trying to put all she had just been told about sorceresses, herself, Meredith, and maybe her mother, into place. It was like someone had told her to complete a jigsaw with no picture of what it was supposed to be and an untold number of pieces missing — i.e. nigh on impossible.

The friends were in the room with the incredibly long tables that almost audibly groaned under the weight of food that they held. There were tall pyramids of fruits, platters of pies, sweet pastries, tiered and lavishly decorated cakes, stacks of shellfish, and medleys of meats. All of this was punctuated with glass jugs of different coloured drinks, decorated with silver craftsmanship.

"I thought your realms were dying," Annie said to Lucan as she and her friends sat together at a table.

"You have seen for yourself that they are," he replied, picking up a porocë leg and tucking into it.

"So, how come there's so much food here?" she asked.

With his mouth full of tambaro, Finwe didn't hesitate to give the answer.

"You are in the palace with the king and all his courtiers. The realms are dying, but the king and his courtiers will not go without."

"Hush," Elva warned. "Be careful what you say, brother."

"Why?" Finwe asked irritably. "I speak the truth. Elves outside of the palace walls struggle to find enough to eat, while their king and his courtiers have the luxury of leaving food on their plates, uneaten."

"I can see it is not stopping you from partaking of such food," bristled Lucan.

Finwe rose to his feet, placed his knuckles on the table top and leaned forward towards Lucan, looking him straight in the eye.

"I have risked my neck, thinking it was a royal command. I am about to risk it again in the Human Realm and then, as if that is not sufficient, I shall be risking it yet again for the very pellopë that got this merry band together in the first place."

"That pellopë is our prince," Lucan warned, standing and mimicking Finwe's hostile stance.

"He is not my prince," Finwe replied. "I like you and Varis as Sun Elves, but I am a Woodland Elf through and through. We work as one with the Sun Elves to restore our realms, but I do not respect any elf who is not honourable, especially one who I thought was my friend. Prince or no prince."

There was that word again, honourable. Hoping no one noticed, Annie winced and her fleck reduced to a pinprick.

Putting a firm hand on Lucan's shoulder, Varis calmed the emotional waters that had, within moments, become precariously choppy.

"It is true, Commander," he said. "Prince Carric did lead us a merry dance into danger without being honest from the outset."

Now Annie and her fleck were positively squirming. She hated Carric being referred to as dishonourable, and yet he had been deceitful. And who was she to bristle about Finwe's indignation? Finwe was right. And she had become far worse than Carric.

She squirmed some more and felt sick.

Mentally, Annie held a mirror up to herself and forced herself to look at her reflection. Like Carric, only worse, she was being deceitful and dishonourable. She was lying to her friends. These elves who she had become so close to, who had grown to trust her, who had defended her. She had no one to share her terrible secret with.

And exactly what would I do, if I did? She wondered.

"Once we have had our fill of food," Lucan said pointedly, "we shall discuss the strategy for our mission into the Human Realm."

And with that he stood and moved to an empty table near the roaring fire. He sat with his back to them.

<><><><><><><><>

Making his own point, Finwe was the last to take a seat at the table by the fire. Lucan and Finwe gave each other curt nods to acknowledge that their disagreement had come to a close. There were bigger and far more important things to focus on. If the two were a Venn diagram, they had far more overlap of commonality than not.

Breaking the ice, Annie set their discussion in motion.

"So, as you know, I think I've seen the Labradorite Amulet."

Lucan, Varis, Finwe, and Elva looked at Annie, stunned. In all the drama of their journey to the Sun Elven Realm, they had quite forgotten Annie's revelation while they were still in the Shadow Realm. Each looked somewhat embarrassed.

Varis was the first to regain the faculty of speech.

"Of course, Annie. I am sorry," he said, his voice wavering slightly, "but are you *really* saying that you have seen the Labradorite Amulet? And if so, how so?"

Her friends continued to look at her intensely, but their stunned expressions had morphed into hope and anticipation for what she had told them before, to be true. She even felt that her golden fleck was doing the same. As always, quite how her fleck did this, she had no idea.

"Well," she started a little nervously, "I believe I saw the Labradorite Amulet not far from where I came through the portal."

With a tacit gesture of his hands, Finwe encouraged her to go on.

"I noticed it while I was at the Necropolis. It is... was one of my favourite places. It was so quiet and peaceful compared with the bustling, noisy city itself."

While they all yearned to know more about the amulet, they allowed Annie to have this moment of wistful memory.

"I would wander among the ornate gravestones, monuments, and memorials, compiling a list of the wide variety of people that were buried there and make up stories about their lives. There were sculptors, artists and architects, shipbuilders and engineers."

Annie was chuckling now.

"There was even a golfer and a magician."

Disregarding this mention of some weird and mysterious vocation known as a "golfer", Finwe eased her back to the point in hand.

"And the Labradorite Amulet?"

Startled from her reverie, Annie said,

"What? Oh yes, the Labradorite Amulet." She adjusted herself in her seat and focused in on her memory of the amulet.

"It was my birthday. I glimpsed something iridescent that glinted with a rich and unusual blue-green tone. When I got closer to inspect it, I realised it a piece of jewellery, about the size of my fist. It was practically glowing. It was clearly valuable. When I got closer, I saw it was carefully cemented into a low plinth at the base of the gravestone. Just looking at it made me smile. It somehow made me feel happy."

A wave of animated excitement surged through everyone at the table. They knew where the Labradorite Amulet was located and they knew how they would get to it. Everyone was talking at once, brimming over with ideas and anticipation. Lucan went to stand at the head of the table and gestured for them all to quieten down.

"We have already agreed that we all go with Annie through her portal," he said. "The question is in what order."

"So, you'll be forming a daisy chain, then," said Annie, thinking out loud.

The others stared at her blankly.

Annie stared back.

Have I grown two heads now, or what? She thought.

"You'll link together in a line," she explained, emphasising with hand gestures that moved in a crablike way across the table top.

"Yes," Lucan confirmed in his strait-laced tone. "We shall form a *daisy* chain."

"I shall go last," offered Varis. "We know from our captured Shadow Elves that Meredith could transport a maximum of six elves at any one time, but we do not know if it is the same with all sorceresses."

So, now I'm not just a human, but a sorceress to boot, Annie thought. Admittedly, she rather liked the idea.

"If Annie cannot transport as many elves, I volunteer to take the risk of being severed."

Wait... what... severed? The idea that she may not be able to transport as many elves as Meredith hadn't occurred to Annie. Suddenly, she was acutely aware of the severity of the situation and how their safe passage was completely her responsibility. Such a weight of responsibility was incredibly heavy.

Lucan vigorously shook his head.

"No Varis," he insisted. "As commander, I cannot expect my elves to do what I'm not prepared to do myself. *I* shall be the last one through. You, Varis, as my second in command, are more than equipped and experienced to lead should I fail to make it through."

A fleeting and unfathomable look was exchanged between the two Sun Elves.

"So," Elva interjected, while coming to stand next to Lucan, "it is decided. Lucan is to be on the end of our daisy chain. Now we just need a portal to go through."

She looked at Annie and gave her an encouraging squeeze of the shoulder.

"The Wise One will guide you Annie and I, for one, have every faith in you."

Each of the others nodded in complete agreement.

Again, Annie and her fleck squirmed at Elva's words. The expectation that she would be able to create her portal was pressure enough, but the shame Annie felt over them each having faith in her, was almost unbearable.

Oh how wrong you are to have faith in me, she thought. *I'm only going to take your faith in me, shred it, and stamp all over it until it is nought, but dust.*

"And so to bed," Varis ordered. "We must recover from our trials of late and ready ourselves for the challenges we have yet to encounter tomorrow."

And with that, bidding each other goodnight, the group dispersed — each to their assigned quarters.

<><><><><><><><>

Despite the luxurious surroundings, Annie didn't sleep a wink.

The dusty pink, silk sheets, alqua-feathered pillows and the softest, yet most supportive mattress that Annie could ever have imagined did nothing to assuage the guilt of betraying her friends' trust, and her worry over Carric.

To remind her of what could happen to Carric if she didn't come through with her part of the nefarious deal, Tathlyn bestowed upon her another visit.

As if she needed reminding.

"How many ways shall I harm your precious Carric if you fail to bring me the Amulet?" Tathlyn's whisper hissed in her ear.

In the darkness, Annie flipped herself onto her belly and firmly planted the pillow over her ears. Within seconds, her pillow was roughly ripped from her grip and Annie whirled round to meet Tathlyn head-on.

She was horrified to be met with a technicolour vision of Carric stripped to the waist and chained to a black-stoned wall. There were deep lacerations across his chest and it was clear that the barbed straps tying him to the chains, were constantly slicing into his wrists.

"You dässträb!" shouted Annie. "You couldn't even wait until I'd got the amulet before torturing him? What kind of monster are you?"

"Why, the very best," Tathlyn smirked nonchalantly. "I just wanted to make sure that you were fully committed to our arrangement, Annie."

"You had no cause for concern, you pathetic, putrid husk!"

Wherever Annie looked she could see Carric being tortured. Enraged, she picked up anything she could find to throw and somehow break the visions — things she shouldn't have been able to lift, let alone throw. Her fury and magic were working in tandem.

Suddenly, Annie's bedroom doors burst open and Finwe stormed in, catching a heavy candlestick, one-handed, before it struck him in the head. Seeing Annie's utter distress, he strode forward and enveloped her in a firm embrace.

Tathlyn and the visions of Carric atomised and vanished.

Annie cried, flailed her arms, and beat her fists into Finwe's chest, but he steadfastly held on. He held on until all the fight and rage in Annie had dissipated. Eventually, she sobbed and sagged, and still Finwe held on. Finally, when Annie was completely spent, he picked her up and lay her among her pillows. She didn't resist. Instead, she pulled all the pillows around her and hung on.

Without saying a word, Finwe left the room, silently closing the doors behind him.

<><><><><><><><>

In the dim candlelight of the black tower in the Shadow Realm, the corners of Tathlyn's mouth arranged themselves into a self-satisfied grin. He retracted a bloodied fist and the lifeless shell of a faithful Shadow Elf slumped to the floor.

The disembodied heart in his palm ceased to beat and he glanced down at the bloody corpse at his feet. The moment the heart stopped beating, the summoned magic deserted Tathlyn. It left him temporarily as weak as a newborn puppy. This act of magic had been particularly difficult and draining to perform. He wilted, and two more of his faithfuls carried him over to his bed to recuperate.

Tathlyn curled into a foetal position while Carric hung lifeless from chains against the tower's damp walls.

Chapter Thirty-One

With the morning came the hustle and bustle of last-minute preparations.

Overnight, the trappings of pageantry had been dusted off and brought out. Garlands of tired flowers and ferns were adorning the foyer and entrance of the palace. The palace was abuzz with anticipation. Courtiers, guards, and servants quietly chattered among themselves, like crickets on a summer's evening.

As they were about to sit and share their last elven breakfast for a while, Annie caught Finwe by the sleeve. She wasn't sure what to say without giving too much away, so she opted for the simplest option.

"Thank you."

"What for?" Finwe replied, smiling with his amber eyes.

"For last night. I was having terrible nightmares about...about..." She was getting herself into deep water now and was grateful when Finwe bailed her out.

"About Carric in Tathlyn's clutches, about deadly crystal shards, about Lilyfire, about the siren, about landing in these elven realms of which you knew nothing? Any one of these things could give one nightmares and you have had them all." His tone was compassionate and sincere, which made her fleck twist with guilt. What he said was true enough, but the primary reason for her terror and anguish was her burden alone. Her dreadful secret.

Without another word, they joined the others at the table.

Each of the elves in the Amulet Retrieval Party had received further rations of the potion-embuded food supplements that the Wise One had given them before they set out on Carric's quest for Annie. There was no telling what reserves of strength they would need to draw on while in the Human Realm and they needed to be prepared.

Annie had explained that openly carrying bows, arrows, and hefty swords around in the Human Realm would be a huge problem. Reluctantly, Lucan and Varis had left their swords in their quarters, and Elva and Finwe had abandoned their bows. However, they were determined not to be left completely vulnerable and, therefore, had secreted a number of elven-sharp, curved knives about their persons. In truth, Annie didn't think any of them would get away with carrying any of their various weapons, but her elven friends had clearly stated that going into the Human Realm completely unarmed was non-negotiable.

The Wise One gave Annie a pouch with a drawstring in which to carry the amulet once she had acquired it. Although it looked velvety, it was actually made of a material that Annie had never come across before. It was a deep, aubergine-purple and when held, its very atoms seemed to rearrange themselves, moulding onto and in-between her fingers — like the peculiar, yet pleasant feeling of playing with cornstarch mixed with water.

"This pouch will prevent the Labradorite Amulet coming to any harm while in transit," she explained.

King Peren was not there to see them off. The group had received a message from him that morning saying,

"I have no interest in your departure from our eleven realms. Should the Labradorite Amulet be returned, there will be much to celebrate. Come back with the amulet or do not come back at all."

Annie snorted, "He's as delightful as ever, I see."

"Hush Annie," warned Elva. "You must be careful. That is the Sun Elven Realm king."

Annie shook her head and retorted, "Like Finwe said about Prince Carric, King Peren is not my king. And, as I understand it, he's not yours either."

Elva blushed a little. It was subtle and hard to spot through her Bambi-bronzed skin, but it was there nonetheless.

"It is true," she nodded. "King Peren is not our king and Prince Carric is not our prince. The Woodland Elves do not have such a hierarchy by birth. We do not have kings, queens, princes and the like. We have no royalty at all. Instead we have a group of elders who make decisions for the Woodland Realm born out of conversation with the nature around us. It is so we, the animals and the plants of the Woodland Realm can live harmoniously. Or, at least it was until the amulet was taken and our realms began to suffer. "

"Hmmm," said Annie, thinking aloud. "So there's an ongoing collaboration with nature, for the good of all who live in a place, whether elf, animal, or plant. I think I like that."

I love it, thought Annie, with her omnipresent guilt painfully nipping at her. *And yet, I'm going to take actions that will continue its demise.* She wondered if she could go through with it, but her mind played back the visions of Carric, injured and suffering. In truth she was being torn, pulled this way and that between the needs of those she loved. On the one hand there were Elva, Finwe, Lucan, and Varis. On the other there was Carric — the elf who had lied to his father and the Wise One, and commandeered a group of top warriors in order to rescue her. The elf who had shown her tenderness and with whom she had shared the ultimate intimacy. With effort, her golden fleck shut the door on these thoughts and feelings. None of these thoughts and feelings were going to help her. They would only serve to tear her apart.

"I said, what do you think, Annie?" Finwe repeated, snapping Annie back to the here and now.

"Sorry," said Annie. "I was away with the fairies."

Her friends looked something between puzzled and alarmed.

"You have been away with the fairies?" asked Lucan. "How can this be? You have been here with us the whole time."

Annie laughed, then wished she hadn't. Her friends were not taking her statement lightly. Not even Finwe, who could often see the funnier side of things, was smiling.

"Oh, I'm sorry. I was just... just deep in thought," she explained. "Away with the fairies, is just a saying that we have in the Human Realm."

The group were visibly relieved.

"For a moment there," said Varis, "we thought perhaps you had actually been with the fairies at some time."

"Wait, is that something that can actually happen here?" Annie asked, incredulously. "You mean to say there really are fairies and you can actually be away with them?"

"Indeed there are and indeed you can," Varis stated, seriously. "But it is not something you would want. The fairies are sly, skilled in sleight of hand, and are not to be trusted."

Exactly like me then, she thought. So as not to be caught out by what she was really thinking, Annie carefully rearranged her face into what she hoped looked like a natural smile.

"Phew!" She said, with forced light-heartedness. "Thank goodness it was just a figure of speech, then."

The rest of breakfast was subdued as each contemplated the task ahead. No one ate very much, apart from Finwe. As ever, Finwe ate plenty and made a point of leaving his plate clean.

<><><><><><><><>

The route from the palace gates to the spot where Annie had first entered the Sun Elven Realm, was lined with elves of all ages and standing. The wealthiest were almost cheek by jowl with the poorest — almost, but not quite, for that would never do.

"Apparently," mused Varis, "this small-scale operation is now a significant, historical event."

The group were on their horses and walking steadily along the designated path.

Now this is a pace in the saddle that I can totally cope with, thought Annie as her completely calm and chill mare, Yavanna, walked behind Lucan on his stallion, Loben. Yavanna's hips swayed rhythmically and Annie let her body flop and fall in with her horse's rhythm. It soothed her nerves, of which she had plenty.

Unlike when she had first arrived in the Sun Elven Realm, the elven children pushed past the adults to get a better view, instead of hiding behind their skirts as they had done before. There was enthusiastic clapping and cheering all the way. It was so loud that the friends couldn't hear each other.

It was clear that the group on horseback had raised the elves' spirits and hopes. Annie was in at least two minds as to how she felt about it. Her fleck swished back and forth in an unsettled fashion. Clouds began to race in and she had to steady her breathing to ensure the crowd didn't get soaked by a vigorous, spontaneous shower of rain. On the one hand, it was exhilarating to be the centre of so many's adulation.

On the other hand, her thought continued, *I feel terrible shame about living a lie with them.*

On another hand, she countered herself, *I feel committed to saving my Carric.*

And on yet another hand, she argued. *I feel guilty that I will raise their hopes further only to dash them completely.*

Annie eventually settled on feeling utterly focused on the current task in hand. Right now, the only thing that mattered was getting to and retrieving the Labradorite Amulet.

One thing at a time, she told herself. *One thing at a time.*

<><><><><><><><>

The Wise One was already at the portal site and ready to greet the group. She would be instrumental in mentoring Annie to create her portal. The crowd fell silent as the group arrived.

Lucan, Varis, Finwe, and Elva dismounted with their usual deft litheness. With a concerted effort, Annie swung her right leg over Yavanna's haunches, momentarily teetered on her stomach in the saddle, and finally slithered down to the ground. Everyone looked away to save Annie from excessive embarrassment.

In a voice that somehow projected to be heard by everyone in the crowd all along their route from the palace, the Wise One broke the awkward silence that had followed Annie's dismount.

"So, the time has come for you to create your portal through which you and your friends will travel."

Before Annie could respond, she handed her some sort of dried fruit, not unlike a medjool date, but cobalt blue. The Wise One gestured for Annie to eat it. Having finished the sweet fruit, Annie began to speak and was startled to discover that her voice easily projected for all to hear, too.

"But... but I have no idea how I created it before. I was running from security guards at the Necropolis, I laid my hand on a gravestone and it all just kind of happened."

"It matters not," soothed the Wise One. "I am here to guide and support you in the making of your portal."

A thought struck Annie.

"You keep saying 'your portal'. Why not the portal?"

"Ah," said the Wise One looking impressed that Annie had noticed this subtle and precise use of language. "We have learned from the two humans that preceded you, that each human with the powers such as those you possess, has her own, personal portal. There is not simply one portal through which you can all travel."

Personal portal, eh? Annie thought, her fleck curling and uncurling its tail casually. *That's actually pretty cool.*

The chance to remain absorbed in her own thoughts was abruptly cut short as the Wise One firmly gripped her shoulder and turn her round.

"Start pacing in a circle," she directed.

Unsure and embarrassed, Annie walked in a tight circle. The Wise One soon grew unusually impatient and started to wave her arms in encouragement.

"A bigger circle Annie, and faster. Pace, girl, pace!"

Annie threw the Wise One a peeved glare, but increased her speed and size of circle, as she was told.

Nothing was happening.

"This can't be right," Annie protested. "Nothing's happening and I wasn't pacing in circles when I was in Glasgow."

Now it was the turn of the Wise One to look peeved.

"This is simply the beginning of the process," she snapped, uncharacteristically.

Everyone in the crowd, from the portal site right back to the palace could hear every word of what was potentially descending into an undignified spat. The Wise One took a deep breath and quickly composed herself.

"Annie," she said in her more recognisable rich, mystic, and plummy tone. "There is a process to creating your portal here in the Sun Elven Realm. We have learned that it is a place rather than a thing that is your gateway between the realms. Keep circling and I shall facilitate the next stage."

With the heavy and melodramatic sigh of a reluctant teen, Annie circled faster. She was getting really hacked off with the Wise One and didn't notice the fat, black clouds that began to shroud the sky. Varis, Lucan, Elva, and Finwe took up positions to create an outer circle to the one Annie was now striding around.

"That's good, Annie," the Wise One called. The hefty clouds brought strong winds that made it hard to be heard, even with the assistance of the blue date-like fruit. "We need you to draw on some of your strongest emotional experiences. Preferably the negative ones as they seem to engender more of the portal creating magic that's within you!"

Well if that's all you need, thought Annie, *I've got plenty of those!*

"Think back, Annie," called the Wise One. "Think back to when you've been hurt or angry, or terribly sad."

Annie's arms clamped to her sides, her hands became tight fists, and she threw her head back to emit a primeval scream as the experiences of strong, negative, emotional experiences flooded over, and through her. They made a dense and weighty scrapbook in her mind and it was as if she was flicking through the pages so fast that they made a sort of flip-book animation.

The sorrow of forgotten birthdays, of the terrible loss of Lilyfire, and of Annie's weeping mother following the beatings of various men. The fear that she wouldn't be able to trade the amulet for Carric, that she may lose her love, and the fear of how her recently won, and so precious friends, would hate her. The anger of unwanted attention from those violent men because her mother didn't protect her, for Tathlyn taking Carric, and cornering her into making a deal that went against everything she valued. Oh there was so much anger that tipped into unchecked rage.

Annie was completely oblivious to the Wise One's encouragement or that the crowd was staggering backwards out of harm's way. The clouds that had shrouded the sky had morphed into a raging storm, yet her friends steadfastly remained in their places, despite their skin being pummelled and lacerated by biting hailstones.

At the event of a particularly savage strike of lightning, in the centre of Annie's trodden circle, her portal sprang open.

"This is it!" The Wise One shouted, her sodden hair and clothes plastered to her face, and body. "You must go now. All of you!"

There was no time to stop and admire Annie's handiwork as she was being naturally drawn to the gaping fissure in the realm, unseeing and unblinking.

"Quickly," ordered Lucan. "We must make Annie's daisy chain. Varis, go first and I will bring up the rear as planned."

The four of them created their elven daisy chain and Varis lead the way towards Annie.

At the last possible moment, Varis connected Finwe's hand with Annie's and broke away to the back of the chain. Staring disbelievingly at Varis, Elva was hand in hand with Finwe.

"Varis!" shouted Lucan. "What are you doing? Get hold of Elva now!"

But Varis vehemently shook his head and looked hard at Lucan.

"I told you, Lucan. I shall go last, not you. I... we cannot risk losing you in the portal, on the most important mission in elven history."

"And I," retorted Lucan, "cannot risk the loss of you either."

For far too many moments, Lucan and Varis were held in a tacit deadlock. Much was being communicated between them, yet neither said a word. From her position a little way off, the Wise One was shouting for them to catch onto Elva before it was too late, but she couldn't be heard above the storm.

Finally, Varis clasped Lucan's forearm and nodded. He made to reach for Elva's hand. But, at the very last moment, with a concerted effort, he swung Lucan round so that Elva caught hold of Lucan's hand rather than his own.

It was too late to change things now. Annie, Finwe, and Elva had already entered the portal. Lucan had partially entered and Varis had secured his place as the last daisy in the chain.

The moment Varis was in, the portal snapped shut and disappeared.

The storm instantly vanished, to be replaced by beautiful blue-skies and the two suns shone down upon the now gently steaming, rain-soaked crowds who stood in stunned silence.

Chapter Thirty-Two

As before, the moment Annie's fingertips grazed the viscous surface of the portal, her vision swirled fast before her.

But that's where the similarity of this journey through the portal with the last one ended. Perhaps it was different because she was doing a return trip. Perhaps it was different because, this time, she had hangers on — literally.

There was a brief moment of utter light-absorbing blackness. There was nothing to feel, emotionally or physically. There were no sounds, smells or tastes.

There was absolutely nothing.

She kept walking, on what, she couldn't tell. She started to feel something enveloping her right hand. It was warm and holding her firmly. She felt it was never going to let go. She felt it would always be there. She realised that it was Finwe. There was no need for a light to see it was him. She just knew. It was then that she remembered that this journey through her portal was a daisy chain, rather than just her travelling solo.

But it was supposed to be Varis who had hold of my hand, she thought, confused.

There was no time to question what had happened to their plan, for a pinprick of light appeared before her. It flickered a few times and then broadened out, like a faulty strip light.

Annie held her free hand out in front of her, but she couldn't make it out. She couldn't see where she ended and everything else started. Her hand was pixelated.

This is all in reverse, she mused while moving forward more confidently. She was surprised at how calm and collected she felt.

Finwe, Elva, Lucan, and Varis were far from calm and collected. They were thoroughly freaked out. Everything around them was pixelated like an atomic soup. They couldn't tell where one thing ended and another started, including themselves. It was impossible for them to process the information. There was just so much of it. They could see everything, smell it, taste it, and hear it. Their senses were overloaded and it was painful.

They hoped their hands were holding on tight.

Suddenly, the atomic soup started to vibrate rather than unhurriedly swirl and purl. Then came the reconstruction of everything. The distinct edges and boundaries between objects, individuals, and their surroundings started to take shape and become defined. Their combined panic subsided.

Annie and her companions saw momentary flickers of memories pass before them. These visions were not shared. Each experienced their own memories. Sometimes they were looking down on themselves, sometimes they were looking through their own eyes. Unlike Annie's first creation of a portal, they each could grasp and hold onto any or all of these moments. All of these moments evoked strong, sometimes overwhelming emotions.

As each member of the party lingered at different moments in their lives, the daisy chain became elongated, to the point of almost breaking.

Annie saw the smiling eyes of Carric. Eyes that seemed only to smile like that for her. She saw them sharing their first kiss, tentative and tender. She saw her arms wrapped around him, the first time he saved her. She saw and felt her first palm bombs, dancing in the village inn and laughing with Lilyfire as they held hands. Now she and Carric were in the barn and she could feel herself blushing as she watched herself make love with Carric. She then giggled as she saw Varis and Lucan standing over them the next morning. Then came the pain of failing to save Lilyfire and Carric. She was watching herself simultaneously cradling Lilyfire and crying out for Carric as he disappeared under the swelling waves.

Finwe felt the exhilaration of being at one with the thriving forest. He was darting between the trees and running with a pack of huarda. There was the joy of sailing with his father and play fighting with his sister Elva as children. Then came the anguish of the ruin of the elder's daughter and his devastation of not being able to prevent it. There was the laughter while dancing in the village inn and the sorrow of losing Lilyfire. Finally he was holding Annie tight to him as she sobbed in his arms. With a shy confession to himself, it was a moment he didn't want to end.

Elva heard the sweet singing of her mother. A sound she hadn't heard for nearly five thousand moons and had never thought she would hear again. She was singing the song of Elva's childhood. It was the song she would sing whenever Elva was afraid or unsure. Her sweet tone and birdlike trills brought tears to Elva's eyes. Her mother was the only one who knew when she was unsure or afraid. Not even Finwe, her twin, knew that. The strength of the bond between Elva and her mother had been indisputable. She had taught Elva everything there was to know about the healing powers of the fauna across the elven realms.

Although Elva had been just a child, she cursed herself for being unable to save her mother while Finwe and their father were away. Elva's family had a small holding some fifty furlongs from the border with the Shadow Realm. It lay well within the realm and was considered to be safe from attack.

A posse of particularly ambitious Shadow Elves had scoped out the holding and waited patiently for Finwe and his father to leave in order to attend a meeting of the elders. Elva could now hear the quickening of breath as the Shadow Elves seized their chance to do damage.

Without warning, they wreaked havoc, slaughtering the family's gatoa and rocco as they made their way to the house. Her mother pushed Elva under her skirts with the order to remain silent at all costs. Her mother stood stock-still so as not to give Elva away.

Elva could hear the Shadow Elves circling and taunting. Her mother remained stoically silent. In the next moment, there was a sickening *shlock* sound as the Shadow Elf axe blade met with her mother's shoulder.

The swish of the Shadow Elf axe that had mortally wounded her mother, played over and over in Elva's ears. She could hear the initial scream, followed by her mother's groans as the poison that had been smeared on the axe, worked its way through her chest and into her heart.

There was nothing Elva could do to make her mother live.

As per her mother's instruction, she had hidden under her mother's skirts until the return of her father and brother. Elva could hear her father retuning and the anguish in his cries.

It was brutal.

It was unbearable.

Annie tried to turn and warn the others of the need to remain connected, but she couldn't. The portal simply wouldn't allow it. All she could do was press on and hold Finwe's hand tightly. She felt the squeeze of her hand being returned by Finwe. She had to hope that the links between the others were as firm as theirs.

Lucan tasted the bitter blood of the fallen, both Shadow and Sun Elves alike. The taste took him right back into his experience of many battles against the Shadow Elves. Looking down he could see himself as a young soldier, first witnessing the fall of his fellow warriors. He clamped his eyes shut, not wanting to see.

But you dishonour them by declining to look, he thought to himself, and forced his eyelids to part.

He saw the loss of his childhood best friend, Thundruil, to a Shadow Elf's barb-tipped arrow through his throat.

Lucan saw the alarm and pain in Thundruil's eyes, his last moments spent clutching at the arrow and trying to pull it out, and the gurgled cry as blood filled his lungs and drowned him. The salty metallic taste of blood spent, danced on the buds of Lucan's tongue.

In that first battle, he had noticed that the taste of Sun or Woodland Elven blood was the same as Shadow Elven blood. Elven blood was elven blood. After that, he had wondered about how the similarities between himself and a Shadow Elf, probably far outweighed the differences.

He never spoke of his reflections.

Such a thing would have been frowned upon by the 'higher ups', especially those in the nobility. And since those early days in the army, Tathlyn had come into power. Tathlyn was a far more insidious, spiteful, and dangerous Shadow Elf leader than had ever gone before. Tathlyn had to be stopped no matter what the cost in lives — Sun Elf, Woodland Elf, Shadow Elf or... or human.

No matter how many moons Lucan clocked up as a soldier, section leader, centurion and now commander or the guard, the smell of post-battle blood mixed with sweat and mud, never failed to take him back to his younger self's thoughts. Back to his friend, Thundruil.

Varis saw his mother, Ellen. She had died giving birth to him, yet here she was, smiling at him, reaching out her arms to him. He'd never really seen her, but there was no mistaking in his mind, as to who she was. Made flesh, she was even more beautiful than her likeness that his father carried with him, close to his chest, at all times. Varis had never felt her embrace, had never heard her voice or seen the lights that twinkled in her eyes as she laughed.

He could feel the pull of Lucan's hand as their link in the daisy chain was put under immense strain. While Lucan was moving forward, but Varis was being drawn back. His mother continued to reach her arms out towards him. There was a soulful yearning in her eyes.

What harm can one embrace do? he thought. *She is my mother. My... mother.*

Lucan's grip on Varis was slipping. His fingers gripped tighter and tighter. The urge for Varis to go to his mother was just too tantalising. He stretched his free hand towards her.

Surely, just to touch with one hand cannot do any harm, he thought.

As soon as their fingertips touched, Varis was steeped in an all-encompassing, unconditional mother's love. He could feel his mother's love filling him up.

He wept with an equal measure of joy and sorrow.

<><><><><><><>

At that same moment his companions felt like they were being unceremoniously thrust into the saddle of a greater gold-tipped soron that was midway through an inverted loop in the convection currents above the Woodland Realm. But Varis's hand slipped Lucan's grip in order to embrace his mother completely.

The link between Lucan and Varis was broken.

Lucan desperately reached for his friend, his comrade, but the virtual giant bird of prey whipped him away with the others. For what felt like hundreds of moons, there was steep rising, falling, and somersaulting. They were completely out of control and unable to scream, for it felt like any air had been brutally punched out of their chests.

They seemed to by headed for another pinprick of light via the most convoluted route known to man or elf. As they came close to the source of light, they each could see that it was a small opening in the fabric of the portal, right at its very edge.

They showed no signs of slowing.

If anything, they were speeding up.

In turn, each of the companions was ejected through the opening and onto damp, grassy ground. The impact of landing was so hard that the forced intake of air just before exiting the portal, was gut-punched out of each of them upon landing.

The exhausted daisy chain laid still and panting, hands still tighly clasped.

Annie's was the first head to raise. She inspected herself for any signs of injury. Apart from a sore shoulder from the rough landing, there were none. Finwe and Elva did likewise. They too were shaken but not hurt.

Lucan's head remained pressed against the earth, face down.

Looking past the twins and Lucan, Annie knew that all was not well.

"Where's Varis?" she demanded. On hearing her question, Finwe and Elva lifted their heads.

Raising his body from being pressed against the earth, Lucan sat up and began to rock backwards, and forwards. He hugged himself tightly and screwed up his eyes, shutting them tightly.

Elva repeated Annie's question, but was more gentle and less accusatory in her tone.

"Where is Varis?"

While continuing to rock back and forth, Lucan let out a heartbreaking howl.

"He is lost!"

<><><><><><><><><><><><><><><>

A Word from Hil

I really hope that you have enjoyed reading the first book in the Annie Harper Trilogy as much as have enjoyed writing it. If you could see your way to leaving an honest review, I'd be ever so grateful — the good, bad, and ugly are all welcome and useful.

If your appetite is whetted for more of what I'm penning, take a gander below.

Prequel Novello of the series:

To get your free copy of **Betrayal**, please go to hilggibb.com

The Golden Fleck Series:

The Dying Realms — Annie Harper Trilogy, Book 1
  The Worst Deceit — Annie Harper Trilogy, Book 2
  The Final Hope — Annie HarperTrilogy, Book 3
  Devotion — Lisa's Story Part 2 (free to subscribers)
  Outsider — Meredith Harwood Story

Books for younger readers:
The Tale of Two Sydneys
Archie Brittle Saves the play

NB:
As I am an advocate for people with dyslexia, I decided to make the print version of my novels in the OpenDyslexic font so that they are more readily accessible.

Printed in Dunstable, United Kingdom